FOUR
ANTHOLOGY 4

FOUR
ANTHOLOGY 4

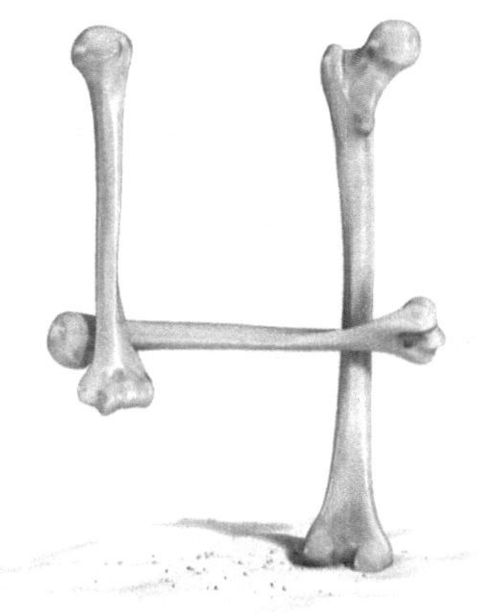

T.K. WRATHBONE

☠ Royal Star Publishing ☠

Skull & Bone is an imprint of Royal Star Publishing
www.royalstarpublishing.com.au

First edition paperback published in 2019
All Rights Reserved, Copyright ©T.K. Wrathbone 2019

Trade Paperback ISBN: 978-1-925683-34-9
Large Print Paperback ISBN: 978-1-922307-09-5
Dust Jacket Hardcover ISBN: 978-1-922307-11-8
Case Laminate Hardcover ISBN: 978-1-922307-11-8
I Spy With My Little Eye e-book ISBN: 978-1-925683-96-7
Knock, Knock…Who's Dead? e-book ISBN: 978-1-925683-59-2
It Creeped At Midnight e-book ISBN: 978-1-925683-61-5
The Bones of Wrath: Monsters e-book ISBN: 978-1-925683-63-9
A catalogue record for this book is available from the National Library
of Australia.

Cover design: Royal Star Publishing and Odyssey Books
Cover photos: istock.com/Koya79
Typesetting in Minion Pro by Royal Star Publishing

CONTENTS

I SPY WITH MY LITTLE EYE

CHAPTER ONE

"And one, two, three, kick," Blake Williamson told his friends.

They side-stepped to the right and fell over each other in a tangle of legs, giggling as they sprawled on the lounge room floor.

"Aw, come on, guys," Blake whined, hands on hips, looking down at his friends. "We're never gonna be the next One Direction if this is gonna happen every time we try the dance routine." He grabbed the remote and hit pause. "We need the practice."

Jarrod giggled and shoved Callum aside to detangle his legs. "I thought we were just doing this for a bit of fun." He clambered to his feet and brushed off his hands. "It's not like we're auditioning for Got Talent or anything. We're not really going to be the next One Direction, especially since they didn't even do dance routines. They were the most unco group on the planet. Just like us tragics." A dead weight grabbed his arm and he looked down to see Jason using him to haul himself up. He helped him, and all four boys brushed themselves off before seeing Blake's angry scowl.

"Dude, calm down," Adam said. "It's just a bit of fun."

"It's not fun if you break anything," Melissa, Blake's stepmother, said from the doorway. "The lounge room isn't big enough as is; it doesn't need five teenage boys trying to dance in it. The new One Direction," she scoffed and placed her well-manicured hands on her slim, yet curvy, hips. Two years previously, at twenty-four, Melissa Dubrey had married Blake's dad, Michael Williamson, after a whirlwind courtship. Michael had been forty-four, Blake was twelve, and she hadn't appreciated having a teenage stepson to deal with. A former beauty queen, her bouffant blonde hair and well made up face made her look much older; the stilettoes and animal print mini dress made her look like a cougar. And she hated Blake as much as he hated her.

Blake seethed inside. It had been three years since his mother had died in a car accident, and two years since Melissa had become his stepmother. He hated her, and wished she were dead, wished he could have his mother back, wished and cried and prayed every day to have his mother back. But nothing changed. Nothing happened, and he was still stuck with the stepmother from hell. Glaring at her, he noticed her freshly manicured nails were rose pink and matched her lipstick. That was all she cared about. Getting manicures and pedicures, facials and massages, blowing through his dad's money like there was no tomorrow. He was glad he had a private trust fund that no one could touch but him, because he didn't want her blowing his mother's life insurance that had gone into the trust for her only son. He noticed the way his friends were eyeing her shapely legs in the animal platform heels and crotch high mini dress.

"What do you want, Melissa?" His scowl deepened and a foot kicked Jarrod who was closest to him.

Jarrod blanched and turned away. He had a bit of a crush on Blake's stepmum. It was hard not to. At fourteen, he was going through puberty and found the female form attractive. He quickly grabbed at the other boys and they turned back to the TV.

"What *I want*, Blake," Melissa said icily, "is for my stepson to be in boarding school, but what *I got* was him and his friends playing pretend in my lounge room during school holidays."

"*My* lounge room," Blake corrected. "*We* lived here long before *you* got here." He had no problem sassing his stepmother; he hated her, after all.

Melissa's eyes narrowed and her lips pursed. "Yes, well, if it wasn't for your father's insistence on living here, we'd be in a bigger home now, probably a house, but we aren't." She hated the fact Michael was so insistent on living in the townhouse he'd shared with his dead wife, but she loved the money he provided her with, so, she sucked it up and tried not to complain to his face. She also tried to remain polite and sweet to Blake when his dad was around, but when he wasn't, it was all-out war.

"My father insists on living here because it's *our* home." Blake eyed her screwed up expression. "*You* just came into it. What do you want? We're busy." He turned back to the TV and DVD, setting the disc back to the beginning of the song.

"What I *want* is for you to not exist. But you do. And there's nothing I can do about it. Yet," Melissa seethed. "So, if you want a place to rehearse your stupid dancing, go to someone else's house, or clear out the attic and do it up there."

"The attic…" Blake's head swivelled around. "Is full of cobwebs and dirt. And probably your junk."

Melissa barely contained her temper. "I *do not* have junk, but all of *your* garbage *is* up there. So, if you want to use it, clear it out. Is that understood?" Stomping her stilettoed foot, she snatched up her bag from the hall table. "I'm going shopping; make up your mind before I get back." After slamming the door, she hit the button on the car key to unlock her car, got in, gunned the engine, and backed out. Peeling down the street, she didn't look back.

"Bloody hell!" Blake's interior furnace blew. His face felt red, and he was sure steam was coming out of his ears. "Who the bloody hell does she think she is, that snivelling money-grubbing—"

"Your stepmother," Callum told him, seeing the redness of Blake's face deepen. "You really don't like her, do you?" He'd been friends with Blake most of his life as they all lived on the same street and went to the same school, so he'd seen what Blake had gone through with the loss of his mother. He'd gone through divorced parents, Jarrod had separated ones, Adam's were still married to one another, and Jason's were married to other people. Most of them knew what it was like to have adults come and go in their parents' lives.

"I don't care who she freakin' is," Blake hissed. "I hate her." Throwing the remote across the room in a fit of anger, he watched it hit an expensive $3000 vase, fall to the floor with a clatter, and have that expensive vase land and shatter on top of it. "Bugger!"

"Bloody hell, Blake. She'll kill you for that," Adam said in shock.

"I'll just say her cat did it." Blake walked over and carefully extracted the remote from the mess. "I'll just tell Dad we were up in the attic clearing it up like she told us to, when we heard a smash and came downstairs to find Snowball running away and the vase smashed on the floor. She won't be able to prove otherwise."

"But you expect *us* to lie to him." Jarrod knew Mr Williamson was usually a nice man except where money was concerned.

"We'd better get upstairs then." Blake switched off the TV and led the boys up the stairs all the way to the top floor. Pushing open the door, they stood gazing at the dirty, dusty mess that was the attic.

"And we're supposed to clean this?" Callum waved a hand in front of his face as if to clean the air. "What *is* all of this?"

"Mum's stuff," Blake said quietly, his mind wandering

back to memories long gone. "Our stuff, old furniture, toys, clothes, whatever doesn't fit in the rest of the house that *she* banished when *she* moved in and remodelled." He walked over to the windows and managed to get them open for light and air. Turning, he caught sight of the old mirror that had hung on his parents' bedroom wall. For years his mother had joked that it was magical and could grant any wish he had, and he'd believed her. His heart heaved at the memories flooding back, and he wondered why it had ended up in the attic leaning against boxes on the floor. The boys started pulling boxes aside and having a look at sporting equipment, photos and albums, plus a bunch of his dad's old school and work stuff.

Jarrod waved at the air. "Dude, the dust is thick up here. How are we gonna clean it?"

"Duster," Adam mumbled. "You'll need a heavy duty one, too."

"I'll get the vacuum cleaner and see if that helps." Blake ran downstairs to the utility closet in the laundry and hauled the cleaner back upstairs along with a bucket of rags. Two hours later, the floor was clean, boxes wiped down, and what furniture there was, was pushed to the walls either side of the back wall window. The attic was the length of the house, but more light came through the two front windows than the one back window. They neatly piled the boxes either side of the two couches and side tables, leaving plenty of room for dance routines in the front of the room.

"I think we've killed about ten spiders." Callum swatted at another one. "Make that eleven."

"And there were a lot of dead bugs." Jason screwed up his nose and sneezed. "It's going to wreak havoc on my allergies."

Blake finished vacuuming the walls for cobwebs and turned off the cleaner. "At least we have a space to practise now without Her Majesty whinging about it. And I found some things I thought were missing, so that's a bonus. All we need now is to set up a TV and we're done."

"And where are we getting one of them from?" Jarrod asked. "You got a spare?"

"Well…there's about fifty in the house," Blake mumbled. "One in every room. We should be able to take *one*. It's *my* house after all."

"Man, you really hate her, don't you?" Adam slumped down onto the floor, his back against the wall beside the open door.

"She's twenty years younger than Dad. Twelve years older than me. If he was going to pick someone, she *should* have been older."

"It probably didn't help that he met and married her just a year after your mum died," Callum said softly. "That would have sucked."

"It did." Blake wearily slid to the floor. "He didn't even give us time to grieve properly. To get used to being without her. He just up and got himself a new wife and expected me to accept a new mother. Well, *I don't. I don't* accept a new mother. I just don't, *especially* her."

Bang. Thud.

The boys' heads swivelled around.

"Did something fall over?" Blake asked, looking at everything they'd spent the last couple of hours moving and sorting.

Nothing had, so they looked out the window.

"Must've been a bird hitting the window," Jarrod volunteered. "They're stupid, they do those things."

Bang. Thud.

Their heads swivelled to the wall adjoining the next townhouse.

"Must be the new neighbours." Adam scratched at a red lump on his arm. "They moved in a few days ago, didn't they? Besides, they've just had *us* banging around for two hours."

Bang. Thud.

A piece of plaster fell to the floor.

"Yeah, but we didn't put holes in the wall." Blake climbed to his feet and hurried over to inspect the damage. "That must've gone through their wall and into ours." He picked at the plaster, and it fell away with ease. After cleaning the hole, he peered through to see what was going on and a gasp escaped him. He stumbled away from the wall and fell to the floor in shock.

CHAPTER TWO

"What did you see?" Adam asked.

"Um…someone…" Blake pointed, and the boys gathered around the hole taking turns looking through.

"There's nothing there," Callum said. "I just see the other wall in their attic."

"I saw someone," Blake managed. "An eyeball. Like someone looking back." He hefted himself up from the floor. "I know someone was there. I saw an eyeball."

"Maybe they were looking to see what damage had been done, like you were," Jarrod suggested. "They probably got a shock too."

"Yeah, maybe." Blake moved to the wall and had another look. There was nothing there, and all he saw was the wall of the townhouse next door. "Oh, well." He pulled away and looked at his friends. "Let's go find a TV and get back to it." After taking the vacuum and rags back to the laundry, they wandered from room to room looking for a TV to use and found one in the bathroom downstairs. They unhooked it, carried it upstairs, and plugged it in. Blake hurried back downstairs for the DVD from the lounge, catching sight of his father and stepmother pulling up at the same time. He raced upstairs and frantically shoved the disc into the TV and turned it on, making sure the volume was loud.

"What's going on?" Adam yelled over the din of pop music.

"The olds are back," Blake yelled back. "Quick, start dancing."

The boys formed a line and repeated the moves they'd rehearsed, not even hearing the shouting going on downstairs.

"Who smashed my vase?" Melissa screeched, seeing the mess in the lounge room, and Snowball, her Persian cat, sniffing around it. "Blake. Blake. Where are you? You smashed my vase."

"You don't know that he did," Michael said, irritated that his wife automatically blamed his son. "Your cat is sniffing around it, *he* probably did it."

"It was *your* stupid son." Melissa's voice hit the high decibels. "He and his friends were playing pretend in here this morning. Probably knocked it over with their stupid dance routines thinking they were One Direction, for God's sake. It was him. I'm sure of it. Blake." The screech came out high and thin. "Blake, you get down here." She marched up the stairs.

"And how do you know *where* he is?" Michael asked. "And don't ever call my son stupid again." Following her up, he watched her storm into the attic.

"How dare you break my vase, you rotten little shit," Melissa screamed, seeing all of the boys stop and stare at her. She didn't even notice the attic had been re-arranged. "You smashed my vase and you're going to pay for it." Storming over to him, she raised her hand to strike.

Michael got to her first and grabbed her by the arm, pulling her back from his wide-eyed son. He stuck his finger in his wife's shocked face, his anger boiling over. "Don't you *ever* raise your hand to *my* son again, do you understand me?" He couldn't believe that the woman he'd fallen in love with and married could do that. "You will *never* hit my son. Do you understand me?"

The shock of having her husband, who normally kowtowed to her, stand up to her with such fire in his eyes, scared her. "I-I wasn't going to," she stuttered and then her lips formed a pout. "But he broke my vase."

"Yes," Michael muttered through clenched teeth. "A ridiculously expensive vase that we *never* should have bought. But for some reason I let you talk me into." His head turned to his scared son. "Did you break the vase?"

"Um…no." Blake's voice came out small and squeaky. "I saw it before, when I went downstairs for the DVD. Figured the cat did it. Besides," his voice grew strong, "she's the one who told us to get out of the lounge room and come and clean up the attic. We've been here for hours."

Michael glanced at all five boys in their dusty

clothes, and then glanced around the room. "Wow. I haven't been up here in what, three years." His hand released Melissa's arm and she rubbed it furiously to get the blood flowing again. Michael's hands went to his hips and he stood staring at the neatly packed furniture and boxes. "You boys do all this?"

"We did," Blake replied, his eyes going back and forth from a furious Melissa to a surprised father, confusion grabbing at his brain over what had just happened. He'd never seen his father so angry, so violent. Except after his mother's death when they had both been angry and inconsolable.

"What sort of stuff did you find? I thought this place was a mess. You boys did a good job of it. It must have taken hours." He wandered over and peered into each box. "I see you kept everything separate."

"Yeah, figured it was easier." Blake wandered after his father and the boys followed. "Sports, crockery, personal, albums. I found the pictures of…" his voice trailed off.

"Yeah," Michael's voice was soft. "I haven't looked at those since…" Seeing his son's anguished face, he put his arms around him and held him tight. A great heaving sigh left his body and he felt his son do the same. "I miss her sometimes too," he whispered. "But she'd want us to be happy again."

"Are you?" Blake whispered into his father's shoulder. "Really? Because I'm not."

Michael pulled away to stare his son in the eye

and released another sigh. "Most days, I am. But not right now. You okay?"

Blake managed a small nod, content that at least he still had his father and his love, no matter what Melissa did.

"Well, I think you boys should be rewarded for your hard work. It must have taken hours." Removing his wallet from his back pocket, Michael thumbed through the notes and handed a fifty to each boy. "Well done, boys, you earned it, and pizza's on me tonight. I didn't want to do this job, but you did, so many thanks." He glanced at how neat everything was and then noticed the hole in the wall. "Did you do that, or was it already there?" He gave a nod in its direction.

"The neighbours," all five boys answered at once.

"We looked through it and you can see into their attic as well," Callum said, super excited at getting fifty dollars from his best friend's dad. It was what he needed for the latest Nintendo game he wanted.

Michael walked over to the wall and peered through, noticing the edges of the hole, and how it was obvious it came from the inside rather than the kids shoving something through. "Easily patched, I guess. Or we just don't worry about it."

A smashing sound came from downstairs and everyone raced down to find Snowball freaking out amidst the broken china of another vase.

"Snowball, how could you?" Melissa tottered over to her stunned cat and lifted him into her arms. "Naughty Snowball, are you hurt, my sweetie?" She nuzzled her cat, allowing it to lick her lips.

"That solves it for me." Michael screwed his face up. "The cat did it now, the cat did it earlier, and you won't ever blame my son for anything again, is that clear?"

Melissa cast a sly glance at her husband, knowing she could make him change his mind later.

"And I'm not buying new vases. Your overspending is going to stop now, and if that cat breaks one more thing, it can go." Michael turned away in disgust. "You can clean up the mess. Boys, let's get pizza." Leaving his wife and her cat to seethe, he took the boys to the local pizza parlour.

After getting home, Blake went to his room, showered, and changed for bed, but sat watching TV. The sound of raised voices intrigued him, and at first, he thought it was the neighbours next door. After turning the volume down to listen, he soon realized it was his father and stepmother, which surprised him. *They've never fought.* Sneaking over to open the door so he could listen, he was unable to hear anything clearly, so he turned off the TV and light, then sneaked onto the landing and over to the bannister. It was hard to hear what they were saying at first, but it soon became clear when Melissa stormed into the ground floor entrance. He ducked back.

"Don't you *ever* speak to me that way again," she yelled. "How *dare you* tell me what to do or what to spend? *I am a beauty queen and you are just my husband.*" Her fists clenched by her side.

"And *you* will *never* raise your hand to my son ever again. Or even *think* about it, let alone call him stupid, or blame him for what *your* cat does, or *you* will be out on your backside."

"And I will take you for everything you're worth," she screamed back.

"You signed a prenup. You won't get anything."

Blake pulled back, disturbed by what was happening. Fear curled its way through his chest and he turned back to his room. *What the hell's going on?* Tears sprang to his eyes and a panic rose in his throat. *Why is Dad so angry? He's never yelled at her, only yelled when Mum died. Since he met her he hadn't ever raised his voice, and now today...* His head moved left and right, his eyes taking in everything in his room. Not knowing what to do, a thought sprang to mind. Shoving his pillows lengthways in bed, he covered them to make it look as if he was sleeping. Going back to the door, he heard them still arguing, so closed his door, sneaked up the stairs to the attic, and closed that door behind him, locking out the world.

Heaving a sigh of relief in the quiet stillness, he glanced over to the boxes containing the photo albums. He wandered over, pulled them out, and sat on the old sofa, turned on the lamp they had plugged in earlier, and flicked through years of memories. Him as a baby in his mother's arms, his parents' wedding, parties, happy times before she was taken.

He sighed, and tears slowly fell in tiny rivulets down his cheeks. "Oh, Mum, I miss you."

Absentmindedly, he stood up and walked around the room, not noticing where he was going, or what he was doing. He spied the mirror that had hung in his parents' bedroom leaning against the wall and remembered how his mother said it was magical. Clutching the album to his chest, he faced the mirror, seeing his legs in the reflection, and he was smiling a little at it when the hissing occurred.

He blinked, breathed in, and looked up. "What's...?"

A green glow flittered through the hole made by the neighbour, and surprised, he slowly stepped over and peered through it. The room was green. A glow the colour of bright green toy slime lit up the neighbour's attic. His lids blinked and he leaned back.

"That's strange," he muttered. "Wonder what's making that?" Another look, but he couldn't see beyond the scope of the hole. "Mmm, well." Heaving a sigh, he sat cross-legged in front of his mother's mirror and spread the album on his lap. "Oh, Mum. How I wish you were still here. We'd be so happy, so alive. *She* wouldn't be here. I wish you were alive and she wasn't. I want you back, Mum. I want you to come back."

The green light streaming through the hole brightened, pulsating to its own beat, hearing the pleas of a lonely, broken-hearted fourteen-year-old boy crying out for his mother, crying out for the family to be together again, crying out for a life to return and a life to be taken.

CHAPTER THREE

The next day was too hot for the boys to be out playing cricket, so they wandered into the cool air-conditioned comfort of the attic to practise their moves.

"Why are we even bothering with this?" Jarrod asked, watching Blake load the DVD into the TV. "Are we even going to do anything with it?"

"We're going to be the next One Direction," Blake said, setting up the right section on the disc.

"But we don't sing, so *how* can we be the next One Direction?" Callum asked.

"And we don't dance well." Adam tried to do a kick ball touch, but his feet became confused and tripped over each other. "We're useless."

"No, we're not," Blake spat. "My mum said I could do anything if I put my mind to it, so I'm putting my mind to it. There's that talent show coming up and I want to enter. Even if we don't sing, we can dance to the song, and besides which, not only is there a huge cash prize, but we get a chance to go to the finals and be on TV. So come on, let's work."

They practised for two hours before grabbing sodas from the fridge and slouching on the couches in the attic.

"So, how was it last night after you got home?" Jarrod asked Blake. They'd all been dropped off after having pizza, so hadn't gone back to the Williamson house.

"They argued." Blake stared at the ceiling. "I've never heard them argue before. But last night, they yelled at each other. It was horrible."

"What did you do?" Callum asked.

"Came up here and looked at the photo albums of Mum and me." The melancholy washed over him, but was gone in an instant at the memory of the green glow. "But get this, there was a green glow coming through the hole, and when I looked, all I could see was green."

"A green glow?" Callum scoffed. "You must've eaten too much anchovy pizza last night."

"Dude!" Blake rolled his eyes. "*I know what I saw*. It was a green glow coming from next door."

"I don't see anything now." Jarrod looked toward the hole. "But let's have a look anyway."

The boys rushed over to the wall and head-butted each other to be the first to look, but Jarrod won out. Peering through, he saw nothing. "Nope, nothing there."

"Give me a look." Adam shoved him aside and stuck his eyeball to the hole. "Hey, I saw something."

"What?" came four times.

Adam blinked. "It looks like something going

back and forth. A bat or something. Something long, up and down." He watched the long cylindrical object rise and fall repeatedly.

"Get out of the way and let me look." Callum pushed him over and peered through. "Nothing there. Probably your imagination."

"Let me." Jason looked into the hole and saw an eyeball looking back. "Argh!" He jumped back in fright and pointed to the hole. "Eye, eye. I saw an eye."

Blake looked through the hole and saw nothing. "There's nothing there, you idiot."

"I *know* what I saw," Jason went on. "I saw an eyeball. There's someone there."

"Probably the new neighbours," Callum reminded him.

"Whatever it is, it wasn't a normal eye. It looked weird," Jason replied.

"Weird how?" the others asked.

"Dunno." Jason shrugged. "Not human, weird."

The boys looked at each other and cracked up laughing. "Yeah, right. Not human," Adam gasped. "Good one, Jase."

"I'm serious," Jason stated. "I saw an eyeball that *did not* look human." He stomped his foot. "*I know what I saw.*"

Blake took another look, but saw nothing. "Whatever it was, it's not there now, so don't worry about it and let's get back to practice."

With Jason still mumbling about seeing an eyeball, they got in another two hours of rehearsal before the boys went their separate ways.

After a refreshing shower, Blake was lying on his bed contemplating what book to read when he heard the thuds. Faint, at first, he wasn't sure if they were next door or outside. But when they continued, he stuck his head out the window and decided there was nothing going on outside that could be causing the sounds.

Thud. Bang.

"Now where is that coming from?" Blake muttered and wandered into the hall. He listened, thinking it was Snowball somewhere in the house breaking more vases. But his ears tuned in and determined the sounds were coming from upstairs. "The attic." Wondering if Snowball had gotten into the room and couldn't get out, he walked up the stairs and slowly opened the door so he wasn't attacked. But, stepping in, he didn't see Snowball anywhere. "Mmm, that's strange." He was turning to leave when the thuds came again.

Curious, he swivelled to face the wall opposite. The wall with the hole from the neighbours. With sweaty palms, the door slid from his hands. His tongue licked his lips, and his feet moved one in front of the other until he was standing in front of the hole. Unsure if he should, he leaned toward the wall and peered through.

An arm flung something up in the air and swiftly down again. An arm in a leathery old coat. The hand was covered in something, and Blake struggled to decipher what he was seeing. An arm swinging a huge knife of some kind, or a sword. Dark liquid flew into the air and the arm stopped. Grunts and groans were heard, and something was moved. It fell with a thud as something else was slid into its place.

Blake didn't have a full panoramic view of the room next door, but he got the gist of it. He placed his ear to the hole and tuned in. Definitely grunts and groans, and thwacks. *Is he cutting meat up?* Looking through the hole to see what was happening, he decided to stick his nose in and sniff the air. Ew, just dirt and mildew, not raw meat.

Wondering about his neighbour, he went to the front window and stuck his head out to see if he could learn anything. He saw nothing. No car in the driveway, no mail in the box, no paper in the yard, and the attic windows were nailed shut.

"Definitely wants to keep someone out," he muttered and shut the window against the early summer heat. Going back to the hole, he peered through, but saw nothing, no one, no arm; nothing. Sighing, he dug into the photo box and pulled out framed photos of the family. "Oh, Mum, why aren't you here with me? Why did God take you? Why did he have to bring Melissa into our lives? Why aren't you here and she's dead?"

*****

"And one, two, three, four, five, six, seven, eight." Blake led the boys into the dance and they managed to make it through without falling over themselves or each other. "Good. We made it through that time."

"Barely," Jarrod huffed and puffed, bending over to rest his hands on his knees. "Is this contest even worth it?"

"If it gets us fame and fortune, why not?" Blake asked.

A crash came from the neighbour's attic and the wall vibrated. The boys jumped and spun around, staring at the wall.

"Bloody hell!" Callum muttered. "What *was* that?"

"Don't know, but let's find out." Blake ran over to the wall and looked through the hole. He shifted slightly, thinking that if he leaned left or right, or up or down he would see more. But he didn't.

"Well?"

Blake glanced at his friends. "Nothing." Looking again, he saw the back of a man. The oily battered leather of a jacket. "Wait," he whispered. "There's someone there." Keeping watch, he saw the man walk out of view and back again. Always with his back to the wall. But that's all Blake saw. Sighing, he moved away. "It's a man, but I can't see anything else."

"Let me have a go." Adam stepped up to the wall and looked through. "I can only see his back."

Blake pulled him and the others away from the wall and in hushed tones told them about the night before. The noises, and the blood, and the man's hand going up and down. "I don't know what he's doing, but it looked like he was chopping something up."

"A body!" Jason surmised.

"Hardly think so," Blake said. "But…"

"But *you* don't know and neither do we," Callum said. "They just moved in last week, they could still be unpacking."

"They?" Jason asked. "I thought it was just a guy."

"Nope. Mum said a couple moved in," Callum replied. "Didn't see the man, but the woman was a bit of a weirdo hippie type. Apparently, they've hung wind chimes and strange stuff on the porch to ward off evil spirits. Or so Mum said."

"I haven't even seen them," Blake told them. "And they live right next door. I didn't see them move in, I don't see them collect their mail, although, I suppose, someone does because the box isn't overflowing, and there are no papers lying around."

"Maybe they go out after dark to bring it in," Callum offered. "Don't want people seeing what they look like."

"Maybe they're vampires," Jason added. "And they're going to suck our blood after dark." He made sucking sounds and bared his teeth.

"Don't be stupid." Blake rolled his eyes. "They're not vampires. Vampires don't exist, besides; maybe they're just private people."

"And maybe they're vampires," Jason reiterated.

Callum punched him lightly in the arm. "Then you'd better not invite them over to your place. They can't come in unless they're invited."

"Better tell my parents then," Adam said. "They

invite everyone over."

"Look, it can't be that bad," Blake interrupted. "Probably chopping up old furniture or something."

"And I haven't seen any reports of missing people, or anything," Jarrod added.

"Why would people be missing?" Jason asked. "Oh, you mean because they're vampires and they'd need blood."

"No, stupid." Jarrod sighed. "Blake thinks someone was chopped up in the attic, which means someone will be missing. But I haven't seen any reports of missing people. So, they can't be chopping people up."

"Doesn't mean they're not kidnapping street people or something," Callum mused. "Plenty of homeless people on the outskirts living in that old warehouse. No one will miss them if they go missing."

"But why would they want to cut up homeless people?" Blake asked.

"Axe murderers," Jarrod said.

"Experiments," Callum muttered.

"Vampires," Jason added.

"That's ridiculous," Adam cried, exasperated by the conversation. "You have no idea what's going on next door, so why worry about it? Just let it go and let's get on with this stupid dance routine for this stupid contest."

CHAPTER FOUR

That night, as Blake lay on the couch in the attic, looking at the old photo albums, he remembered back to every time depicted until he was in tears, sobbing his heart out at the pain of losing his mother. The last couple of days had been tense. His father may have been back to his old self, something he was sure could be attributed to Melissa in the marital bedroom, but he sensed something. Melissa was still nasty to him when his dad wasn't around, but saccharine sweet to his face when he was. Dinnertime was tense, but at least he had his friends, and at least he had his mother's memory. Moving over to sit in front of his mother's mirror, he started talking to her.

"Mum, I wish I could see you one more time. I wish you were still here with me. I've missed you so much in the last three years. Dad married that horrible Melissa and she hates me. I hate her and I wish you were here so badly." Gazing from the mirror to the album in his lap, he didn't notice the green glow coming through the hole in the wall.

"Mum," he whispered, his finger touching her face in one of the last photos taken. "Please come back, please come back to me."

Sleep overtook him and he lay down on the floor, flicking through the album until his eyes closed and peace came.

"Blake, Blake, time to get up, sweetie."

"Mmm, Mum?"

"Blake, time to get up."

He rolled onto his back and opened his eyes to see his mother standing over him in his bedroom. "Mum?" His eyes snapped shut and open and he quickly took in his surroundings. His bed, in his room, with his mother. "Mum? You're alive? Oh, my God, you're alive," he yelled, hugging her as she leant over him.

"Of course I'm alive, silly. Why wouldn't I be?" She returned the hug, fiercely holding her son as if her life depended on it.

"Oh, Mum. I thought you were dead. You've been gone for three years," he sobbed.

"It's just a bad dream, sweetie. Just a bad dream."

Blake cried on his mother's shoulder, but felt a strange sensation. He looked up and saw her figure fading before his eyes. "Mum, no. Mum, no. Don't leave me, Mum. No."

Blake thrashed out at the disappearing version of his mother.

"Blake, Blake, wake up."

"Mum, don't leave me. Don't leave me," Blake sobbed.

"Blake, it's okay, it's okay." Michael held his sobbing son in his arms, seeing the old photo albums that had brought the tears on. He'd gone to check on his son and say goodnight, only to find him gone. Thinking he'd be in the attic watching videos, he'd gone upstairs to find his son asleep on the floor in front of his mother's favourite mirror. The one she'd told him was magic. He knew that it wasn't real, but wasn't about to let Blake down by telling him. Although, he guessed Blake knew. "It's okay, Blake. It's okay. I miss her too. It's okay to miss her, it's okay to cry."

"I miss her so much," Blake cried into his father's shoulder. "I want her back."

"I know, I know." Michael soothed his son. "I know, but she can't come back, so all you have is memories and photos."

With his heart broken into a million pieces, he allowed his father to help him downstairs and tuck him into bed.

*****

"Dude, are you *still* crying over it?" Jarrod asked the next day.

Blake had told them about his dream and sobbing in his father's arms. "Can't help it. It still hurts and I miss her."

"Yeah, I guess you would," Callum murmured. "We miss our olds when they're not around, but at least they're alive."

"At least you get to see your dads," Blake mumbled. "I don't get to see Mum in real life, just in videos and photos and dreams. I don't get to hug her, talk to her, nothing. You all get to do that. And Adam's parents are still together."

"How's it between your olds?" Adam felt a little self-conscious that he still had both parents, and ones that were together at that.

"Dad's relaxed, Melissa's smug as usual. She's got Dad wrapped around her little finger and he can't see what a cow she is."

"I heard that, Blake Williamson." Melissa stood in the doorway of the attic, hands on hips, her red manicure matching her red lipstick.

"Don't care if you did, Melissa," Blake retorted. "You may have Dad up your butt, but you don't have me. And we both know full well we don't like each other. You want to send me to boarding school, and I wish you'd drop dead." Blake glanced away, staring out the back attic window, no longer interested in what his stepmother had to say.

"Ooohhh, why you little disobedient brat," Melissa growled. "If it's the last thing I do, it's sending you off to boarding school."

"Yeah, yeah," Blake mumbled. "What.ev.ah. Dad won't allow it. Me and this house are the last attachments he has to Mum. Why do you think all of her stuff is still here? Because he can't bear to throw it away. He can't bear to throw *her* away because he still loves *her* and *you're* just a substitute." The anger had risen from Blake's chest to his throat and out through his mouth. The hatred and anger he had for her had been growing in recent days, and he wasn't sure what was causing it. He wondered if it had always been there and he'd just dampened it down for the sake of his father.

"You hateful little brat." Melissa stomped over to them in her silver stilettoes. "Just you wait until I tell your father what you said. That will get you sent off to boarding school quick smart. As for your mother's things…" She waved a neatly manicured hand at all of the boxes and saw the boys, except for Blake, cowering on the couches. "I'll get rid of it. One day when you're not here and your father's at work; I'll just get rid of it. Lock, stock, and bloody box." She spied the mirror leaning against the wall. "Ugh, and that vile thing is still here I see. God knows why you kept it, it's ugly and so last century."

"We kept it because it was my mother's." Blake flew from his seat toward her. "You just want to eliminate everything about her. Her stuff, her past with Dad, even me. You want it all gone so you don't have any competition to worry about." With her in heels, she was a bit taller than him and he couldn't match her in height, but he didn't care. "Well, you were *never* competition. If Mum were alive, he never would have looked at you and you'd still be a money-grubbing—"

Thwack.

Melissa's hand sped across Blake's face, making him spin around.

He clutched his face, shocked, astounded,

disbelieving that she had actually done it. Even though his father had threatened her if she ever did.

"Don't you *ever* speak *to* me or *about me* that way ever again," she spat. "Who the hell do you think you are, you little toad? I'll have your guts for garters."

"Go to hell," Blake yelled, turning back to face her, his fists balling up at his side. He so desperately wanted to hit her, but his father had taught him not to, although, given the circumstances…

"I *will* get rid of you, Blake Williamson." Melissa stepped closer. "Just like I got rid of your mother." She saw the confusion spread over his face and smiled her saccharine sweet smile. "That's right, I'll get rid of both of you." Turning, she spied the mirror, stormed over to it, and planted her ten inch heel right into the middle of the glass.

"No," Blake screeched. "No." Racing over to the wall, he fell to his knees and scooped up the glass. "No, no, no, no, no."

"That's what you get for your bad behaviour," Melissa sniped from behind. Spinning on her heel, she headed for the door.

"No," Blake screamed with every ounce of fury he had. He picked up a large shard of glass, ran after Melissa, grabbed a handful of her blonde bouffant, raised the glass, and sliced off the hair.

"Ah," she shrieked and spun around. Seeing the chunk in Blake's hand, she frantically grabbed at her hair, realised what he'd done, and saw the evil in his eyes.

He held the hair in his left hand, the shard in his

right, blood dripping from grasping it so tightly.

The other boys were in shock, jaws hanging, eyes wide, unable to say or do, let alone move.

"Blake," she screeched. "What have you done? My hair, my hair." Stumbling out the door, her stilettoed feet buckled underneath her, and her arms flailed for balance.

Snowball chose that moment to race up the stairs and around his mistress's legs.

"Snowball, no, argh." Melissa lurched, unable to grab the bannister, and tumbled down the flight of stairs from the attic to the first floor landing.

Snowball screeched like his mistress, bolted into the attic, and hid under one of the couches.

"Bloody hell!" Jarrod whispered, and the boys raced from the room and down to the landing to hear Melissa groan. "Better call the ambos."

Callum grabbed the phone from the side table and dialled triple zero, giving the address and condition of the patient.

"Where's Blake?" Adam asked, looking from friend to friend. The boys shrugged and he raced upstairs to see Blake still standing there, hair in left hand, glass in right. "Blake?" He touched his arm. "Blake?"

Mesmerised, Blake lowered both arms, silently turned, and walked over to the shattered mirror where he slumped to the floor and burst into tears.

Unsure of what to do, Adam left him and went back downstairs to the boys. "He's gone nuts. Now he's crying and his hand's bleeding from the glass."

"I called his dad after the ambulance. He's on his way," Callum said. "I'll go down and wait for them. Do we need to get our parents?"

"No, let Mr Williamson deal with this," Jarrod told him. "Blake clearly needs help dealing with his mum's death."

Five minutes later, the ambulance arrived and strapped a groaning Melissa onto the stretcher.

Five minutes after that, Michael arrived home to see his wife being wheeled out and the boys hovering around on the landing. He noticed Blake wasn't with them. "What happened, and where's Blake?"

They quickly told him and he raced upstairs to see his son sobbing in a heap surrounded by glass. "Blake, Blake. Oh God, son, are you okay?" Running over, he saw blood on Blake's hand and hair in the other. Recognising his wife's hair, he knelt down and wrapped his arms around his son. "Oh, Blake. What have you done?" Even though the boys had said she'd fallen over the cat and tumbled down the stairs, he'd also seen the chunk of hair missing from his wife's head. He saw that chunk fall from his son's hand along with the glass shard.

"She broke it," Blake sobbed. "She broke Mum's mirror. The one she loved. She did it on purpose. I hate her. I hate her and wish she was dead." Blood poured from the two long cuts on his hand, but he didn't notice.

Michael did, and pulled a handkerchief from his pocket and wrapped it around Blake's hand. Kissing his head, he gently helped his son to his feet and led him downstairs and out to the car, telling the boys to lock up and go home, as he was taking his son to the hospital.

CHAPTER FIVE

Seven hours later, in the dead of night, Michael drove into his driveway and turned off the ignition, glancing at a morose Blake leaning against the window. It had been a long seven hours. Seven hours of explanations *to* the doctors, *from* the doctors, *to* the police, who had been called, and from Melissa who had woken briefly to complain about his son and how he had assaulted her. When Michael repeated what the boys had told him, she relented and turned saccharine sweet, claiming a moment of frustration. Michael had told her they would talk when she was home, which wouldn't be for a few days. Those few days gave him time to spend with Blake.

Laying a gentle hand over his son's right bandaged one; he heaved a sigh and got out of the car. He helped Blake out and led him inside. Blake was comatose and silent. He hadn't spoken at all at the hospital, not to the doctors, the police, not even to him. Upstairs, he tucked him into bed, pulled the easy chair over from the window, and sat beside his son. They would be having a serious talk tomorrow.

Sometime in the middle of the night, Blake woke and saw his father by his bed, saw his bandaged hand, and remembered the events of that day. Melissa's nasty words and attitude, slapping him, smashing his mother's mirror. The blood in his veins bubbled, warming quickly to surge around his body, making him angry and hateful and full of vengeance.

He slipped out from under the covers, left his room and ascended the stairs to the attic. The room was lit by a faint glow from the moon, but it was enough for Blake to find his way to his mother's mirror and sit cross-legged in front of it. The glass had been swept up by the boys before they'd left, so he needn't worry about cutting himself. Again.

A deep sigh from the pit of his stomach escaped him and he closed his eyes to breathe. In and out. In and out.

"Mum," he whispered. "I need you, Mum. Please come back, Mum. I need you and want you here with me. Please come back." Tears welled in his green fourteen-year-old eyes. Eyes that his father said looked exactly like his mother's. The hot liquid rolled down his face, under his chin, and slid into the neckline of his t-shirt. "Mum, please come back."

Gasping, he wiped his face with the back of his left hand and looked up. The green glow was coming through the hole in the wall. The hole he'd completely forgotten about, considering everything else.

He got up, put his eye to it and looked. A hand was waving something around. He wasn't sure what; the green made things fuzzy. A person walked past and around whatever was in the centre of the room and waved their arm. The person was shorter than the other one, wasn't wearing an old leathery coat, and he could see long grey hair.

Wiping his blurry eyes, he saw another hand raise a large bowl of some kind. More things were sprinkled, he couldn't tell what, and the bowl was lowered. The person stepped aside as the green glow turned to yellow, to orange, to red, and a small explosion made it white.

Blake pulled his head back and blinked rapidly. His eyes were fuzzy and he rubbed them before looking again. He saw a raised arm, the one covered in the old leathery coat from days previously, and it swung what looked to be a machete downward. Two more chops and the other arm held up a severed head by its blonde hair, its eyes bulging out of their sockets.

"Argh." Blake stumbled backwards. It had been Melissa. But it couldn't possibly be. She was in the hospital, not being chopped up next door.

"Blake?" Michael came through the door and flicked on the light to see his son on the floor in front of the frame. "Blake? I heard you yell and saw you weren't in bed. What is it? What's going on with you?" He slid to the floor beside his son and took him into his arms.

"Head," Blake stuttered, pointing to the hole in the wall. "Cut head off."

"What?" Michael looked up at the hole. "What

do you mean, cut head off?"

"I looked; he cut a head off and held it up. He had a head." Blake stared in horror at the hole and watched his father get up to look. "No, don't."

"Don't be silly, Blake," Michael said, seeing the crazed expression on his son's face. "You were probably sleepwalking and dreamt it." He peered through the hole and saw nothing. "The room is dark and there's no one there."

"I know what I saw. We've seen it before," Blake stammered. "Eyes and hands and people and a green glow. We've seen it. The boys and me."

Michael looked again. "Well, there's nothing there now, and I have to wonder if you've been watching horror movies late at night to see stuff like that." He sat beside his son and took his left hand. "Tell me what happened today."

Fear travelled up Blake's insides. He'd never been scared of his father, and had no idea what he was going to do about the fact he'd cut his stepmother's hair off. Sighing, he looked down in shame. "I didn't mean to. She was being hateful and broke Mum's mirror."

"The boys told me the basics." Michael noted his son's shame-filled expression. "You called her a cow and she heard and threatened you with boarding school, you got into a screaming match and she slapped you then broke the mirror, to which you picked up a glass shard and cut her hair off. She stumbled out the door, tripped over the damn cat, and took a tumble down the stairs. Of course," his laugh was mechanical, "she blamed you. Made it all about how you did her wrong, and when I told her the boys had told me what happened, she relented. I can't believe she slapped you when I warned her not to."

Blake finally had the strength to look at his father. "I'm sorry. She hates me. I hate her. I didn't mean to. It's not something I planned; it just made me so angry when she stuck her stupid stiletto into Mum's mirror." He gazed forlornly at the empty frame.

"You know it wasn't really magical, right?" Michael gazed at his son's face. "She told you that as a kid when she made up stories."

"Yeah, I know. But it was a connection to her and now it's gone. She used to stand me in front of it and tell those stories. We'd travel into it and it took us to magical lands for exciting adventures." Blake's mind travelled back to happier times. "It was our time…" his voice trailed off and tears poured forth. "And now *she's* taken it away from me. She broke it." He blubbered like a baby, falling apart in his father's arms.

"Oh, Blake." Michael held his son. "It's been three years, but, I guess, I didn't consider how you were affected in all of this. I just worried about me and being happy again and finding someone to take care of us and be a mother to you."

"I had a mother," Blake managed through his tears. "I was still dealing with it when you met Melissa, and then you married her and it was all so quick. It was horrible. It made me think you didn't love Mum anymore."

"Of course I loved your mum, Blake," Michael soothed. "And a part of me still does and always will because she gave me you." He lifted his son's head and looked into his eyes. "She gave me you. And you're right. It did happen quickly, and maybe it shouldn't have."

"And maybe you should've married closer to your own age." Blake wiped his face with his bandaged hand. "She's not much older than me and wants me gone. She says so when you're not around."

"I know, the boys told me. But I'm not about to let her send you away. Okay?" He touched a thumb to his son's cheek to wipe away a tear. "This is your home before hers, and that's all there is to it."

"Doesn't make me feel better." He miserably stared at the frame. "What will we do about that?"

"It can be replaced," Michael replied. "Not the first time, either. I think it's broken about three times over the years. I'll take it to the shop tomorrow, but in the meantime, how about you get back to bed. You need your rest." He helped Blake to his feet and down to the bedroom where he tucked him in. "Try and get some sleep this time and not wander off."

"I'll try." Blake's smile was small, unsure, afraid. Had he sleepwalked before? He didn't think he had, had remembered getting out of bed and going up to the attic. Remembered the glow come through the hole. *What was that? Was that really a severed head? Are they killing people? The new neighbours? What do we really know about them?* They had moved in over a week ago and didn't interact with anyone else. While that may not have been weird to some, it was to him, especially when that weird green glow came through the hole and they saw arms flying through the air holding machetes and holding up heads. Heads that looked like Melissa's. *Why had it looked like Melissa's? I had to be dreaming, right? Melissa is in the hospital, so how would she have been next door? Not possible, right?* She wasn't dead, unless he was being lied to and she *was* dead and he wasn't being told. But then wouldn't the cops be all over the place? And should he call the cops on the house next door? But then he didn't know exactly *what was* going on next door. What were they actually doing? Experiments? Witchcraft and sorcery? Were they demons, zombies, vampires?

"Oh, for God's sake, don't be ridiculous," Blake muttered. "Now you sound like the boys with their stupid comments." Sighing, he rolled over and snuggled under his summer bedspread, hoping for a sweet dream to come.

*****

Next door, the couple shuffled into the attic and got back to work. Their job was to bring back the people needed most, and to get rid of those not wanted. They lived on the prayers and dreams of youngsters, feeding on them every night; hearing the cries and tears as the kids sobbed themselves to sleep in pain of heartbreak and depression. Depression over the loss of a favourite cat or the family dog. Or, more importantly, the loss of a parent or sibling. They fed on the emotion, and it was strong from next door. His cries swirled around the attic as they added a dash of wolfsbane to the potion in the brass bowl and watched it turn to smoke and rise upward.

The woman added a few herbs and spices to it, murmured a few words, and a green glow radiated from the potion, lighting up the whole attic and penetrating through the hole in the wall to next door.

They know he looked, had counted on it when they'd made the hole, knowing curiosity would get the better of him, knowing his attic was where his memories were kept hidden. They knew, they sensed it. It was strong within the boy. So was the hatred and anger, and they fed on it, making them stronger with each day. And soon they would be able to do the job they had come to do. Bring back what Blake wanted most, and take what he wanted least. For that was their job. That's what they had moved in to do. Give back what had been taken, and take what had been rejected. And Melissa was a bad, bad girl who had done some bad, bad things to get what she wanted.

CHAPTER SIX

Blake opened his eyes to another day. He was empty, unfeeling, unsympathetic. He had no sympathy for Melissa. No, he shouldn't have done what he did, but in his mind, she deserved it, especially after slapping him and then breaking the mirror. *Wonder what she's going to do now,* he thought. *She'll probably be real angry when she gets home and hate me even more. Try and convince Dad to send me off to boarding school until I'm twenty-one.*

"Is he awake?"

"Dunno. Find out."

Blake frowned and looked over his shoulder to see his friends. "Why are you whispering? And what time is it?"

"Ten," Jarrod said. "Your dad let you sleep in."

Callum threw back the curtain to let the bright sun flow in. "What are we doing today?"

Blake piled his pillows behind him and leant back, watching his friends jump onto the double bed either side of him. "I'm not really in the mood to do anything. And my hand kinda hurts." He glanced at the bandage.

"Did you get stitches?" Adam asked. "Can we see?"

"Yeah, a few," Blake replied. "I gotta take the bandage off for a shower anyway. Why are you here?"

"Come to see you, drongo," Jason told him. "Yesterday was not cool, dude."

Blake had the decency to look ashamed. "Yeah, I know. I ended up in the attic in the middle of the night and Dad found me. We talked. Not sure if it's better, though. Hey, guess what?" He went on to tell them what he'd seen through the hole, and that when his dad looked, he saw nothing. "I can swear I saw them hold up a severed head that looked like Melissa."

"Maybe you were sleepwalking and dreamt it. After what happened yesterday you would have her face in your mind," Jarrod suggested.

"I thought about that when I got back into bed, but it doesn't make much sense. I was awake; I *know* I was awake when I went up there. I *know* I was awake when I looked through the hole. I *know* I was awake when Dad came in because we talked about Mum and Melissa and what happened yesterday. I *know* I was awake. So, why did it look like Melissa? Why were they chopping off a head that looked like hers?" He sighed and slid down into the bed. "I dunno. I'm confused, and in a couple of days I'll need to deal with her when she comes home."

"Will your dad sort it out?" Callum asked, glad he didn't have the same issues as Blake.

"Hopefully," Blake said. "I doubt he'll divorce her, but things might be better."

"Will you have to apologise?" Adam swung a leg over the edge of the bed.

"Probably, but then so will she."

"Boys," Michael called from the landing. "Come downstairs while Blake has a shower and then you can do whatever." He stopped at the bedroom door. "Blake, I need to check your hand first."

"Can we see?" Jarrod piped up excitedly.

Michael grinned and walked over to the bed. "I guess." He unwrapped the bandage. "The doctors said it will take a few weeks to heal, but to clean it every day and put antiseptic cream on it. I'll do that after your shower." The bandage fell away to reveal Blake's war wounds. Two long parallel rows of black zigzagging stitches through angry red blotches. While the cuts were deep, they hadn't severed any nerves or arteries.

"Ew." The four boys screwed their noses up.

"Gross, dude," Callum added.

"And now you can go downstairs while Blake freshens up." Michael ushered them out while Blake wandered into his adjoining bathroom and carefully showered. Using his left hand, he managed to dress, and found everyone down in the kitchen snacking on cookies. They were the disgustingly healthy kind that Melissa allowed in the house. "So, what are we doing today?" He snatched a cookie and sat on the stool at the island bench waiting for his father to clean and wrap his hand.

"Nothing, unless you want to watch TV all day." Jason reached for another cookie. "Or practise that stupid dance routine of yours."

Blake munched the last bite of cookie and flinched. "Ow." He pulled his hand away. The pain had been like a thousand searing hot needles going into his hand.

"It might sting a bit." Michael dabbed the cuts with cream and then covered them in two Elastoplast strips.

"A bit." Blake frowned. "That was more than a bit." He watched his father wrap a clean bandage around his hand and pin it.

"As long as you stay inside, I don't really care what you do. I've got the next few days off to deal with this, and I'm taking a bag in to Melissa. We'll discuss how things are going to be. I'm going upstairs to pack a bag. Behave yourselves." He kissed the top of his son's head. "And have a better breakfast than a cookie."

"Yes, Dad," Blake mumbled and watched his father walk out of the room. Waiting until he heard footsteps and a door close upstairs, he turned to his friends. "I want to find out what's going on next door. Who's with me?" He looked expectantly at his friends.

"Uh, should we be going next door?" Adam asked. "If all of that really *is* going on, then they're the kind of people we need to stay away from."

"All right, we won't *go* next door, but we'll go and have *a look at* next door," Blake replied and stopped talking as his dad came clomping down the stairs.

"I'm off, boys. Stay out of mischief today," he told them and walked over to Blake. "Mel and I have a lot to talk about, so I might be awhile." He kissed his son and ruffled his hair. "And if you see Snowball, feed it."

"Yes, Dad," Blake mumbled. Snowball wasn't a bad cat; he just got treated better than Blake when it came to its owner. He waited for his dad to get in the car and back out of the drive before heading out the back into the garden.

"What are we doing?" Jarrod asked, following his friend to the back fence.

Blake turned around and stared at the townhouse next door. "Look. Attic windows are blacked out so you can't see in them, and the others are covered in thick curtains." He grabbed the fence, stepped onto the bottom railing and peered over. "Even on the ground floor the curtains are closed." Studying the backyard, he added, "And look. There's fresh dirt, like something's been buried."

"Or dug up. Maybe they planted veggies." Adam was beside Blake and looking over the fence at the fresh dirt patch. "Could be a garden."

"Could be a burial plot for dead bodies, too," Blake said. "I can't see anything. The backyard's completely clean, they don't have junk outside, and all the windows are covered. Let's go and look out the front." He carefully got down from the fence and the boys followed.

"Won't it look suspicious if we stand out the front of their house looking at it?" Jason asked, traipsing after the boys. "They'll know we're looking."

"Then we'll stand in my yard and look." Blake led the way through the house and out the front door, making sure he chained it back so it didn't slam shut. They walked down the drive to check the mailbox, and then wandered along the inside of the front fence until they reached the side fence. They could easily see that the neighbours' front yard was as clean as the back. No papers, no mail, and very short green grass.

"The windows are covered here, too," Blake said. "You can't see through, so the curtains must be black. But why would they have them closed on such a nice day?" His gaze travelled up to the attic. "And the attic windows look like they've been painted black. They're nailed shut, too. I saw it the other day when I stuck my head out the window. So, that's painted and nailed attic windows, curtains at all the others, nothing lying around to make people think they're not home, but we never see them. *What is* going on, and who the hell are these people?"

"Dunno. But I say we stop staring in case they see us," Jarrod said. "It's getting warm; let's go inside."

"Let's go next door," Blake suggested instead and took off for the driveway. He hurried along the street and into the neighbours' yard.

"Blake, what are you doing?" Callum muttered from behind him. The boys had rushed after him and all stood awkwardly on the front porch while Blake knocked.

"Introducing myself and welcoming the new neighbours to the hood," Blake replied. He knocked again. Silence echoed back.

"I don't think they're home." Jason backed away. "Let's go before they answer and invite us in."

"They could be vampires with all of that black paint and curtains," Adam suggested. "That's why they're not answering. They sleep during the day."

"Vampires don't exist." Blake knocked a third time and waited. "Did anyone see them go out?"

"Nope."

"Nope."

"Nope."

"Can we go?"

Sighing, Blake stepped away from the front door and stared out at the street. It was an ordinary neighbourhood in an ordinary suburb, in an ordinary city of Australia. Demons, vampires, werewolves didn't exist, but axe murderers did and might be right there. He still couldn't explain why he'd seen Melissa's head in the hand of the person in that house, or whether he'd dreamt it and been sleepwalking. One last glance at the door, and he walked down the stairs with the boys following and made his way down the driveway to the street. But something made him turn around. Something was making the hairs on the back of his neck stand on end and his gut pulsate.

He swept his eyes over the house from bottom to top, taking in each window until he saw one on the second floor. The curtains had been moved aside, as if someone was peering out, yet there was no one there. "Look." His finger extended.

The boys looked in the direction of his finger and saw the parted curtain, but saw no hand holding it back, saw no face peering down at them. Saw... nothing.

"Do you...?"

"Is there...?"

"There's no one," Adam stuttered. "The curtain's being held back, but there's no one there *to* hold it back. This is creepy. Let's get out of here." He rushed off with the others, but Blake stayed where he was, looking up at the window transfixed in place, unable to move, unable to breathe, unable to do. It's not that he didn't want to; he did. He wanted to move back to the house and barge through the door and up to the room that had the curtain pulled aside, because, as afraid as he was, and as reluctant to admit he was oh so wrong, he couldn't get over the fact that a person, a being, had appeared in the window, peering down at him, as he was peering up. And even though the others would think him crazy, and maybe he was, he could *and would* swear on a stack of bibles, even though he wasn't religious, that the person now standing in the window looking out behind the curtain was his mother.

CHAPTER SEVEN

"Blake, *come on*," Callum muttered from the Williamsons' front porch. "Come on."

Blake's eyes flicked from the window to Callum and back, but there was no longer anyone at the window, and the curtain was back in place as though it hadn't even been moved. "What the hell?" he breathed, desperately looking from window to window searching for his mother's face.

She wasn't there.

"Blake, come on," the boys urged, waving him over. "Come on."

Slowly, as if being washed along on a warm ocean wave, Blake drifted down the street, up his driveway, and into his home.

"*What the hell was that?*" Jarrod gabbled as they moved into the lounge room and sat down. "The curtain was back, but no one was holding it. Is the place haunted?"

"Maybe they were hiding," Callum suggested. "To freak us out."

"Which they did," Adam replied. "It looked like

there was no one there."

"There was," Blake said softly, staring into the distance, not connecting with the other boys.

They stopped talking and stared at Blake. "You saw someone?"

"My mother." Blake's eyes glazed over, and his brain worked overtime to explain what he's just seen.

"Dude, what?" Callum glanced at the others. "You couldn't have."

"But I did." Blake's voice was whimsical. "I saw her, after you'd run away. She was staring down at me, like I was staring up at her. I saw her. She was there, next door, looking down at me." His fingers absentmindedly picked at his bandage. "She's alive."

"Dude…no…" Jason mumbled. "Your mum's not alive. She died."

Blake focussed. "Then what the hell did I see next door?" He got up and moved around the room. "I saw her, like I see you numbskulls right now. I *can't* be seeing things?"

"You haven't been in your right mind lately," Adam gently reminded him. "You cut your stepmother's hair off, for God's sake, and cut your hand in the process. You've been crying a lot, and you're probably depressed."

"My mother's alive, I saw her. She's supposed to have died three years ago, but that could be a lie. I never saw her body after the accident. Dad wouldn't let me. I *never* saw her dead." Frowning, he stopped pacing around the room and remembered back to yesterday. "Did anyone else hear Melissa say she'd gotten rid of Mum and she'd get rid of me, too?"

The boys thought back. "I vaguely remember something," Callum said.

"What was it she said?" Blake muttered. "*I will get rid of you, Blake Williamson, just like I got rid of your mother. That's right; I'll get rid of you both.* Oh, my God, does that mean she killed my mother?" Blake spun around to his friends. "Does that mean she killed my mother? And then latched onto my father? Oh, my God, we're living with a murderer?"

"Calm down, dude." Jarrod put his hands up, palms out, to pacify his friend. "It means no such thing. She probably just said that to get you riled up, which you are. She just probably wasn't expecting you to do what you did."

"Neither was I," Blake replied. "I didn't know I'd ever do that. That freaked me out. But so has seeing my mother next door. I need to get into that house." He spun around and headed for the attic.

"What! No, you don't," the boys cried and followed him. They found him peering through the hole. "Dude, you don't need to get into that house."

"I do. I need to know what's going on. Why I saw my mother in the window, where the green glow's coming from, and what the hell they do in that room." Blake pulled away from the wall. "We could break it down and get through."

"Dude, seriously?" Jarrod said. "You're considering breaking down the wall just to see what they do next door? Are you nuts? You need to see some sort of grief counsellor. You've gone nuts."

"I'm not nuts, I just want my mother back," Blake yelled then burst into tears, falling to the floor and sobbing. "I miss her. I want her back."

"Ah, geez. What do we do?" Jason scratched his head, perplexed by the situation. "We can't fix this."

"Watch him until his dad comes home, I guess. We can't leave him alone," Adam replied. "Maybe we should practise our dance routine, get his mind off it." He looked at the others who all shrugged.

Blake wiped his face. "I don't want to. Just leave me alone." He got to his feet, stumbled over to the couch, picked up the photo album that had been left there, and hugged it to his chest. "Just leave me alone." Curling up on the couch, he sobbed some more.

"We can't leave him alone," Jarrod whispered. "We have to stay here until his dad gets back."

"But that could be ages." Jason watched his friend bawl his eyes out.

"We could go downstairs and wait. Make sure he doesn't leave, or go next door, or something," Callum added. "What if he tries to break in next door? They'll call the cops."

"I doubt it," Adam told him. "Not if they're as secretive as we think they are. They won't want the cops in there."

"Won't want a bunch of kids either," Jarrod muttered and looked over at his best friend. "Let's give him some privacy." He led them down to the kitchen where they grabbed sodas and sat around talking.

"Should we call his dad?" Adam asked. "He said

he'd be a while, but still, it looks like he's on the verge of a breakdown. He needs to get help, and what will happen when Mrs Williamson gets home? It will be all-out war for those two. Especially if he accuses her of murder."

"We need to tell his dad before she comes home, so he can do something about it." Callum fidgeted in his seat. "We sure can't fix it. And he'll want to know."

"So, do we wait until he gets home or not?" Jarrod asked.

The boys glanced at each other then looked at the clock.

Blake flicked over the page in the album, coming to the last page. It was from his tenth birthday and his mother and father were in all of them. His friends were all there, he was showing off his presents, and his mother was kissing him on the cheek. A small smile lit up his lips and he closed the album and picked up the next one. His eleventh birthday started it off and he and his parents had gone to the local theme park with his friends. There were pictures of them eating hotdogs and ice creams, and on all of the rides. There were three double pages of photos, all with dates and small messages underneath as his mother had kept records of everything. He was smiling his toothy grin, as were his parents. All happy, all healthy, all together in the one photo. All together in the one house, the one time, the one place in their lives before it all went to hell.

He flipped over the page and came to two pages

of photos of his twelfth birthday. That's all there was. Two pages of photos. Not the usual six, just two, because his dad hadn't taken many that year. The year he turned twelve. Because his mother was gone. Had *been* gone for nearly a year. She'd died two days after her son's eleventh birthday, so on his twelfth, he knew it was almost a year since his mother had passed. It wasn't a happy occasion; he was quite depressed in the photos. They'd had it at the house, a few streamers and balloons, a cake, not the usual festive fare his mother would set up, but his father had tried the best he could. And his friends' mothers had helped, but it wasn't the same. He was spending his twelfth birthday without his mother. His rock, his guide, his parent. She was his whole world and she was gone, and he was miserable and depressed. It showed in the photos. The light and laughter in him was gone. It was the same with his dad. He studied the photos of him and his father. His father's smile was grim, his was non-existent.

He flipped to the next page and found his thirteenth birthday. He still looked depressed; not just because two days later it would have been the second anniversary of his mother's death, but because Melissa was in the picture. She'd married his father not quite a year earlier and insinuated herself into their lives, changing the décor of the house, blowing through his father's money. She was smiling, but it wasn't a bright happy one, more of an 'I hate my stepson' kind of one. His dad was definitely happy in them; he had a new wife that was nearly half his age, not much older than his son. And, of course, *he* looked miserable. He was turning into a teenager without his mother. The woman who gave birth to him. Meanwhile, the woman who had married his father was taking over the whole family. His whole life. Boarding school had been constantly brought up, especially since he'd turned thirteen, and she always wanted to flit off somewhere on holiday, completely forgetting Blake existed until his dad reminded her.

Two pages, one double page spread; that's all his thirteenth birthday had taken up.

Flipping the page, he found them blank, remembering that they hadn't even had them printed yet.

She had been gone for three years, and it had been two years since Melissa had moved in. Too damn soon as far as he was concerned. He remembered back through the last few birthdays, wishing his mother was still alive, dreading his birthday every year since, because it meant two days later was the anniversary of her death. The day she had left him, this earth, this mortal coil, his father, this house, their life together as a little family.

And then…*Melissa.*

Melissa turned up out of the blue to woo my father and take his love away from my mother, Blake seethed inside. *She took my father away from me just like she took Dad's love away from Mum. And if you did have anything to do with my mother's death, so help me, Melissa, I will take you down. You don't get to take my mother and then my father from me. No, you don't.*

He thought back a few months to his birthday. She hadn't bothered, but his father had. Balloons, streamers, a huge racing car cake. His friends had all been in the backyard playing. It had been better, a better birthday than his thirteenth or twelfth, but not as good as his eleventh. The last birthday he had with his mother. The last birthday that mattered. The ones since hadn't and probably never would. No other birthday would matter except for that one. The last one. The last one with his mother. The woman who raised him, loved him, held and cuddled him. The one who took him on adventures in her mirror and told stories to keep him amused and send him to sleep. The mother who kissed his scrapes better, packed his school lunches, helped him with homework. The mother who turned up to parent-teacher night, helped out in the school canteen, volunteered for school fetes, and sewed costumes for school plays. She was the world. She was perfect. She was his mother.

Going back to his last birthday with her, he slid a photo out of the album and kissed it. "I love you, Mum. I miss you so much. I want you here so badly. Why did you have to leave? Why did God have to take you? Why did you have to leave me, Mum? I want you back, come back, Mum," he sobbed, clutching the photo to his lips and letting the rivers of tears flow freely. "Come back."

He was so busy crying, he didn't notice the green glow through the hole in the wall.

"Mum." He wiped his face with his arm and bandaged hand. "Mummy, come back." Falling back onto the couch, he stretched his legs to ease the cramps, sobbing until he fell into a restless sleep.

CHAPTER EIGHT

"Blake," whispered softly through the attic. "Blake."

"Mum?" His eyes blinked open. "Mummy?"

"Blake."

"Mum, is that you?" He leaned up on one elbow and cast a glance around the room. "Mum?"

"Blake, come to me, sweetie. I'm here."

"Mum?" His legs swung to the floor and moved him into a standing position, his eyes frantically looking around the space. "Mum. Where are you? I'm coming, Mummy."

"Blake. I'm here, sweetie. Come to me. Mama's here."

"Where? Mum, I can't see you."

"Look into the hole in the wall, sweetie. Come to me, Blake."

"Mum." He moved over to the hole in the wall and peered through. Seeing nothing at first, he said, "Mum, where are you? I can't see you."

The green glow burst forth from the attic next door, blinding him. His hands flew to cover his eyes and he looked away, stumbling back. "Mum," he yelled. "Where are you?"

"I'm here, sweetie. Come to me."

"Mum?" Blake peered around his arms, trying to see, but saw nothing except the green glow growing bigger and bigger.

"Let go, Blake. Let go and come to me."

Blake lowered his hands and looked head on. "Mum, where are you?"

"I am here, Blake. Come, sweetie."

"Argh." The green glow hooked into his eyes, stabbing through them. A slither snaked out and stabbed him through the chest, lifting him until he was levitating and swathed in green.

"Was that Blake?" Jarrod asked, and they all looked at the ceiling.

"We'd better go find out what he's done now," Callum replied. "Come on." They headed out of the kitchen, but hadn't made it to the stairs when they heard Blake yell again. They raced up the stairs, and tried to enter the attic, but the door wouldn't budge.

"Blake." They banged and yelled. "Let us in."

"Argh." Blake had no control over what was happening. He was levitating mid-air, being controlled by the green glow that grew bigger and bigger.

"Blake," Callum yelled, slamming his hand on the door and twisting the knob. "We need to get in there. On the count of three, altogether. One, two, three." The boys all hit the door with their shoulders.

It budged, but didn't open.

"Again. One, two, three." The boys lurched into the door. It flung open, and they all landed on the floor sprawled behind Blake as he floated in the air.

"Whoa," Jason gasped, watching as the adjoining wall gave way, the hole growing bigger to envelop the whole wall. The glow came through and slowly reeled Blake towards it.

"Argh." Blake struggled, his breath harder and harder to control. "Argh, Mum."

"It's okay, sweetie. We'll be together in a moment."

"Mum." He couldn't see. His eyes were full of green, his arms and legs flailed.

"Blake," Jarrod yelled. "Blake." He tried to get up, but an invisible force kept him down. There was a breeze swirling around the room and he saw a couple standing in the attic next door. Flinging his arms up to his eyes to block out the light, he tried to focus on the room, but could barely make out the people. "Stop it," he yelled. "Let him go."

Blake floated through the hole in the wall unable to see anything, just hearing his mother's voice beckoning him.

"Blake," the boys yelled and tried scrambling to their feet as their friend disappeared into the house next door. "Blake."

The green glow disappeared. The wall was back to normal. And the boys fell to their hands and knees.

In the neighbours' attic, Blake collapsed to his feet as the glow dwindled. "Ugh." He slumped to the floor on all fours, gasping in air as the pain dissipated in his chest. His eyes burned, and squeezing them shut, he sobbed, "Mummy."

"Not yet, dear. But soon," the woman said, watching him collapse on the floor. "Soon."

"Mummy." He curled up into a ball. His body ached, his vision hadn't cleared, and he had no idea of what was happening.

"Blake?" Adam called. "Blake." The boys looked at the wall in front of them. "Did we just…? Did he just…? Did we…?"

"Could *not* have just seen that," Jason mumbled, scratching his head in disbelief.

"Blake?" Jarrod scrambled over and peered through the hole. "Blake?" he yelled, banging on the wall. "Blake."

The other boys joined him, banging and yelling Blake's name.

"What do we do? We did just see that, right? I mean, we weren't seeing things, and that didn't really…did it…did it really just happen…?" Callum mumbled.

"Well, he's not here anymore." Jarrod stood back and scanned the wall. "So, he's got to be somewhere, and we all just saw that green glow, right?" He got nods all round. "Did we…*really* just see that?"

The boys traded glances.

"Seems so," Adam said. "What are we gonna do about it?"

"We have to get him back," Jason said. "How do we do that?"

"Break down the wall," Callum suggested.

"Don't think Mr Williamson would appreciate that," Adam replied.

"Go next door," Jarrod said. "Break in if we have to, and if anyone says anything, we'll say they kidnapped Blake."

"And *how* do we break in?" Callum asked.

"Through the door or window," Jarrod replied. "Come on, we have to find Blake. So, do we go front or back?"

"Better go back so no one sees us," Callum said. "Let's go."

The boys raced downstairs, out the back, and found lawn chairs to stand on to give them a boost over the fence.

Jarrod landed on all fours and quickly stood, brushing off his hands as Callum and Adam came after him. "Wait." He stopped Jason. "We don't have anything to break in with. Go and find something from the garden shed."

Jason jumped down and ran over to the shed, glad it wasn't padlocked. He found several hammers and a crowbar and ran back to the fence. Standing on the chair, he threw them over. "Here." He jumped the fence and the boys took their tools to the back door.

"Let's try the door before we break a window," Jarrod suggested, and they tried opening it with the crowbar.

"Damn it, it won't give," Callum sputtered. "Looks like window it is." After trying to jimmy the lock, they decided to just smash the glass and crawl in.

Praying that no one heard, they tapped the glass

until it shattered, swiped around the edge with their tools, and pulled the curtain aside. Light flooded into the room and they saw no furniture, no rugs, no person. Using the curtains to cover the window pane so they didn't cut themselves, they boys climbed inside.

*****

Upstairs in the attic, Blake lay resting on an old couch.

The man and woman had been getting everything ready for the spell to work. They had their herbs and spices, their fancy ingredients, and knew it wouldn't be long.

"Mmm." Blake stirred and opened his eyes. "Mum?"

"Not yet," the woman said, coming over to him. "It will take some time for the spell to work, and even then, she won't be back in full."

Blake saw the woman and scrambled backwards. "Who are you? What are you?" He glanced around the room and saw the man towering over him. "Argh. Who are you? Who are you people? Where am I?"

"You're in our attic," the woman said. "We are Dream Gifters. We make children's dreams come to life. Make them a reality. Bring back your loved ones when you cry out for them. But," she glanced at the man, "it doesn't always go as planned. So, you must be ready for the consequences, Blake Williamson. Are you ready for them?" She sat on the end of the couch watching him intently.

"Who are you?" Blake's eyes moved from one to the other. "What do you mean; you can bring loved ones back? Can you bring my mum back? I saw her in your window earlier. I heard her voice." His heart hammered in his chest, the blood raced in his veins, but he wasn't sure if it was from fear or excitement. He quickly caught glimpses of their attic. Dead animals hanging from the rafters, a large bench in the centre of the room. Lamps dully lit the place since the windows were painted black, and shelves were full of bottles and jars filled with fluids and weird things. He gulped, and looked at the man and woman. "Why have I seen Mum in your window?"

"We are Dream Gifters," the woman repeated. "We bring back the dead to make children happy. We make dreams come true by bringing back their loved ones. But it does come at a cost."

"What cost?" Blake blurted. "Tell me what I need to do to bring my mother back."

The woman looked at the man. "For every action, there is a reaction, for every choice, there is a consequence. And if we bring your mother back to life, then there *must* be a consequence."

"What? What is it? I just want my mum back," Blake pleaded.

*****

Downstairs, the boys made their way into the hallway off the ground floor. The whole house was dark, but they were able to make out the outline of the stairs and find their way up to the first floor.

"I wish we'd brought a torch," Adam whispered. "It's so dark."

The light came on overhead, and they blinked in surprise, standing stock still in case they'd been caught out.

"Shoulda just turned the light on." Jason shrugged and the others looked at him. "Do we really have time to waste in the dark?"

*****

"Tell me what I have to do," Blake pleaded with the woman. "I just want my mother back."

The woman laid a hand on his arm. "If we bring your mother back, there will be a consequence. For one to come back, one must go. Who will that be?"

Blake frowned, trying to understand what the woman was saying. "You mean, if Mum comes back, then someone else must die in her place?"

The woman nodded.

It only took a second for Blake to think. "Melissa. Take her. She killed Mum."

"Do you know that?" the woman asked.

"Not for sure. But she said something the other day, that she got rid of my mother and she'll get rid of me, too. What did she do?" He swung his feet to the floor and faced them both. "Did she kill my mother? Do you know?"

"The vibe is strong in her," the woman muttered.

"The vibe is strong around you, Blake. Your mother has been gone just on three years, and things will have changed. Your mother may not be the same, but you will have her back just the same."

*****

The boys made their way up to the top floor and the attic door. The whole house was a replica of Blake's, just a really old derelict version of it.

Jarrod tried the handle, but the door wouldn't budge. "We'll have to shove it open," he whispered to the others.

"Can you hear anything?" Adam kept his voice low and his ears pricked.

Jarrod placed an ear against the door. "No."

"Why won't she be the same? She looked the same and sounded the same. I want my mother back," Blake sobbed.

"Because she has been gone for three years. She will *never* be the same. So, you must weigh up whether you want the memory of how your mother was, or the body of what will be." She cast another glance at her companion. "And it may not work out for the better."

"S-so," Blake stuttered, wiping his face. "She'll end up a monster?"

"One, two, three, heave," Jarrod cried and the boys went sailing through the doorway to land at the feet of the giant.

"Guys," Blake cried out.

"Hey." The boys looked up, but saw the man, screamed, and backpedalled.

"Wait, it's all right, stop," Blake yelled. "It's okay. They haven't hurt me."

Keeping an eye on the man who hadn't moved, Jarrod slowly climbed to his feet. "What have they done?"

"Nothing, but they're going to give me my mother back," Blake told him.

"What!" Callum studied the man. He was well over six feet, and broad like a house, with an old, leathery weather-beaten oilskin coat, long grey matted hair down his back, long grey beard, and grizzled features. "*How* are they going to do that?" He and the boys inched their way around the room so they were closer to Blake.

"I don't know." Blake's head swivelled to the woman. "How?"

"We need a picture of your mother. We put it into a brew, cast a spell, and within a week she'll be back."

"Why a week? And will that mean Melissa will die and Mum will be back and we can be a family again?" Blake asked.

The woman's hand gripped his arm. "Understand this, Blake Williamson. Your mother *will not* be the same. She *will not* be the way you remember her. And for her to come back fully, one must die in her place. And the consequences I mentioned; it may not be the one you want to die. Whoever answers the door to her, will be the next one taken."

"What do you mean, whoever answers the door?" All of this was freaking Blake out, confusing him, raising him with hope at having his mother back, and then letting him go with the idea of another dying in her place.

"When souls come back they need to be invited. When they knock three times, whoever answers the door will be taken in their place," she explained.

"So, Mum will come back and knock three times," Blake said. "As long as she comes back, I don't care."

"You might," the woman told him. "You have to be absolutely certain you want this."

"Blake, what are you doing?" Adam asked. "You know you can't bring your mother back. She's been gone for three years."

"She'll be a zombie," Jason added. "Not all there, and not the mum you used to have."

"I don't care. I want my mother back," Blake said stubbornly, looking from his friends to the woman. "Bring her back. I want my mother back."

"No, Blake, you can't." Jarrod looked at the couple. "Whatever you're doing, stop it now. It won't work. Don't do it. Blake, you can't."

"I want to," Blake spat crossly. "I want my mother back."

"And if she isn't the way you want her? Or Melissa doesn't die? What then? Isn't that it? You want Melissa dead and your mum back?" Adam wished they could get out of there and it all be a dream.

"Yes, I want her dead, and I want my mum back."

Blake looked from Adam to the woman. "Do it. Do it. I want my mum back."

The woman nodded and got to work, throwing herbs, spices, and dead animals into a huge brass bowl. She murmured words from an ancient book of spells and stirred until the green glow spread around the room.

"Whoa," Jason breathed. "There's that green glow." The boys stood wide-eyed, staring at the bowl as the glow grew.

"Blake, don't do this," Jarrod whispered fiercely. "What if it backfires and all goes horribly wrong? What if your mother doesn't come back, or Melissa doesn't die, or someone else does. Like you or your dad?"

"I don't care. I want my mum back and Melissa gone." Blake walked over to the table to watch, waiting until the woman had finished.

"We just need a picture and we are done," she said. "Are you sure you want this? Are you sure you want your mother back regardless of the consequences? Regardless of who will die?"

Blake nodded. "I want my mother."

"Then remember. She will come hunting for you. She will knock three times and then three more. She will knock on every door she comes across until she finds the one she seeks, and the one who answers will be sacrificed for her return."

Blake gulped. "Okay."

"No," Jarrod yelled and pulled Blake away. "No. You can't do this. This is not happening. This can't be real. These people can't bring the dead back. They can't bring your mother back. Hell, we didn't know they existed until now. And what are they? Witches?"

"Dream Gifters," the woman told him. "We heal broken hearts by bringing back what broke them."

"What utter rot," Jarrod went on, grabbing Blake by both arms. "Let's get out of here. This is garbage, and you're being tricked. Let's go." He pulled Blake toward the door and the boys hustled around them.

"No, I won't go, I want my mother," Blake yelled, flinging his arms around to fend off Jarrod. "Let me go."

"No, let's go. Grab him, boys," Jarrod instructed.

But before they knew it, they were levitating, surrounded by the green glow that had held Blake previously, in front of the table and the couple.

"Do you want this, Blake?" she asked.

"Yes, yes. I want my mother," he yelled.

"Then remember, she will knock three times and then three again. Do not answer it, or you will die. *She* must answer." The woman opened the hole in the wall so all five boys could fit through. "Remember, she will knock three times." Flicking her hand, she sent the boys through the hole to land with a thud in Blake's attic.

From his hand, the photo of him and his parents fluttered to her feet and she picked it up, ripped out Blake's mother, and threw it into the bowl.

"Oomph!" The boys groaned and sat up. Looking around, they found themselves back in Blake's attic.

Blake checked his bandaged hand. "Oh, no, the picture. It's missing. The picture of Mum, Dad and me on my eleventh birthday. I had it when they took me." He quickly checked the floor and his pockets, realising he must have dropped it in the neighbours' attic.

"Oh, no, Blake," Jarrod whispered and they all stared at him in horror. "What have you done?"

KNOCK, KNOCK...
WHO'S DEAD?

CHAPTER ONE

"What do you mean, what have *I* done?" Blake's head whipped around to face Jarrod. "*I* want my mother back. *I* want Melissa gone. Do you think *I* magically took myself through the wall?" He pointed to it. "Do you think *I* conjured that green glow and spiked myself with its tentacles, then opened the hole in the wall and took myself through it? I had *no* control over that," he spat. "All I want is for my mum to be alive." Breathing hard, he deflated. "I just want my mum."

"We know you do." Callum felt sorry for his friend. "But she's been gone for three years. People die, Blake. We *all* will one day. Your dad will, *our* parents will. It's just life even though it sucks."

Blake sobbed through his words. "I know. I just want her back so bad."

"And maybe if your dad hadn't married Melissa so quick, you'd be doing a lot better and dealing with it," Jason added. "But bringing her back won't make it better, and that's even if those whack jobs next door manage to do that, because she won't be the same. Even *they* told you that." He slid over to his friend and put an arm around his shoulders. "Dude, we are so sorry you lost your mum after your birthday three years ago. We know what you went through, we saw it, we were there trying to help you through. But if it's still killing you, maybe it's time to talk to a professional. Try and talk it out, work through it. It might make you feel better. Might help you and Melissa sort your problems out."

"I don't want to sort out my problems with Melissa. I want her gone." Blake looked at his friend through watery eyes. "She's done nothing but ruin what we had. What we were going through. We didn't even have a chance to deal with Mum being gone before she came along and hooked her claws into Dad. And she *never* wanted me. Never wanted me around, never paid me any attention unless Dad was around. And even then it was all fake. As fake as she is. It's pathetic. The way she dug her claws into Dad so soon after losing his wife. She didn't even give him time to grieve. And then he didn't give *me* time to grieve before marrying her. She just messed everything up and I hate her for it. And if her dying means I can get my mother back, then so be it." He got to his feet, ran out of the attic and down to his room, slamming the door behind him. Throwing himself face first down on the bed, he wept for three years' worth of pain and heartache, despair and heartbreak. He would never get over losing his mother. Not in a million years.

"So…what do we do now?" Adam asked sombrely

as the boys got to their feet. "Do we tell Mr Williamson about all of this?"

"What? About those crazy kooks next door?" Jarrod returned. "What *would* we say? That a big green glowing thing stuck its tentacles through Blake, opened up the wall in the attic, and carried him through? Yeah, he'd believe that. Or the one about us breaking in next door to get Blake back? Or how the old kook next door opened the wall again and flung us all back through? Which story do you want to tell him, and which one do you think he'll believe?" Jarrod looked from Callum to Jason to Adam. "Huh? What will he believe?"

Adam shrugged in defeat. "I dunno. But we need to tell him something. Blake's really going off his rocker, and now those kooks, as you called them, have him believing they'll bring his mother back. Whack jobs galore next door."

"Maybe we could call the cops and tell them what happened? That they're making magic potions in their attic," Jason suggested.

"Yeah." Jarrod rolled his eyes. "Coz that'll be better for them to believe us."

"Well...I don't know." Jason shoved his hands in his shorts pockets. "At least it's an idea. What's yours?"

Jarred sighed and ran a hand through his hair. "I dunno either. Maybe we should just tell Mr Williamson Blake's not doing well and should see a counsellor. He'll probably think it's a good idea."

"I suppose," Callum said. "The whole family needs it."

Knock. Knock. Knock.

The sound on the front door startled them.

Knock. Knock. Knock.

The boys raced out the door to peer over the bannister and saw Blake bolt from his room.

He looked up at them before flying down the stairs for the door.

"You can't open the door," Jarrod yelled. "Remember what they said. The person who opens the door will die." The boys raced down the stairs.

Blake had come to a screeching halt in the entrance foyer, excited, but scared at the prospect of seeing his mother again. He saw the shadow on the other side of the door move.

Knock. Knock. Knock.

A frown crossed Blake's face. *They didn't say it would knock again.* Walking over to the window, he peered out and sighed in relief. "Just the mailman." He opened the door and added, "Hey, Mr Rockwell."

"Hello, young Blake. How are you today? I have some mail for your mum and dad." Mr Rockwell had been the mailman for twenty years, long before Blake's family had even moved in.

"Dad and Melissa," Blake corrected. "My mum's dead."

"Ah." Rockwell froze. "Yes, sorry. Your dad and Melissa. Are they home? They need to sign for these."

"At the hospital. I'll do it." Blake took the machine and signed his name, and was then given the thick wad of envelopes. "Thanks, Mr Rockwell. I'll make sure Dad gets them when he gets home."

"Okay, Blake. Have a good day, boys." Rockwell nodded to the group that crowded behind Blake and received waves in return.

Shutting the door, Blake flipped through the mail, but most looked like bills. Walking into the kitchen, he slapped them onto the counter and grabbed a soda from the fridge. "Help yourselves." He then wandered into the back sitting room and settled into an easy chair.

"Are you going to tell your dad what happened?" Jarrod asked, sitting on the couch opposite.

"Tell him what?" Blake shrugged a shoulder. "There's nothing *to* tell."

"About the crazy kooks next door," Jason replied, noting the frown on his friend's face.

"What about them?" Blake looked at him. "Do you think anyone will believe a word we say about any of that? Hell, for all we know, they don't actually exist. So, *what would* I tell him?" He set his can on the side table and rubbed his weary eyes. "I dunno. I'm exhausted, and Dad'll be home soon and he'll want to talk about Melissa, and *I don't* want to talk about Melissa, but we can hardly talk about what happened next door today, can we?" Sighing, he added, "Maybe you boys should just go home."

"We're staying until your dad gets back, so you're not alone," Callum said.

They heard the car in the driveway.

"*And* he's back." Blake wearily got to his feet and padded down the hall to greet his father.

"Hey, there you are." Michael closed the door

behind him. "Have a good day?"

Blake moved into his father's arms and wrapped his around his father's waist.

"Hey, what's going on?" Surprised, Michael hugged his son, seeing the equally surprised expressions on the boys' faces. "What is it? What's wrong?"

"Just tired." The words left Blake's mouth, but he barely heard them. "Tired of Mum not being here. Tired of missing her. Tired of the fights with Melissa. Tired of being hated and unwanted. Tired of not dealing with all of it."

Michael felt the exhaustion seep from his son's body into his and match his own. "I know." He rested his chin on Blake's head. "That's why I've set up counselling for all of us. Together and individually."

Blake looked at him in surprise. "Did Melissa agree to that?"

Michael's smile was grim. "She had no choice. It was counselling, or a separation."

Pulling out of his father's arms in shock, Blake added, "What? You're leaving her?"

"No." Michael's voice was firm. "I told her we all needed counselling, and if she didn't agree and attend every session, we would separate for six months while we sorted our issues out. And she would have to find a job to support herself and a place to live."

"I'm surprised she didn't threaten to kick us out instead." Blake's brows rose, more surprised by the moment.

"She can't." Michael's smile turned to a grin. "This townhouse belongs to you in trust. I just pay the mortgage."

"What!" Blake's brows came down and his mouth turned into an o shape.

"That's part of what we need to talk about," Michael told him then looked at the boys. "Time to go home. I'll see you back here tomorrow."

"Uh, okay, Mr Williamson," Jarrod muttered and led the way out the door. He lightly punched Blake on the arm as he passed, as did the other boys.

Michael closed the door behind them and turned to Blake. "It's dinnertime; you hungry?" Sliding an arm around his shoulders, he led him down the hall and into the kitchen.

"Not really," Blake muttered and watched his father walk over to the fridge. "What did you mean when you said, this house is mine?"

Sighing, Michael turned around with a pack of meat and a bag of frozen vegetables. He pointed to the island bench seats. "Sit down and I'll tell you while I make dinner." He removed the wok from the cupboard and turned on the stove, then started frying the meat *and* telling the story.

"When your mum and I met, we were both starting out at the law firm I'm now partner of. We were in our early twenties, fresh out of law school, and we both wanted to make a big difference in the world. That's what drew us together. We worked for two and a half years together before dating, and then dated for another two and a half years. At thirty, we were associates and on the up and up. But your mother didn't want to go farther with her career because she wanted to be a mum. Especially when I proposed *after* we became associates." He added the vegetables and set the cooktop to low.

"We were married within a year and fell pregnant with you straight away. Your mum was so happy that she resigned from the firm to be a full-time mum and she loved it." Slowly stirring the food, he took a slow deep breath before continuing.

"Two years later, she became pregnant again, and was so ecstatically happy. But…" He glanced at his son who sat fascinated. "She lost the baby due to complications and that also meant she lost the ability to have more children." Fetching two bowls from the cupboard behind him, he stopped a moment. "She was devastated at not being a mother again, so she threw herself into looking after you."

Turning, he set the bowls down before looking at his son. "You were the only one we were able to have, and while that devastated her, she knew that made you special in every way. She doted on you." A small smile lit up his face. "You were her everything. Her whole world. And she spent all day every day with you and loved you every minute of it. And that's why she wanted to make sure you were set for life." Michael gave the meal a stir and tasted it. "Just a bit longer." He opened the cutlery drawer and then paused, the spoons in mid-air. "That's why she made me set up a trust fund for you."

CHAPTER TWO

"She *made* you what?" Blake repeated.

Michael's smile grew soft. "Didn't take a lot of convincing, if any. As a lawyer, I knew she was right, and as our only child, we had to protect you in case something happened to one or both of us."

"It did," Blake's voice was low. So was his frown.

"Yes," Michael replied sadly. "And that's what we planned for. We were living in a small two bedroom apartment. Well, more a one bedroom and a study-turned-nursery apartment and knew it was time for a home of our own. Your mum found this townhouse and we renovated it before moving in. We had saved good money and had it paid off in two years. Then we invested in a property west of here, and two years after, in another east of here. But your mother didn't want to move, she loved it here and so did you."

He dished out the stir fry and carried the bowls to the table, waiting for Blake to seat himself before continuing. "Your mother insisted on taking out life insurance for both of us. With me moving up the corporate ladder and taking on bigger cases, it was important if something happened to me."

"But it happened to Mum instead." Blake raised his spoon, looked at the food, and put it down again. "It happened to Mum instead."

"Yes…it did." Michael's voice was soft, almost whimsical. "And I'm sorry for how things have turned out since. I haven't handled that well at all."

"Nope, you haven't," Blake replied. "You said this place was in my name?"

Sighing, Michael went on. "Yes. Your mother insisted that to take care of you, if anything should happen to either of us, one of the life insurances should go straight into a trust fund for you. No one could touch it without a parent, guardian, or judge's signature. You can't touch it until you're eighteen, and even then, it's under supervision until you're twenty-one. All of our estates, like this townhouse, is in trust for you. Everything is in your name upon your parent's death. No one else can touch it."

"Melissa?" Blake raised a brow at his father.

"Not even Melissa," Michael replied, relieved at that fact.

"You said you were paying it off before, but then you said you and Mum paid it off in two years. Is it paid for or not?"

"It was," Michael conceded. "And then I met Melissa. I stupidly mortgaged it so I had money to impress her. Now my salary is paying it off, *again*. Should be done by early next year."

Blake sighed. "Always comes back to bloody Melissa."

"Yes, and I'm sorry for rushing things with her." He laid a hand on Blake's arm. "I was so desperately lonely after your mother died, and I wanted a mother for you so you didn't finish growing up without one."

"She's too young to be a mother, and she doesn't care *about* me, or in raising me. She only cares about herself and her stupid cat."

"Speaking *of* Snowball, have you fed it?"

Blake glanced around looking for it. "Don't even know where it is and don't care. It knocked over six thousand dollars' worth of vases."

Michael grimaced. "Yes, and I had a good chat with her about that today."

"About what?" Blake was curious as to how much they *had* talked about.

"All of it." Michael ate another mouthful and swallowed. "I went back to the beginning and started from scratch. How I wasn't made of money even though I was partner at the law firm. And while we had nice holidays, and I'd allowed her to redecorate this place, I was reining in her spending."

"How'd she take that?"

"She didn't, at first. Became argumentative, haughty, nasty about you, and then when I mentioned counselling or separation, she became sweetness and light." He sighed deep from his gut. "I really don't know her, do I?"

"Did you before? You got married quick."

"No. I guess I didn't," Michael murmured. "I was sad and lonely, and she brought laughter back into my life. Didn't really give much thought to the timing, did I? Just wanted to set up a family home for you again."

"I had a family. You." Blake pushed his bowl aside. He wasn't hungry.

"Yeah, I know, and I'm sorry." Michael glanced at the remains of his meal and pushed it away too. "But it can be fixed. I hope. With therapy and lots of talking and understanding."

"*She* was never understanding before. Why would she be now?"

"Because it's that or separation," Michael replied. "We're cutting down on our spending, cutting back on our holidays, cutting down on ridiculously priced vases, and we're going to *try* and get along. Deal?" He held out his hand, but his son just stared at it.

"What about Mum's mirror? And the photo albums and her stuff? She said that one day, when we weren't here, she was going to chuck it all out. She said that the day she slapped me in the attic."

"Well…" Michael stared into his son's worried eyes. "I've thought about that. How about you and I go up to the attic, go through everything, and whatever you want of your mum's you can take into your room. And I'll get the mirror redone so you can hang it on the wall. Then you can remember all the good times you had every day and night."

Blake's interest piqued up. "Really? I get to have all of Mum's stuff?"

"It is yours by inheritance rights. I don't want it, except for the photos, but I have no problem with you having them now instead of when I'm gone. So, what do you say? Deal?"

Reluctantly, Blake extended his hand and grasped his father's. "I want all of Mum's stuff, and I'll go to therapy as long as Melissa does. And I'll *try* and tolerate her as much as she tolerates me."

"Okay then. How about dessert?" Michael shook his son's hand and got up to clear the table.

"How about we go clear the attic now?" Blake returned.

Michael stopped what he was doing. "Eager pup, aren't you?"

"Yep." Blake grinned, feeling a light happiness lift his spirits. As it hadn't in three years.

After cleaning up, they hurried upstairs to the attic and flicked on the light.

"I take it you know which boxes your mother's things are in?" Michael walked over to the mirror frame on the floor and picked it up. "This will be the fourth time it's had the glass replaced." He set it against the wall outside the door so he remembered it.

"How come it keeps needing repairs?" Blake lifted boxes onto the couch.

"It was broken when we bought it." Michael opened a box of sporting equipment. "But your mum loved the frame so much she wanted it and had the glass replaced. That was when we were in our old apartment. It broke a second time when we moved in here and were trying to hang it in the bedroom. It fell off the nail and cracked. The third time was when you were four or five and you'd thrown something at it. Again, it cracked."

"And the fourth time Melissa stuck her ten inch stiletto through it," Blake muttered and opened a box. "Oh…"

Michael turned from his old football cleats and moved over to his son. "What?" Looking over his shoulder, he saw what Blake had found. "Oh…your mother's wedding gown." Gently lifting it out, he held it up. "Your mother looked so beautiful in this." The sadness washed over him and he settled it back into the box. "I think I donated most of her clothes and shoes, and what not. But I kept the important pieces like this dress, her jewellery; a few precious pieces she thought you'd want one day, maybe to pass on to your wife or daughter." He squeezed his son's shoulder. "I don't know if you want it, but we could have it cleaned and properly packed so it's preserved. Her jewellery was in a wooden jewellery box I bought her as a wedding present."

"I think it's under the dress." Blake dug under the white satin froth, pulled out the box and turned the key which was still in the lock. Lifting the lid, he heard the tinkling sound of music and the memories came flooding back. Memories of him sitting on his mother's lap and watching the little dancer spin around, hearing the music, watching it all disappear when she shut the lid. He would look up at her with his big questioning eyes and gurgle. She would laugh daintily and open it for him to be fascinated all over again. She'd shut it a second time, and a third time, making him look up and gurgle and giggle at the game.

Sighing, he came back to his senses and made note of the jewellery in it. Her favourite amethyst earrings, some studs and hoops, a few chain and bead necklaces and bracelets, and a few sparkling rings. Three of those were her engagement, wedding and eternity rings. He gently touched a finger to them.

"Sadly, you're not married for an eternity," Michael barely whispered, in awe at the overwhelming feelings it was bringing back for him. Memories of him considering proposing, of deciding to propose, and how he was going to do it. How he took months finding the right ring set, months figuring out where and when and how to propose, and then trying to make it all go off like clockwork at the right time in the right place. It was military precision. One after the other came together after months of hard work. He took her out to a picnic lunch at her favourite spot, and a romantic dinner by the water at her favourite restaurant where he took her out on the balcony, got down on bended knee, and pulled out the ring box and opened it. She'd squealed and said yes in an instant, demanding he place the ring on her finger immediately. He had, and she had made him the happiest man on the planet.

"Oh, Blake." Michael wiped his tears away. "Your mum loved everything I ever gave her, including you." He wrapped his arms around his son and cried with him. "She wanted you to have those things.

She wrote it in her will. That's why I kept them. For you. She wanted you to have them for your wife or daughter one day."

Blake gave a hiccupping sigh through his tears. "I want them. I want to remember Mum."

"Okay. You take them and I'll have the dress cleaned and packed properly. Let's see what else we have. Maybe we can sell some stuff and make some money. I don't need the sporting equipment anymore." He went back to the boxes and sorted through the stuff. No, he definitely didn't need any of it anymore, so he hauled the four boxes to the door and stacked them for removal. It was the same with his old clothes and football collectables. He hadn't played footy since high school over twenty years ago. Searching through another box, he came across his Beatles memorabilia. "Hey. How come this stuff if here? I forgot I had it; it should be in my office." He pulled out gold and platinum album plaques, signed posters and album covers, and CDs.

Blake looked over his shoulder. "Who are they?"

Michael laughed. "What do you mean, *who are they?* They're the Beatles. One of the world's biggest bands from the '60s and '70s. Google them."

Blake shrugged and went back to searching through the boxes, leaving his dad happier than he had been in a long time that he and his son were not only getting along, but spending quality time together.

CHAPTER THREE

The next day, Michael took the frame to be repaired and the dress to be cleaned, and offloaded his four boxes of sporting equipment at the local pawn shop. The money he got would more than cover the costs of dry cleaning and new glass.

While he was out, the boys were with Blake helping him sort through the rest of the boxes.

"So, what are you gonna do with it all?" Jarrod asked, glad to see his friend was better than the last few days.

"Keep it in this trunk." Blake cleared out an old wood trunk that sat under his window. It only contained a few toys he didn't use anymore, so he pulled them out and laid an old towel on the bottom. "Here, hand it over." He took the box from Callum and went through the contents; books, notebooks, art books, legal notes, all belonging to his mother. He stacked them neatly on one side of the trunk. "Now, the albums."

Jason pushed the box over and Blake pulled out ten photo albums, laying them on the books, oldest to newest, so he could look at the pictures of him with his mother first. He set the music jewel box on the right, and placed knick-knacks down the middle between the two sides to divide the spaces. That left space for the dress when he got it back.

"You really gonna keep all your mum's stuff?" Adam asked, glad his friend seemed to be doing better.

"Of course. It's all I have of her." Blake finished the trunk and shut the lid. It had an old-fashioned key in the lock, which he turned, then pulled out and hid behind his bedside cupboard. Dusting off his hands, he turned. "And I know exactly where the mirror's going." Walking to the wall opposite his bed, he lifted a huge print down and set it on the floor against the wall. "Right here so I can look at it every morning when I wake up, and every night when I go to sleep." Backing up until his legs hit the bed, he sat, not taking his eyes off the spot. "I want to see it every time I open my eyes, every time I close them, and every time I sit on the window seat and face it." His smile was small. "I want to remember her every day for the rest of my life."

"Will you even be living here the rest of your life?" Jarrod asked, sitting beside his friend.

"Yeah, won't Melissa want the house to live in?" Callum threw himself into the beanbag in the corner. "She's married to your dad; doesn't that make it hers?"

"Nope." Blake's smile grew into a large grin. "Dad told me last night the house is mine in trust, along with another two houses, and Mum's life insurance. It's all mine and Melissa can't touch it."

"Whoa." The boys' eyes went wide at that bit of news.

"She's not gonna be happy," Jason murmured.

"And Dad told her, if she didn't do counselling they'd separate while we sorted out our problems and she could get a job to support herself," Blake regaled them.

"Jesus. Your dad's serious," Jarrod said. "Wonder how you two are going to get along."

"We'll find out tomorrow." Blake stood and gathered the empty boxes. "Dad's going to sell more stuff in the morning, and bring her home after lunch. Our first therapy session is next week."

"Looking forward to it?" Callum rolled out of the beanbag and followed Blake out of his room, as did the other boys.

"No, especially with her." Blake led them up to the attic and set the boxes on the couch. "As you know, I wish she was dead, but she's not. Yet. So, we'll have to see how it goes. I dunno. Let's stop talking about it and pack some more stuff up."

"To chuck or sell?" Jarrod eyed the boxes still left.

"Both." Blake dug into a box and pulled out his dad's old legal papers. "Hey, these shouldn't be here, they should be in his office." He rifled through them to see what they were about, picking up a manila folder to look underneath. The papers slid out and across the floor. "Bugger!"

The boys helped pick them up and Blake tried to

put them back in order. A name caught his eye. "Hey, what?" Peering closely, he noted the name on the paper and quickly read through them, seeing the date they were filed. He went back to the name. "Bloody hell."

"What?" The boys crowded around, wondering what he'd found.

"Melissa's name is on Dad's legal papers," Blake muttered.

"You're kidding!" Jarrod exclaimed. "From when?"

"From a year before Mum died, so four years ago."

"How come her name's on them?" Callum tilted his head to read the papers.

"It would have to be because she worked for the law firm." Blake read more of the paperwork.

"In what capacity?" Adam asked. "I thought she was a former beauty queen."

"She is, *was*." Blake finished scanning the papers and rifled through the rest of the box. "Oh, my God. Her name's on other papers as well." After dumping the box's contents on the floor, he flipped through folder after folder, and of all the files in there, Melissa's name was on at least half.

"She worked at the law firm?" Jarrod was confused about the circumstances before them.

"She would've had to for her name to be on so many files," Blake said, and quickly went through the other boxes of his dad's papers. "She's not on any of these, but they are dated before five years ago."

"So, her name's only on papers from *four* years ago," Callum murmured.

"Through to when they met." Blake went back to the files on the floor. "But Dad said they only met *after* Mum's death." Puzzled, he glanced at each of his friends. "Did he lie?"

"Maybe they didn't actually *work together*," Jason suggested. "Maybe she was in a different part of the office to him, so they didn't *technically* meet?"

"Mmm, maybe. But I'm gonna ask him about it and let him know his papers are here. Let's pack them back up and take them downstairs to his office. He said to clean it all out." They packed up the boxes and took them down to Michael's office on the ground floor, opposite the lounge room at the front of the house.

"Let's leave them here and get back to it. It feels good to clear all the junk out," Blake told them and grabbed the bannister to go back up. His foot landed on the first step.

Knock. Knock. Knock.

The boys halted and turned in fear.

Knock. Knock. Knock.

The old kook's words came back, floating through their heads, and they fearfully glanced at one another.

Knock. Knock. Knock.

"Ah," the boys collectively sighed, and Blake went over to the window to see who it was.

"It's Mrs Baker from next door." Blake opened the door to see his middle-aged neighbour standing there with two dishes in her hands.

"Hello, Blake dear. I brought you and your dad a quiche and chocolate cake. I figured you wouldn't want to cook for yourselves with *her* in the hospital." Mrs Baker may have still gone by Mrs, but she was a widow who was still in good health in her late forties. And she had an eye on Michael Williamson.

"Thanks, Mrs Baker. Come in." Blake waved her in and closed the door. They walked down the hall into the kitchen where he made room in the fridge. "Is the quiche microwavable, or does it have to go in the oven?"

"In the oven for twenty-five minutes on 130 degrees. It's freshly made today. So's the cake."

"Thanks for that." Blake settled the dishes on the shelves. "We'll bring back the containers when we're done." He closed the door and waited for her to leave. There was no way they'd leave that cake alone.

"Okay, dear, when you're ready." She turned, but said, "Are you and your dad doing okay?" She fell into step beside Blake as he escorted her back to the entrance.

"We're getting there. It's tough, but we'll work through it when Melissa comes home." He opened the door for her.

She stopped in front of him. "If you ever need anything, I'm just next door. Remember that." She stared intently into his eyes. "You *or* your dad."

Blake hid his grin and nodded. "Thank you, Mrs Baker. For the food *and* the kind words."

She squeezed his shoulder. "You're welcome, dear. Bye boys." With a wave of her hand, she left.

Blake closed the door and let his grin grow wide.

"Let's attack that cake." He raced back to the kitchen and pulled the container out of the fridge.

Jarrod grabbed the plates, Jason the forks.

Pulling off the lid, the boys oohed and aahed over the chocolatey goodness. Blake grabbed the knife and slid it through, eliciting groans from the boys. He cut five slices, passed them out and they dug in, savouring every bite.

"Where'd you get that from?" Michael asked from the doorway.

Blake jumped. "Ah, Dad," he managed through a mouth of cake. "Where'd *you* come from?"

"The hospital. Where'd *that* come from?" Michael pointed at the cake then sliced himself a piece.

"Mrs Baker. She brought a quiche too." Blake swallowed another bite. "Oh, my God, this is so good."

"Mmm, it is," Michael agreed. "It's been a while since we had cake in the house. Melissa normally has us on some weird diet where good stuff like this is banned."

"Maybe we should change that," Blake mumbled, not looking his father in the eye. "Life's too short to go without chocolate cake."

Michael looked at his son thoughtfully. "You may be right." He took another bite. "It's time to make a lot of changes and set things right again." After finishing off his cake, he packed up the rest and put it back in the fridge. "I'm picking Melissa up tomorrow. She's made an appointment at the hairdresser to fix the damage. It could be a while before we get home. Do you mind?"

Blake shrugged and gathered the plates. "It's not like she doesn't go to the hairdresser any other time. We'll be fine." He loaded the dishes into the dishwasher.

"I know. But those visits will be cut down from now on." Michael changed the subject. "Did you boys clear out the attic again?"

"Just Mum's stuff, and four boxes of your papers. I put them in your office," Blake said, not wanting to discuss Melissa's name on them until later when he and his father were alone.

"Four boxes? Blimey, didn't think I had that many. How 'bout I start going through those and you boys finish off upstairs," Michael suggested. "And then I'll order pizza for dinner."

That got the boys excited and they hurried up to the attic.

"Why didn't you mention Melissa's name on his papers?" Jason whispered.

"Because I want to do it later tonight when we're alone," Blake replied. "And why are you whispering?"

CHAPTER FOUR

After several hours of clearing up, they finished off the attic and hauled all of the boxes downstairs for the stuff to be thrown out or sold. Then they washed and ordered pizza.

Knock. Knock. Knock.

The boys froze, cold tendrils of fear slicing through them. The old kook's words flowed through their ears. They hadn't discussed that in two days, and during the cleaning, they had forgotten all about it.

Knock. Knock. Knock.

"Boys, can you get that? It's probably the pizza guy," Michael called from the kitchen.

Blake padded over to the side window and looked out. The lights automatically come on with every little movement, so he clearly saw the pizza guy under it. Heaving a sigh, Blake opened the door. "Dad, pizza guy." He took the boxes as his dad came with the money.

"Twenty-five fifty, right?" Michael handed over twenty-six dollars. "Keep the change." He smiled at the delivery guy and shut the door. "Let's get into it. Ice creams for dessert." They headed for the kitchen and sat around the table, munching on pizza and garlic bread while talking about the stuff they'd found in the attic.

Afterwards, the boys scurried home to avoid any ghost or ghoul, and Blake locked and bolted the door. Seeing his father in his office, he decided to broach the subject. "Ah…Dad…" He wandered into the room and saw his father scanning the papers from the boxes into his computer before shredding them.

"Mmm?" Michael glanced up from the scanner.

Blake had purposely put the box containing the papers with Melissa's name on the bottom of the pile, so his father hadn't gotten to them yet.

"What is it?"

"Um." Blake glanced at the boxes. "Today, when we were going through the stuff, I came across your boxes and looked through them." His eyes scanned the room nervously. "I dropped some papers, and as I picked them up and put them back, I noticed Melissa's name on them."

Michael frowned. "Melissa's name?"

Blake gulped. "Um, yeah. So, I went through the rest of the files in the box and found her name on at least half of the papers. I didn't know she worked at your law firm? We thought she was a beauty queen."

"She is, *was.*" Michael's frown grew deeper. "But I vaguely remember her working a job to supplement her pageants. I met her in the business district, the mall where my office is." He paused, and then added, "You said her name was on the papers?"

"Yep, like she worked the cases or something."

"Which box?"

"The bottom one."

Michael moved the box he'd been going through, shifted the others, and lifted the bottom one onto his desk. He pulled out files and quickly flipped through them, finding what Blake had said to be true. Her name was on at least half of the papers. "Well, I'll be. I didn't know she worked for the firm."

"Did she?" Blake watched his father rifling through the papers. "I didn't understand if she did or not."

"Yes, but in a lower capacity." Michael noted the accreditations. "Down in the trenches. She was a legal assistant. Huh. Well, I'll be." Throwing the papers back in the box, he slumped in his seat. "They were dated a year before your mum..." Looking at Blake, he went on. "But they only go up until we met, not long after your mother..." He calculated the time in his head. They'd had a ten month courtship, although not really that. They'd actually met two months after his wife's death when he'd gone back to work. But they hadn't dated, just continually run into each other before or after work. After a few months, he'd found himself attracted to her and smiling. Finding himself falling in love again and wanting companionship for himself and a mother for his depressed twelve-year-old son. So, he'd proposed, she'd said yes, and they'd made it legal in the registry office. And he'd stupidly taken out a mortgage to impress her with presents and holidays. Clearly, life hadn't been as rosy as he'd thought.

"Dad?"

"Mmm?" Michael came out of his reverie. "I rushed it, didn't I?"

Blake smiled sadly. "Yeah."

"Oh, Blake. I'm so sorry." Michael went to his son and held him tight. "I'm going to try and make this better. I promise."

*****

The next morning, while Michael went to get the mirror and his dead wife's wedding dress, Blake was going through his stepmother's things.

"What *are* you doing?" Jarrod watched his friend go through cupboard after box after container.

"Looking for clues, papers, anything that says she set my dad up, or my mum up for that car accident."

"You don't actually know she did that," Jason reminded him, keeping a lookout from the window for Blake's dad.

"She said, in front of all of you, that she would get rid of me just like she got rid of my mother. *That's right, I'll get rid of both of you,*" he quoted, looking through a box of papers in her bedside cupboard.

"I don't think she meant anything bad by it," Jarrod piped up. "She was just angry, and you *had* called her a cow."

"And you've got a really bad crush on her, yeah, we get it," Blake snapped and got to his feet. Scratching his head, he wondered where else to look. "You're going to defend her regardless of what she does. Meanwhile, *I'm* her stepson."

Jarrod blanched and shut his mouth. They all knew he had a crush and it wouldn't help the circumstances right now.

Blake walked into the closet and looked through her clothes for things hidden in pockets, in drawers, in containers, and finally, his eyes lit upon a box in the far corner of the top shelf, not so subtly hidden by a hat box. Using the small ladder they had for reaching the top shelf, he checked the hat box and found nothing but hats, and then checked the box behind it. In the plain A4 sized box, he found a small jewellery box and a few mementoes that meant nothing to anyone but Melissa. And in the jewel box, the only thing he found was a key. Holding it up, he recognised it immediately. It was a key to a storage locker at the local facility. And he knew because his parents used to have one for when they were renovating the townhouse. Blake remembered going with his dad to finish emptying it out when he was eight or nine.

"He's home," Jason called, moving from the window.

Blake closed the jewel box, then the box, and carefully put everything back the way he'd found it, including the ladder. "Let's go," he told the boys and they dashed across the landing to his room in time to hear the door open.

"Boys, can you give me a hand?"

They turned around and ran down the stairs to see a white box on the hall table, and Michael bringing in the mirror.

"All done?" Blake asked, eager to see the mirror on his wall.

"All done." Michael shut the door with his foot. "Where do you want it?"

"On the wall across from my bed." Blake grabbed the box and started up the upstairs, his dad and the boys trailing behind. He set the box on the bed and turned, pointing to the wall. "There."

Michael lifted the mirror and carefully hung it on the two nails, and once it was steady, stepped back beside Blake, grinned, and slid an arm around him. "How's that?" They stood staring into the mirror.

Blake's grin was the happiest it had been in a long time. "It's good."

"Good." Michael ruffled his son's hair and kissed his temple. "I'm off to get Melissa. We'll have lunch out and go to the hairdresser. We'll see you at dinnertime."

"Okay." The light and happiness in Blake's grin dimmed somewhat and he waited for his father to leave, watching the car pull out of the drive before turning to the boys. "Guess what I found?" He pulled the key out of his pocket and held it up.

"A key?" Jason said in mock surprise.

"Not just *any* key," Blake replied. "A *storage locker* key. In fact, I know exactly where the storage locker is because we used to have one at the same place."

"Sure it's not the same key?" Callum asked, wondering what his friend was going to suggest next.

"Nuh! You have to give it back when you finish with it," Blake said. "Which means, Melissa has a storage locker hiding all her secrets."

"It's probably all her beauty pageant stuff," Jarrod suggested, having not said anything since Blake's mocking.

"Most of that's on show in the house, or hadn't *you* noticed," Blake sneered. "The pictures cover the walls, and the trophies cover the shelves. She wants everyone to know she was a pageant queen. Miss Australia, Miss World, miss thinks her own shit don't stink," slid out of Blake's mouth. His expression turned into a deep scowl. "What could she have that she needs to hide in a storage locker? She's been with Dad for two years, been living here, didn't move in with much, just a fancy wardrobe full of stuff and all of her pageant rubbish, nothing else. No furniture, no housewares, nothing."

"That doesn't mean much," Adam remarked. "A lot of people don't have a lot of furniture when they get married. Or they give up their stuff because the other has everything already."

"True," Blake conceded. "But if that was the case, why have a storage locker?" Turning the key over in his fingers, he considered another possibility. "She's hiding something."

Jarrod scoffed. "Why would she be? She's not that old to have secrets."

"We get it, Jarrod," Blake spat. "You have a crush on her. Stop defending her for God's sake." He noticed the blush creep over Jarrod's shame-filled face. "She's *my* stepmother and *I know* she's hiding something. You don't let it slip that you got rid of someone's mother for no reason. Or without some sort of guilt of doing so. Otherwise, why did she say it? Was she after my dad from the moment she met him?" He started pacing. "It was a year before my mother died that her name was on those papers of Dad's. She clearly worked at the same law firm. She would have known him, maybe gotten a crush. But he was married with a son, so, what's a girl to do, but get rid of the wife and maybe the son. Get the wife first, the son later. Then, she'll have her prey all to herself." He stopped as a thought hit him. "What if there's evidence in the storage locker?" Spinning to face his friends, he noted their disdain. "What? She *could* have done it, and the evidence *could* be in that locker. Why else would she have one except to hide the evidence of her crime?" The idea excited him and maybe it would finally get rid of Melissa out of their lives forever.

"Dude, are you even listening to yourself?" Callum asked, fearful for his friend's mental health.

"Yes, *I am.*" Blake stared at the boys. "And *I* plan on finding out tomorrow. Who's with me?"

CHAPTER FIVE

At five that afternoon, Michael pulled up outside of their home. "I hope you plan on being polite to my son."

A scowl lit up Melissa's face at the mere thought of being polite to the bratty fourteen-year-old she had as a stepson. But she'd have to hide it. For now. Putting on a fake smile and tone of voice, she said, "Of course. You've made it abundantly clear that we need to get along, so we will get along." Reaching out her right hand, she slid it over Michael's leg. "I'll do anything for you, my darling."

Michael, sensing she wasn't being completely sincere, smiled tightly. "And Blake has promised he'll get along with you. Our first counselling session is on Monday. We'll be going as a family."

The saccharine smile tightened. "Of course. You've booked it into my diary, haven't you?" Her fingers trailed higher up his leg.

He grasped her hand and lifted it off his leg. "Yes, I have." Releasing her, he got out and walked around to open her door.

She alighted daintily, swinging both legs out together and standing upright. Glancing around the neighbourhood, she waited while Michael shut the door and retrieved her bag from the backseat. They'd talked a lot in the hospital, about everything. And she hadn't liked it one bit. She knew she was losing her grip on her husband, and had to fix it and fix it soon. The problem was…Blake. What was she to do with him?

Taking her husband's arm, she walked to the door with him, which he opened for her, allowing her to walk in first.

He placed her case beside the stairs and turned to close the door. "Blake, we're home."

Silently, Blake walked down the stairs to face his stepmother with the boys following. Reaching the ground floor, he stared at her. The new layered bob haircut and colour made her look like blonde bombshell Marilyn Monroe and a good deal younger than her previous style. *Damn it, it makes her look better than she was,* Blake thought. "New haircut?"

"Yes." Melissa stared icily back. "I needed one after what you did."

"Melissa," Michael warned, watching the exchange between the two.

Melissa cast her eyes at her husband then back to Blake. Through clenched jaw, she added, "I really must thank you, Blake. I had been considering a new hairstyle for a while, but kept putting it off. You made the decision for me. Thank you." She had all but spat the last two words.

Surprised, Blake could only stare in shock. She had thanked him. *She* had thanked *him*. For cutting her hair. Bloody hell, that was a new one.

Even Michael was surprised. "You were? Well, that's a very nice thing to say, Melissa. Thank you. Boys..." He glanced at the stunned faces of Blake's friends. "Why don't you head on home now. Blake will see you tomorrow."

"Ah...okay..." One by one the boys trailed out the door, casting glances at Blake and Melissa, before the door shut.

It was a Mexican standoff between the two. Melissa scowling and tight-lipped, now looking like Marilyn Monroe, and Blake scowling and cross-armed, looking like the angry teenager he was.

"Okay." Michael looked from one to the other. "How about we go into the kitchen and make something to eat? I think Mrs Baker's quiche is still there as we didn't eat it last night." He put a hand on each of their backs and guided them down the hall.

"Mrs Baker was here? She gave you food?" Melissa asked, annoyed that another woman was feeding her husband. Her brat stepson she didn't care about.

"Yep, and a chocolate cake too," Blake replied innocently, watching Melissa smooth down her very tight and short animal print dress while his dad pulled out a chair for her. "It was de.lis.cious."

Michael grinned at his son and slid Melissa's chair in as she sat. "And there's some left for dessert. Unless you boys ate it today?"

Blake's grin matched his father's. "We managed to refrain from gorging on it."

"You know I don't like sugary junk food in the house," Melissa complained. "Especially chocolate."

"And you don't have to eat it." Michael grabbed the quiche from the fridge and set it on the counter. "How high did Mrs Baker say for the oven?"

"She said 130 for twenty-five minutes," Blake replied, leaning on the back of a kitchen chair. "It just needs to reheat."

"Why was she bringing my husband food? Especially food we don't eat?" Melissa went on. "I don't keep this figure by eating junk food."

"Mrs Baker brought the food for Dad *and me*, because *you* were in the hospital. *And* because she was being a polite and caring neighbour." Blake gripped the back rung of the chair. She was already grating on his nerves.

She glared at him as if he repulsed her. Which he did. "Or was she trying to take my place?"

"Like you took Mum's?" Blake shot back, noting the alarm spread over her face.

"Enough, both of you." Michael stood between the two. "Civil. And then we will hash out our issues in counselling." He looked at his wife. "We've known Mrs Baker, like the rest of the residents in the street, since we moved in over ten years ago. They were all very kind and caring when Adalind died, and I'm not going to turn away their kind offerings now. She was being helpful."

"I'm sure she was." Melissa tone was icy, and she

arched a perfectly groomed left brow. But seeing the unhappy expression on her husband's face, she reached up and grabbed his hand, deciding to change the subject. "And Snowball? Has he been looked after?"

Michael glanced at Blake who shrugged. "We don't actually know where Snowball is. We've called and set out food, which gets eaten, but we haven't seen him in days. He's probably hiding until you call him. He'll be around somewhere." He patted her hand and went to check on the quiche.

"You probably killed him," she muttered under her breath to Blake. Standing, she straightened her dress.

"Wouldn't care if I did," Blake muttered in return, and saw her stunned expression. "How about I cut up the rest of the chocolate cake? I take it you won't be having any, Melissa?" He walked in front of her and around the kitchen counter.

Scowling, Melissa stomped through the ground floor calling for her beloved pet. "Snowball. Snowball, my darling, where are you?"

"Funny how *she's* the one acting like a petulant child," Blake murmured, slicing through the cake. There was only a quarter left, so he cut it in half knowing Melissa wasn't having any.

"I heard that," Michael said, turning off the oven. "Twenty-five minutes is done. I'll just let it go a bit longer while Melissa freshens up. I'll see if she's found the cat." He left Blake and went in search of his wife, finding her on the first floor landing cuddling the cat. "Found him, I see. Dinner's ready. Do you want to freshen up?"

Melissa's face was buried in her cat's fur, but her eyes flew up to look at her husband. "I don't eat quiche. And I want that cake out of the house."

"Then you can make yourself a salad, since you made no mention of not wanting it half an hour ago, and the cake will be out of the house when Blake and I eat it," he said firmly. "Are you coming down to dinner?"

"No," she replied haughtily. "I'm going to lie down. I'll make myself something later." Storming into their bedroom, with Snowball still in her arms, she slammed the door in his face.

Sighing, Michael remembered all of Blake's words. And he was right. Melissa never *had* liked having a stepson, and she certainly *was* acting like a petulant child. Regardless of what she'd told him after the last few days of talking.

He walked downstairs and into the kitchen. "Melissa's resting. She'll eat something later."

"Ah, huh," Blake muttered, getting the plates and forks ready. "Refuses to eat at the same table, slams the door—"

"Don't say it," Michael warned. "Just don't say it."

Behind his father's back Blake mouthed, *like a petulant child.*

Michael cut up the quiche and they sat at the table. "Maybe a divorce would be better," he mumbled to himself before putting a piece of quiche in his mouth.

Blake stared at his father incredulously. "What did you just say?"

Michael's fork stopped in his quiche and he looked at his son. "Just thinking out loud. Don't read anything into it. Don't take it seriously."

"*Can* it be serious?" Blake dared not hope that his father had seen the light.

"Blake…I'm not saying it *will* happen. We will have our six months of counselling and see how it goes. And if it doesn't, then we'll see. *Do not* get your hopes up."

But Blake's hopes already *were* up. Clearly, his father was starting to see the light about Melissa. How nasty, cold, and mean she was, how much she hated him, and, if he could prove it, how she'd killed Adalind Williamson to get Michael all to herself. Maybe the queen of the castle could be brought down after all. Maybe, he could change his dad's mind completely and they'd get a divorce. She wouldn't get the house, as *that* belonged to him. And he had his mum's life insurance, so she couldn't touch that either. So, it would just be his dad's money she would get some of, and even then, it wouldn't be much. *Oh, how delicious!* he thought, finishing off his quiche. How delicious if he could get his dad to divorce Melissa. But he'd have to figure out a way to do it.

Getting up, he put his plate in the dishwasher, and felt something jab his leg. Reaching into his pocket, his fingers brushed against the key he'd found in Melissa's jewel box. *Yes, that's it.* He got the cake out of the fridge and plated it up. He would go to Melissa's storage locker and find evidence. Evidence of murder. The murder of his mother. She'd have something lying around, surely. Diaries, photos, papers, *something*. Don't murderers keep trophies from their victims? He tried to remember all of the crime shows and documentaries he'd watched and whether they talked about murderers keeping any proof of their crimes. Wouldn't she keep something? If she stalked his father for a year before they met, or she had them meet *accidentally*, then surely she would have had some sort of plan, and surely she would have kept those details if she'd written them down.

Sitting at the table, he ate a forkful of cake. God how he'd missed cake. They hadn't had it in the house in two years except for his birthdays. Not since Melissa had banned all junk food in the house except for the diet sodas in the fridge and those disgustingly healthy cookies she kept in the glass jar on the kitchen bench. He didn't know what they were made of; they were nothing he'd ever seen, but they tasted okay and he knew it would annoy her if he'd been eating them. Not that he cared anymore. If he could just get his dad to divorce Melissa then they could be happy again. A family again. Dad, Mum and me.

Mum... His eyes widened. Jesus, he'd forgotten about his mum. He was still waiting for her to come back, but she hadn't knocked yet. Maybe because she knew Melissa wasn't home until today. Now, all he needed was for her to answer the damn door.

CHAPTER SIX

The next day, being a Saturday, Blake decided he was going to the storage yard to search through Melissa's belongings. He told his dad at breakfast he was going out with the boys.

"Will you be out for lunch, or home?" Michael asked, wiping down the bench.

Melissa was sipping her tea at the table and feeding Snowball, who was in her arms, pieces of her wholegrain toast.

Blake screwed his face up at that. "We'll have lunch out. I'll be home for dinner."

"And where are you going?" Michael watched Melissa hold her cup of tea up for Snowball to drink from it. "That's disgusting, Melissa."

She arched a brow at her husband and kept on doing it.

Blake noticed his father's displeasure and couldn't stop a sly grin from spreading across his face. "We'll head out to the skate and bike park. There's a snack bar nearby, we'll get food there."

"You got money?" Michael turned from the sight

of his wife and her cat which was licking her lips, disgust all over his face. Putting an arm around his son, he ushered him to the front hall. "God, I hope she doesn't do that before I kiss her." Shaking his head, he repeated himself. "You got money?" He slid his wallet from his pocket and pulled out two twenty dollar notes. "Enough for two meals and drinks, and a bus or cab home if need be."

Blake grinned. "Thanks, Dad, but um, could I have a bit more in case one of the boys doesn't have much. Some of them are from single-parent families after all."

"Mmm, that's true, and I probably do give you more than they get." He handed over another twenty. "Make sure everyone is fed."

Blake took the note. "Yes, Dad." He turned for the stairs, but stopped. "Oh, um, Dad. If someone knocks on the door three times and then three times again, don't answer." He wasn't sure how else to warn his father.

"And why's that?"

"Um, something on the news about a murderer going around knocking on people's doors three times, and then killing them when they answer." His gaze wandered over to the door. "Please don't answer. I lost Mum, I don't want to lose you, too."

"Oh, Blake." Michael pulled his son into his arms and hugged him. "You won't lose me, too. Besides, I always look through the side window to see who it is. It's Melissa who answers without checking."

And that was exactly what Blake was counting on.

"Okay, Dad, just be careful." Blake started up the stairs.

"Ah, hang on." Michael stopped his son. "If there's a murderer in the neighbourhood, why should I let *you* go out?"

Blake's bottom lip caught between his teeth. Crap! He'd stuck his foot in it. "Well, because he's knocking on doors, not taking kids on bikes. And I'm not sure which neighbourhood he's in, just that there's one around."

Michael shook his head in bewilderment. "Okay, then *you* be careful, too."

Blake's lips turned into a smile. "Yes, Dad." He went upstairs, grabbed his backpack, skateboard, and helmet from his room, and then ran down to the basement and took his bike from the rack on the wall. Melissa had insisted on the bikes not being on display anywhere any guest would see them, so they were stored in the basement since they didn't have a garage, just the shed in the backyard. Carrying it upstairs, he looked out the window to see if anyone was at the front door and then opened it. Leaning his bike against the wall, he closed the door, clipped on his helmet, and strapped his bag on his back.

Seeing Adam ride out of his yard across the road, Blake clipped his skateboard to the back of his bike, stood on one pedal, and rolled down the drive to meet him. "Hey."

"Hey." Adam nodded down the street. "I see Callum and Jarrod waiting."

"And I'm here." Jason pulled up beside them. "Had to ride down the other side of the street so I didn't pass the old kooks' house next door. Have you heard anything from them since the other day?"

"Nothing." Blake hiked a leg over his bike and they pedalled down the road to meet the others.

"I just asked Blake if he'd heard anything from the kooks next door. He said no," Jason informed them

"What? Nothing?" Callum asked as they headed off down the road.

"Nothing," Blake repeated. "I'm beginning to wonder if that happened at all. I've forgotten all about it, and then someone will knock on the door and freak me out. I had to lie to Dad so he wouldn't open the door today."

"What did you tell him?" Jarrod asked as they turned the corner and rode for the skate park down the road which was before the storage facility.

"The first idiot thing that popped into my head. That I'd heard something on the news about a murderer knocking three times, and then another three times on people's doors, and then killing them when they answered. I told him not to answer the door. He says he always looks out the side window, and then, get this, he reminded me that it's *Melissa* who opens the door without checking. That's perfect."

They stopped to cross at a red light, then biked over and down the road.

"Do you really think that your mother's coming back to life and will knock on the door? And do you really think that Melissa's going to answer the door and die?" Adam asked.

They turned the corner and headed for the park.

"I don't know anymore." Blake shook his head. "I just said I don't even know if the other day *actually* happened. I haven't remembered it except for the knocking. I don't know if it's true. I don't know *if* it will actually happen. All I know is, I want Melissa gone and Mum back. But get this...Dad muttered something about divorce last night. Melissa didn't have dinner with us, slammed herself in her room with the cat. Didn't come out until about eleven after I'd gone to bed. But Dad was not happy whatsoever with Miss Beauty Queen last night, or this morning when he saw her let Snowball drink out of her teacup and then lick her lips. Ugh, gross." He screwed his face up and shivered at the memory of it.

"So, if you can get your dad to divorce Melissa instead, you'll be happy again?" Jarrod asked, a little disappointed that she wouldn't be around to look at.

"Close to it," Blake said as they passed the park and kept on down the road. "Let's go faster; I want time to search before they shut."

"What time's that?" Callum asked and they sped up.

"One p.m. on Saturdays. And it's nearly nine. Let's go," Blake urged.

They rode in silence the rest of the way, only pausing to check for traffic at intersections.

The storage facility was ten blocks from the

skate park and two streets over, but they finally found it.

After pulling up at the gate, they stopped for a drink and a breather. It had been a few years since Blake had been there and he was hoping the rules hadn't changed. Back then, on Saturdays, you unlocked the gate with your locker key, and as Blake read the instructions on the huge metal sign, he realised the rules were still the same. "Aw, that's good."

"What?" Callum closed his drink bottle and shoved it into his bag.

"Still the same rules." Blake dug the key out of his zipped up cargo shorts pocket and scanned the plastic tab top over the electronic gate lock. It clicked open and he rolled it back. "No guard. Easy to get in. Let's go." He shut the gate behind them then checked the number on the key. "354," he murmured and slowly rolled down the main drive, checking the large numbered signs that directed clients to each set of numbered lockers.

"0-50, 51-100, 101-150, 151-200, 201-250, 251-300, nearly there, 301-350, and 351-400. It's down here." Blake rode part way down the lane and found 354. "Here." Jumping off his bike, he let it fall to the ground, eager to get into the locker. He slid in the key, turned it, and the lock popped open with little sound. And even if it did have a sound, it would have been obliterated by the pounding of Blake's heart. He wiped his sweaty hands on his shorts and breathed in. He had no idea what he'd find in there, if anything at all. But it was worth it if it meant taking down Melissa and getting her out of their lives. Grasping the handle, he pulled.

The door slid noiselessly open and the boys all stood gaping into it.

"Well?" Jarrod asked from behind Blake.

"Boxes." Blake pulled his backpack from his back and dug for his torch, flicking it on before entering the locker. "Let's do this. But be careful, and put it all back where and how you got it," he warned as the boys turned their torches on. "We don't want her to get suspicious that someone's been in here if she comes."

They set to work, carefully going through one box each at a time. Melissa had stacked them three boxes high down the side of one wall, leaving space for them to stand and search. She had also written on each box what was in it.

"Old clothes in this one," Callum muttered. "Looks like little kid's clothes. Maybe hers from when she was little?" He glanced at the label. "Yep."

Blake had carefully read each label and picked the one box that didn't have one. After lifting off the two boxes on top, he pulled the bottom one out and spun it around, looking for anything written on it. There was nothing. Intrigued, he opened it and found a bunch of A5 books with locks and keys. "Diaries," he breathed, knowing he'd hit the jackpot. Pulling them out in turn, he laid them on the other boxes and continued searching, finding a black trench coat, black pants and turtleneck top, black boots, gloves and a wig. A set of car keys fell to the floor when he lifted the coat. "What the hell?" He picked them up and looked at the insignia. "That's definitely not the car she has now. I wonder why she kept the keys and not the car."

"Sentimentality?" Adam shrugged, staring at the objects in Blake's hands. "Anything in the pockets?"

Blake set the keys down on the diaries and searched the pockets of the coat, only finding something in the right hip pocket. His fingers brushed a small hard lump attached to some kind of cord, and grasping it, he lifted it into the light of four torches.

"Whoa, a necklace." Jason held his torch closer to illuminate it better. "Why would she have that in the pocket?"

"She wouldn't unless she didn't know it was there. Maybe it fell off the last time she wore it and she didn't notice," Callum suggested. "It's small, maybe it caught on something and fell."

"Into her pocket?" Jarrod frowned in thought. "That's a big jump to make. A necklace falls from your neck and just *happens* to fall into your coat pocket? I don't think so. It would have fallen down, not out, sideways and down. It was more than likely taken off and put in there for safekeeping and then forgotten about."

"No." Blake gulped down the hard lump rising from his chest to his throat. "The clasp is broken and it has hair and blood on it. There." He pointed to a small tangle of brown hair. "Melissa's blonde, so it's not hers."

"How do you know the necklace isn't hers?" Adam asked, curiosity itching him.

"Because." Blake breathed in to steady his voice. "It's my mother's. It belongs with the amethyst earrings she left in her jewel box. The police couldn't find it. Neither could the hospital. We thought it was lost. But this proves Melissa was telling the truth that day in the attic. She *did* get rid of my mother."

CHAPTER SEVEN

"But…" Jarrod licked his dry lips. "Can you be sure? Maybe your dad gave it to her?"

"No!" Blake's fingers curled around the necklace tightly. "Everything that Mum owned was left. Her jewellery was in her box that I now have. The earrings are there, the matching necklace isn't because it went missing. After the crash they couldn't find it, no one could. Not the cops, the doctors or nurses, not even Dad. Everyone figured it just got lost in the crash or the rescue. But here it is." He unfurled his hand and stared at the small oval amethyst surrounded by diamonds. The pendant was only the size of an adult thumbnail, but he knew it was his mother's. Tears fell silently down his cheeks, and his eyes welled with countless unshed ones waiting their turn to fall. His vision blurred, his chest heaved, his heart broke, and he sobbed as his hand closed around the pendant and went to his chest.

"Ah…dude…" Jarrod murmured, looking at the other boys to see what they should do. But all he got were wide-eyed shrugs. "Um…oh…dude…we're so sorry." He awkwardly placed a hand on Blake's shoulder, not knowing if he should hug him, slap him on the back, or what.

Blake heaved in a breath and slowly let it out. Swiping the back of his hand across his eyes, he sniffed. "We should ah…pack this stuff up. I ah… brought bags." Laying the coat across the box, he pulled large Ziploc bags from his backpack. "We can put the clothes in these in case they need forensic testing later, and ah, we'll have a look at the diaries to see if they're worth taking." Opening a bag, he handed it to Jason who held it while he folded the coat and put it in. They did the same with the top and pants, shoes and wig, and then packed it all in Blake's backpack. "Glad I brought my big one, but if there's no room, I'll have to use your bags."

"Not sure I want to get caught with her stuff on my person," Adam muttered.

"Just until we get home. Then we get up to my room and I'll unpack it all and hide it," Blake said. "Let's check the folders and diaries." Handing the diaries out so they went five times faster, he chose to look through a folder, finding photos of his father, mother *and* himself, all close-up, outside of their home, his dad's office, eating out, and spending time together. "She was stalking us," he muttered, his brows slowly descending. "She stalked us and took pictures." Turning to the second folder, he found detailed notes of when his dad arrived at work, left work, and what he did in between. When his mum went out, what time she picked up Blake, who

Blake's friends were and when they went to his house for dinner or visits. There was even a list of their weekend activities, and it was all detailed for the year before Blake's mother had died.

"Bloody hell." Blake breathed in, not quite comprehending what it all meant. That Melissa, or someone she'd paid, had stalked his family for a year. "This can't be happening, this can't be true. This can't be happening, this can't be true," he murmured.

"Maybe you should read this?" Jason handed over the diary he'd been reading.

Blake took it and read from the top of the page. *"Today I met a man who's perfect for me. Tall, brunet, sparkling green eyes, in great physical form, and is a partner at a law firm. And not just any law firm, but the one I just started working at. We'd be perfect for each other. He's older, at least twenty years older than me, and has chest hair, not that I've seen him without his shirt, but his tie was loose and I saw the hair poking out. He's broad and muscular with a chiselled jaw, and I'm sure I saw the definition of abs under his shirt. His name's Michael Williamson and he's perfect. That's why I started working there. I saw him in the business district and followed him. The only problem is...he has a wife and son. Not to worry, I can get around that. Melissa Dubrey always gets what she wants."*

"Bloody hell!" Callum murmured, and slammed shut the diary he'd been reading. "I don't think we should do this anymore. We're getting in way over our heads."

"We can't stop now," Blake complained. "We have to find out what she did."

"Then do it at home." Callum handed over the diary. "That one's got number one on the cover. She probably numbered them, so pack them up. We'll look in the rest of the boxes, but let's get out of here. I don't want to be here anymore. I don't want to be caught."

"We won't be. She's at home with Dad." Blake took the diaries and put them into a Ziploc bag and managed to pack them in his backpack. "Okay. I'll read them when I get home. Let's check the rest of her stuff." They quickly scanned the rest of the boxes and then carefully put them all back in the right order. Finished, they made sure nothing was left out, then shut and locked the door.

They rolled back to the gate where Blake let them through and locked it behind them, then they rode for the park.

"What are you going to do with her stuff?" Adam asked. "Are you going to tell your dad?"

"Not yet. I don't know." Blake wasn't sure what to do first, or second, or third. He wanted to read those diaries and get a proper look at the folders, which meant everything would have to be carefully packed away so Melissa wouldn't find it. Or anyone else for that matter. Not that Melissa went into his room, so he didn't really have to worry about that. But when should he tell his dad? Should he show him the folders and diaries? And what would his dad say? How would he justify finding them in

Melissa's storage locker, technically a place he had no right being, especially without permission? How would he explain that to his dad? Would his dad even understand, or would he demand Blake give Melissa's things back to her *without* looking at them? He couldn't give them back before his dad had a chance to read them, to see for himself that Melissa had been stalking him for a year before his wife's death.

"What about the cops?" Jason asked as they arrived at the park.

"Dunno." Blake pulled up to a shady table near the snack bar and slid off his backpack and helmet. "Should I even go to the cops? I haven't read the diaries yet. I don't know what the rest say. She might detail her crime. I don't know. But then again, she might not. So, better to find out *before* telling the cops or my dad."

"True." Callum took a swig of water from his bottle. "When will you read them?"

"Now." Blake sat at the table and dug into his backpack for the bag of diaries. "What better place to do it since she's not around. You guys go skate or ride. I'll be here." Pulling out the first diary, he checked the number and put it back, then searched for number one and started reading.

The boys glanced at each other, shrugged, dropped their bags on the table and rode off to the bike ramps.

"I think he's obsessed," Jarrod told the others and rode over the edge of the bike track. "Maybe someone should tell Melissa? I'm sure there's a simple explanation to why she has all of that stuff. She should be asked."

"And what?" Adam asked, circling around his friend. "*You'd* tell her? Because *you're* the one with the crush on her. Would you really go against one of your best friends, go behind his back, to tell his wicked stepmother that he found her storage locker key and went through her belongings, and there just *must* be some reasonable explanation of why there's evidence that she committed a crime?" Adam stopped his bike in front of Jarrod's, making him come to a halt. "Do you have it *that bad* for her that you would dob in one of your best friends? To what? Not only get him in massive trouble with Melissa *and* his dad, but to possibly be sent to boarding school, or worse, be killed himself?" He stared incredulously at his friend who turned bright red in embarrassment.

"No-no," Jarrod stammered. "I just thought—"

"Thought what? That you'd get on Melissa's good side by dobbing in your best friend? That's *so not cool*, dude." Callum adjusted his hat and sunglasses. "You dob him in and I'll punch your lights out."

"Me too," Adam added. "Keep your crush to yourself from now on, Jarrod. This is none of your business, or ours, for that matter. We may be helping him, but at the end of the day, Melissa is *Blake's* stepmother. Married to *his* father. And this is *their* business to sort out. *Not* ours."

Jason flicked one of his pedals to make it spin.

"Besides, you could just end up making things worse, and they're seeing a counsellor on Monday, Mr Williamson has already made that decision to sort his marriage and relationships out. He doesn't need you and your crush on his wife butting in. Does he even know that one of his son's best friends has a massive crush on his very young wife? Maybe we should tell him."

Jarrod's eyes widened to the size of saucers in fear. "No, no, don't, please don't tell him. No, don't. I'll do anything. Just don't tell him that. Please don't."

"Promise you won't tell Melissa what we did today, or that Blake has her stuff." Adam removed his sunglasses to look Jarrod straight in the eye. "Promise us, Jarrod. Or we tell."

"No..." Jarrod panicked. "Don't tell him...oh... oh bugger...okay. I promise I won't talk to Melissa and tell her. Just don't tell Blake's dad."

"Swear it on the head of your best friend, Blake," Callum told him. "Because if anything happens to him because you told, then it's on *your* head."

"Ah...guys..." Jarrod pleaded. The fear attacked his chest, convulsing it and making his breath come in spasms.

"Are you having a panic attack?" Adam asked. "Get a grip, dude. This isn't about you. It's about Blake and not getting him into trouble. Let him and his dad and Melissa sort it out."

Jason punched Jarrod in the left arm.

"Ow! What'd you do that for?" Jarrod furiously rubbed his arm to stop it hurting.

"To snap you out of it." Jason leaned over and raised his arm again. "Promise you'll stay out of it and not get Blake into trouble."

Seeing Jason's raised arm, Jarrod reluctantly sighed. "Okay. I promise not to tell Melissa and get Blake into trouble."

"Are his fingers crossed?" Callum checked Jarrod's hands. "Nope. Good. You'd better keep your promise, Jarrod, or you'll have us to deal with. Now, let's get a couple of hours of riding in."

CHAPTER EIGHT

They rode around the bike tracks until twelve when they pedalled back to their table. There were more kids around, but not as many as there normally were because of the heat of the day.

"Phew, I'm hot and thirsty." Callum knocked back the last of his water. "Anyone know if the water fountain works? I don't have enough money to keep buying drinks. I'll have to fill up my bottle from the fountain all day."

"Same here."

"Same here."

"Mum only gave me ten dollars," Jason said. "That's all we could scrape together."

"Same here," Callum replied. "So, it's free water for me all day, and I'll spend my money on food."

Blake closed the diary he was reading and reached into his cargo shorts pocket for his wallet. "Here." He handed over two twenty dollar notes knowing it would come in handy. "Go buy us all burgers and chips, and the largest bottle of drink each, then we can make them last. You can spend your money on drinks later."

"Cool." Callum snatched the notes. "Thank your dad for us."

"I want the change," Blake yelled. Waiting for his friends to come back with lunch, he finished the diary he'd been reading and put it away. It was only number three, and he was still in the year before his mother's death, when Melissa was talking about her crush on his dad, and how she watched him from afar. She'd discussed her feelings for him, how she was falling in love, and what she'd discovered about his life. The family's routine. She mentioned the detailed list she kept of their comings and goings, and all the times she'd run into Michael.

But why didn't he recognise her? Blake thought. *Why didn't he know her from before and not just from when they'd supposedly met?*

"Here's your change." Callum dropped $2.45 in front of Blake. "Sorry, not much." He sat down with his burger and drink.

"From forty bucks?" Blake complained.

Jarrod handed him his burger and drink. "Nothing's cheap these days, and you said to get the biggest bottle of drink each." He sat next to Blake with his own food.

Adam dropped his food on the table and unrolled the extra extra large serve of chips they'd bought. "Dig in."

They inhaled their burgers and chips, and drank half a bottle of soda each before heading back to the snack bar for an ice cream dessert. After sating themselves, the boys finally asked Blake what he'd found out.

"Not a lot so far. Just her growing obsession with my dad. I've only read three diaries, they're long and detailed and she wrote a lot. Each diary covers about three months each, so I'm not up to the months where Mum died, or Melissa actually *met* my father."

"What will you do when you do get to that part?" Jason asked.

Blake shrugged. "Dunno. But I'm wondering if I should make copies of them all, just to be on the safe side."

"Take photos or photocopies of them?" Callum asked, feeling sleepy from their big lunch and the hot afternoon heat.

"Both?" Another shrug. "Dad's the only one with a photocopier, though, and I can't use it while they're home because they'd hear and want to know when I'm making copies of. If I take photos, they may not turn out properly, so I don't know."

"You gonna come skate with us?" Jarrod picked up his skateboard and stared at the specially built park.

"Nah. It's a bit too warm for me, and I don't want to be sick after the food we just ate. But you go. I'll read another diary," Blake told them.

"Not sure I want to skate either." Adam looked up at the burning sun. "I might just watch from the sidelines for a while."

The four boys wandered over to the skate ramps

and sat on a bench in the shade watching while Blake went back to reading. At five, the boys called it a day and packed up.

"Learn anything else?" Adam asked while gathering his stuff.

"A year and a bit down and Mum's still not dead yet. But that's probably in the next diary. There's a few to go." Blake zipped up his backpack and hauled it over his arms. "I'm pooped. It's been a long day."

"You didn't do anything except sit and read." Jason clipped on his helmet. "But yeah, I'll be glad to get home. This heat has done me in."

"Me too," Callum said. "I need a long cold shower and an early night."

The boys slowly pedalled back to their street where they parted ways.

Blake stopped in his driveway looking up at the townhouse. The one that he owned. The one that was in his name, all for him. Thanks to his mother. Wondering whether or not anything had happened, he slid off his bike and walked it to the front step. He let himself in, rolled in his bike, and quietly shut the door behind him. Hearing voices coming from the sitting room down the hall on his left, he chose not to yell out, but left his bike leaning against the staircase and quickly went up to his room to hide his backpack in the closet. He'd look at everything later. Leaving his helmet and skateboard in his room, he went down to collect his bike and rolled it to the basement door under the stairs.

"Blake? Is that you?" Michael called out, stepping

into the doorway. The sitting room was at the back of the house opposite the kitchen dining. "There you are. Dinner's around 6:30."

Blake glanced over his shoulder. "That's fine. I'll just put my bike away."

"Enjoy your day?"

Blake grinned. "Yeah, I did." He carried his bike down the stairs, lifted it onto the hooks on the wall, and went back up and shut the door. Seeing he still had an hour before dinner, he went up to his room and locked the door behind him.

After a refreshing shower and a clean set of clothes, he carefully unpacked his backpack and found an old sports bag he didn't use anymore. He packed the clothes, shoes, wig and car keys into it, moved his closet ladder over to the wall, and climbed up to the ceiling. He pushed on the corner of the ceiling and a section dropped down. It was a secret hidey-hole his parents had put in for him to use as extra storage for all his toys. He scurried down the ladder for the bag, climbed back up, and slid it into the space. There was no way Melissa would have any idea to look there. After setting the ceiling door back in place, he descended and found another old sports bag to hide the diaries and folders in. He had to finish reading them before hiding them, and he had to get the key back to Melissa's box.

Bugger! The key!

Startled, he patted his pockets and realised it was in his other shorts. He went to his ensuite, where he dug his shorts out of the wash basket and retrieved the key. Sighing in relief, he left it with the diaries in the sports bag, not sure when he'd be able to get it back.

In the distance, thunder rumbled, an ominous prelude to the main show.

After a reasonably calm dinner of chicken and salad, Blake retreated to his bedroom and locked the door. He and Melissa had spoken about ten words to each other, and he'd noticed his dad wasn't any happier. So, whatever they had been doing or talking about all day, it hadn't made things any easier or relaxed between them.

Thunder rumbled overhead and the first spattering of rain began.

Summer showers didn't last long in Australia; normally they just blew over within a few minutes, but at least it would cut down on the heat for the next day or two.

Blake settled on the floor of his closet, the doors to the bedroom and bathroom shut, and the light on. He didn't want to be disturbed and have to quickly hide anything.

He pulled out the diaries he had left to read, and started on number six.

CHAPTER NINE

Dear diary,

I can categorically say that I am head over heels, madly, truly, deeply in love with Michael Williamson... and his money. He's partner at the law firm, making a motza, and I overheard today that he owns three properties. They can also afford an overseas holiday once a year for at least a month, and two smaller holidays within Australia. I love travelling, but I love money more, and he has loads of it!

Disgusted, Blake scanned page after page until he came to the date of his birthday.

I wanted to see Michael today, but was told he wasn't in. Apparently, it's his son's birthday, and it's one of the days he takes off every year religiously. I didn't know he was religious. Oh, well, hope I don't have to convert when I marry him. Oh, yes, diary, I will marry him one day. You can bet on that.

"Jesus Christ," he muttered, sickened to his core. "She was going to go after Dad, and that was my eleventh birthday, just three years ago. That bitch!" The anger simmered along with the thunder, pounding in sync with the storm brewing outside. He flicked the page.

Dear diary,

It's all planned. I let him have his day with his brat, but come tomorrow, it's all over. I'll get them on the way home. I know the routine. She picks up the brat at 7:30 on a Thursday night after soccer practice, and they go and get takeout. No wonder she's fat if she eats takeout all the time. Definitely not svelte and athletic like me. Oh, yes, diary, Michael will prefer me over her. He has a sporting background and I'm a pageant queen. He'll definitely want me over her, especially when I show him what a good little wife I can be in bed. He won't be able to resist me, diary. Not one bit.

Just reading the words made him want to vomit, but so did the thought of what was coming next. He wasn't sure if he wanted to read it. Wasn't sure if he wanted to know it. Wasn't sure what he would do about it if it was true. Wiping his sweaty hands on his shorts, he breathed in and counted as he released.

The thunder cracked so loudly the house trembled. The lights flickered, but remained stable, and it made his head ache and the hairs on his arms stand on end. If only it would all be over. If only Melissa was gone and his mum was back. Clearly nothing had knocked on the door that day, otherwise, Melissa would already be gone and his mother would already be back. And where had the neighbours gone? He hadn't seen them since that night. And how long was this supposed to take?

Within the week, they'd said. He didn't want to wait any longer.

Turning the page, he kept reading.

Dear diary,

Oh, how exhilarating. It ended up being a rainy day today. Perfect for my plan to work. And I dressed for it too. Black turtleneck top, black pants, shoes and trench coat. Even a black wig so no one would recognise me. I wrapped a scarf around my neck and partly covered my face with it, and wore black gloves. I'd managed to steal an old boyfriend's car, he won't miss it, and I was using it to fulfil my destiny. Except my destiny didn't go according to plan.

First, I followed the wife and brat to soccer practice after school and sat there in my car for four hours while the brat did his practice. Four hours for God's sake. Who practises for that long? Anyway, at 7:30 the brat decided to go home with one of his friends which was out of routine. But I still followed her; it was her I needed out of the way so I can marry Michael. I followed her to a 7/11 and waited while she went in. I waited for another hour. Seriously! I just wanted to get home to my nice warm apartment. Finally, she came out and left. And this is where it gets interesting.

While my plan had changed with the circumstances, I knew the area well and also knew how to do a little somethin' somethin' to a car to make it stall. While she was in the 7/11, I had popped out to pour water in her tank. She didn't even notice the petrol tank lid was busted. Oh, well. So, I followed her, and she stalled right where I wanted her to, at the end of a steep road where there were lots of posts and poles to smash her into.

I had been tailing her, at a distance, of course, and passed her to turn left up the steep road. When I got to the end I did a U-turn, hit the pedal, and raced down the hill at a hundred miles an hour. She saw me right before I hit her. I smashed into her with the bullbar. Thank God my ex's car was a four-wheel drive. I kept on driving until I smashed her car into the poles and kept on hitting the accelerator until I couldn't move it any longer. Once I was satisfied that I could do no more, I got out, leaving nothing behind, of course, and walked around the back of her car to the driver's side.

Her seat had bent back and her head was at an odd angle. Her body was all crushed and broken and battered. I leaned in for one last look, and you know what that bitch did, she turned her head and looked at me. She even moved her lips as if she were talking. I leaned closer and could swear I heard her say, 'help me'. Well, like I was going to help her! I was there to kill her, not help her.

While contemplating what to do next, I saw that pretty amethyst pendant she wears around her neck sometimes. I bet that was a present from Michael. Well, no way was she going to keep that. So, what did I do? I ripped it from her neck free and clear and then I told her, you'll never guess what I said to her, I said, 'I'll be taking this like I'll be taking your husband. But don't worry; your son will join you soon. Pity he wasn't with you tonight, I would've got two birds with one stone. Oh, well.'

And then you'll never guess what I did, diary. To make sure she was dead, I held her nose while she choked on her own blood. You should have seen it. Her eyes widened when she realised I wasn't there to help her, but to take her life. Just as well she died. I made sure of it. There was no way I was letting her live. Once she was dead, I walked away. Happy and free. Everything I've ever wanted is going to be mine. I just have to get rid of the brat of a son first.

With trembling hands, Blake dropped the diary into his lap. And his hands weren't the only things shaking. His muscles, his bones, his heart, his lungs, his head, his mind. Every single cell in his body was trembling with every single emotion he knew. Fear, anger, hatred, mixed with love for his mother, and fear for his father, but the anger was what fuelled him most.

The thunder rumbled with loud claps of sound. The rain pelted down on the roof, slapped against the windows on every level, poured down on his soul like nobody's business. It raged around inside him in a way he had never felt. He'd never felt the rage like that, anger like that, hatred like that. Not ever in the fourteen years he'd been on this planet. Not even when his dad had introduced him to Melissa. Not even when his dad told him he had married Melissa. Not even when she had moved into his house, his father's bed. Not even when she slapped him, or stuck her stiletto through his mother's mirror, had he felt rage like this. Yes, he had been full of anger and hatred, and wanted her dead. But not like this. Not to this extent.

He was raging inside and wanted revenge.

He got to his feet, opened his closet door, walked through his bedroom, opened the bedroom door, and stepped onto the first floor landing.

The house trembled with more than the thunder. It trembled with the hatred, anger and rage that drove Blake down the stairs to the entrance hall. It made his chest heave with a raging heartbeat; made his lungs burn with gasping air. Made every fibre of the being he was shake and rattle and tremble.

Knock. Knock. Knock.

It was slow, loud, monotonous.

Through the tears that welled in his eyes, he looked at the door, knowing in his soul of souls it was time.

It was his mother.

Trudging over to the window beside the door, he glanced out, but saw nothing. Blinking rapidly to rid his eyes of the flood that matched the one outside, he flicked on the front porch light. It illuminated the figure standing there.

The head turned to look at the window and Blake knew exactly who it was.

"Mum." His voice barely broke through the noise. "Mummy." He knew her face, knew her hair, knew her touch. "Mummy." His hands lay against the window, his face squashed against them watching the figure of the woman he loved and wanted back so desperately.

The figure turned its head back to the door and raised its hand.

Knock. Knock. Knock.

Slow, loud, monotonous.

Blake knew what he had to do.

Wiping his eyes, he moved down the hall looking for Melissa, whom he found with his father in the kitchen.

Michael was mixing the pot of tea when he saw him. "Hey. Was someone at the door? A bit strange on a night like this."

"Ah...yeah." Blake sniffed and wiped his nose with the back of his hand.

"Who was it?" Michael poured two cups of tea. "Want one?"

"Ah...no...it was...*is*...for Melissa."

"Did you invite them in?" Michael noted the red puffy eyes on his son. "Blake?"

"Ah...no." He saw them both watching and took a breath. "They wanted to wait on the front porch. Didn't want to come in."

"Oh, for heaven's sake." Melissa sighed and got to her feet. She moved past Blake and stormed down the hall to the front door.

He watched, his heart pounding in his chest, waiting, hoping she didn't look out the window.

Melissa flung open the door. "Who are you and what...do...you...?" Her eyes widened with recognition. Her jaw dropped. Her heart almost stopped. "Adalind... no...you're..." She knew the face. Knew those eyes.

The eyes she'd looked into as she snuffed the life out of them. "Adalind…no…"

Adalind Williamson took a jerky step forward.

Blake saw his mum's face over Melissa's shoulder. He hadn't moved. He was still standing in the hallway outside the kitchen. "Mummy," barely whispered out of his mouth. He saw Melissa's body double over with a jerk. Saw his mother pull her arm away. Saw Melissa's heart in his mother's hand. Saw Melissa take a faltering step out the door. Saw the door slam shut behind her.

"Mummy."

IT CREEPED AT MIDNIGHT

CHAPTER ONE

"Mummy," Blake screamed, not even daring to believe it had finally happened. "Mummy."

"Blake." A concerned Michael moved to his son's side and grasped him by the arms. "What is it, Blake? You know your mother's not here."

Looking at his father through tear-filled eyes, Blake pointed down the hall to the front door. "Mummy."

Michael glanced at the door and saw it was closed. "Where's Melissa? It's Melissa, Blake. Who was at the door? Whoever it was, it is *not* your mother." He felt the vibrations shaking his son. "Are you okay? Are you coming down with something?"

"Mummy," Blake yelled. "Mummy's back." Jerking from his father's hands, he bolted down the hall and flung open the door.

There, on the doorstep, shrouded by the porch light, lay two women.

One blonde. One brunette.

One dead. One alive.

"Melissa?" Michael saw the prone figure of his wife and raced down the hall. "Melissa?" Pushing

Blake out the door, he fell to his wife's side. "Melissa? Are you okay?"

Through the pouring rain and lightning cracks, Blake glanced up at the sky and saw the neighbours from next door standing on their porch watching him. They smiled in the light, but disappeared in the dark, and when the lightning came again, they were gone. Looking down, Blake's heart pounded in his chest. He was staring at his mother and stepmother.

"Melissa, Melissa, oh, my God, she's not breathing. Melissa." He slapped her face and set her on her back. "Melissa?" Laying his head on her chest to listen for a heartbeat, he watched Blake fall to his knees beside the other woman and gently roll her onto her back.

"Mummy." Blake gently pushed away her hair from her face. "Mummy."

"Blake," Michael raised his head, "That's not your…" He stared at the woman lying next to his wife. "Adalind?" His brows moved downwards and his eyes couldn't take themselves off the woman. His heart pounded, and his blood raced. He knew his wife's face anywhere. Regardless of her being dead for three years.

"Mummy." Blake gently shook her by the shoulders, not daring to believe it was really her. "Mummy."

The woman groaned lightly, and her hand shifted to her face to find Blake's.

Blake felt the warmth. "Mummy."

Swallowing hard, Michael turned his gaze from his wife to his wife. "Melissa?" Pulling out his cell phone, he dialled triple zero and asked for an ambulance, giving them the details. Checking Melissa's pulse, he started performing CPR as directed by the call centre operator. "1, 2, 3, blow. 1, 2, 3, blow." He pushed on her chest; he blew into her mouth, and continued doing so until the paramedics arrived.

Blake had run inside and brought back a blanket for his mother whom he cradled in his arms, watching it all until the ambulance arrived which made several houses come alive with lights and open doors. People were standing on their porches and front steps being nosy and wondering what had happened now.

"What's going on?" one paramedic asked, setting down his bag and pulling out his stethoscope.

"We don't know," Michael huffed, stopping chest compressions while the paramedic listened to his wife's chest. "She answered the door and then we found her like this." He glanced at the other woman. "Both of them."

The paramedics pulled out their defibrillator and strapped the electrodes on Melissa's chest. "Shock at 100 CCs…and…clear."

Melissa's body jerked up, but her heart didn't start.

"Charging 200 CCs…clear."

That didn't help either.

"Charging 300 CCs…clear."

Not even 300 could jumpstart Melissa's cold, dead, heart.

"We'll need to give her Epinephrine," the female paramedic said, and pulled out a needle and glass vial. Inserting the needle, she pulled the plunger back and watched the fluid seep into the plastic tube of the syringe. "1mg of Epinephrine." Handing it over, she watched her colleague squirt some out and then plunge it into Melissa's cold, dead heart.

They waited.

Nothing.

"Let's charge 400 CCs…and…clear."

Melissa's body jerked up, relaxed, and sighed… But it wasn't the sigh of a live woman. It was the rattle of a dead one.

The male paramedic switched off the machine and removed the electrodes from Melissa's chest. Looking Michael square in the eye, he said, "I'm sorry, sir. There's nothing I can do for her. She's gone."

Confused, Michael's head shook back and forth in slow jerking motions. He had heard and seen everything through a fog. Unable to comprehend, to understand, fully, that his wife was gone.

Another wife was gone.

"Sir…can you hear me?" The paramedic reached across Melissa's body and grasped Michael by the arm. "Sir, your wife is gone."

"Not completely," Blake muttered, gently rocking back and forth, his mother still in his arms. "She's still here." His eyes flickered back and forth from his mother's face, which still looked exactly the same as it always had, to Melissa, his dad, and the paramedics.

The paramedics turned, finally remembering the other woman, and quickly checked her over. "Pulse is weak, body cold, unconscious. Do we know what happened?"

"No. Melissa answered the door," Blake quietly told them, seeing his father was still in shock. "I saw my mother over her shoulder and freaked out. The door slammed shut and we came to see what was happening and found them both on the ground."

"Well, she's soaked to the skin, but holding up well," the female medic said.

"Which is surprising." Michael finally spoke, making everyone look at him. "Since she's been dead for over three years."

The two medics looked from Michael to the woman in Blake's arms. "What?"

Blake shrugged a shoulder. "If that *is* true, then why is she lying in my arms?"

"Yes, why?" The male paramedic frowned and turned to his partner. "Get the stretcher and we'll get her to the hospital. I'll call it in." Stepping a few feet away, he called in to the ambulance centre. "This is paramedic 125 called out to 225 Huntington Way, Knightsbridge. We have two women down, one deceased and, apparently, one *no longer* deceased."

"Excuse me…" the operator cut in.

"Ah…apparently she died three years ago, but here she is lying in her son's arms. Strange story, probably. The husband is weirded out by it, lost his wife, other wife back from the dead. Might wanna get the cops down here in case it's a whack job posing as a dead woman, or maybe she didn't really die and escaped from an asylum." He watched Michael slump over the body of Melissa in tears, and the son rock his mother back and forth. His partner rolled the stretcher over and he spoke into his radio. "We'll be taking the former wife to hospital. We'll need a truck for the deceased."

"En route, about ten minutes."

"Over." The medic helped his partner lift the woman in Blake's arms onto the stretcher, cover her in blankets, and strap her in. "There's another truck coming for your wife," he told Michael, laying a hand on his arm in comfort. "They'll take her to the morgue for confirmation."

Michel just gave them a vacant stare.

The medic turned to Blake who seemed a lot calmer than his father. "Your dad said she'd been dead for three years. Is she your mum?"

Blake brushed her hair aside and tucked the blanket under her chin to keep warm. "Yes. I guess."

"You guess?"

Blake's gaze moved to the man standing across the stretcher from him. "My mother died three years ago in a car accident. I never saw her body, have grieved ever since. And yet, here she is on our doorstep, passed out. Is she my mother or not?"

Poor kid, the medic thought. *What a confusing time.* "I don't know, son, but it's something you'll have to have tests for to find out. What about a twin sister? Your mum have one of those?"

"No," Michael managed from his almost catatonic state, and they turned to him. "No, she didn't. Only three brothers. I saw her body in the morgue. It was her." Slowly rising from Melissa's body into a kneeling position, he looked down at her. "And now..." He brushed her newly blonded hair aside. "I've lost another wife. How does that happen?" Confused, he glanced up at them. "How do I lose one wife and then three years later she turns up to scare my new wife to death? Melissa was only in the hospital a few days ago after a bad fall. She was fine, but now look…" His eyes turned to his dead wife. "What the hell did this to an otherwise healthy twenty-six-year-old?"

The paramedic opened his mouth to answer, but the arriving ambulance cut him off. Unsure of what *to* say, he waited for his comrades to walk up to the front step where he informed them of what had happened and what needed to be done. They nodded, and started dealing with Melissa's body while the others loaded the woman into the ambulance.

"I want to go with her," Blake said, having followed them over to the driveway. He saw two police cars pull to a stop at the curb and frowned. "What are the cops here for?"

"Procedure," the male medic told him. "We have one deceased and one back from being deceased. It's unusual, and procedure. We'll wait while you get things sorted out." He touched Blake's arm lightly. "You need to have a chat with your dad."

The frown still in place, Blake followed the officers and a detective over to the door. "What do you want?"

The officers glanced at Blake then his father, still kneeling on the porch. "And you are?"

"Blake Williamson," Blake piped up. "He's my

father, Michael Williamson, head partner at *King, Cavill and Williamson*, the law firm."

"Ah, lawyers," the detective muttered. "Think they can get away with murder."

CHAPTER TWO

"My father didn't murder anyone," Blake snapped, stepping aside for the stretcher to be removed. "She answered the door and dropped dead."

"Likely story," the detective continued.

"Why do you think she's lying here on the doorstep, you moron?" Blake's venom rose. "That's where both of them collapsed."

"Blake, stop." Michael rose to his feet and grasped the doorjamb. "That's not the way to deal with this." He heaved a sigh and gathered his strength. "You may as well come in so we can explain it."

"What! No. I want to go to the hospital with Mum," Blake cried. "I don't want to be here talking to the cops."

"Blake, enough," Michael demanded. "She is *not* your mother. *That, that* woman *is not* your mother. Your mother has been dead for three years. She's been gone three years and now Melissa's…" He sobbed and collapsed against the door frame, sliding down to the floor, his body racked with sobs.

"Aw, Dad." Blake moved to his side. "Mum's back.

It *has* to be her. She looks just like her. Aw, Dad." He wrapped his arms around his father hoping to comfort him. "I know Melissa's gone, but Mum's back."

"And you know she's your mother how?" The detective held a hand out to Michael and pulled the weary second time widower to his feet.

"I just do," Blake replied stubbornly, watching the detective lead his father into the lounge room and into a chair. "Why aren't we going to the hospital with Mum?"

"She's not your mother, Blake." Michael sighed. "Stop saying it."

"I think this situation is going to need some legalities to back that up," the detective said and motioned to an officer. "Get the ambos back in here."

The officer went and collected the paramedic who came to see what was going on.

"Do you have those swab sticks you test DNA with?" the detective asked.

"Yes." The medic saw where the conversation was going.

"Do a swab on the kid." The detective waved a hand at Blake. "Then give it to the doctor at the hospital and tell him to do the same on the woman who's still alive."

The medic nodded. "Not a problem." He left to collect a swab stick, came back, and wiped it around the inside of Blake's mouth, then left without a word.

"Where is she being taken to?" Blake asked, arms crossed and scowl on his face at not going with her.

"St Joseph's is closest," the detective said and turned to Michael. "Mr Williamson, I am Detective Hanahan. Why don't you tell me what happened tonight?"

Emotionally exhausted, Michael told the story. How there was a knock at the door, Blake had said it was for Melissa, she went to answer it, and Blake freaked out that it was his mother. "I ran for the door to find Melissa, since it was raining, and we found them both on the ground. Melissa wasn't breathing. I called triple zero and performed CPR until the paramedics arrived. They couldn't bring her back either."

The detective turned to Blake. "And why did you tell Melissa it was for her?"

Blake shrugged. "I looked out the window and thought it was one of her friends. She'd stopped by before and I thought it was her, so I said it was for Melissa."

"So, when did you think it was your mother?" Hanahan pressed on.

"Melissa opened the door and I saw the woman over her shoulder. She looked exactly like Mum." He wasn't about the mention the neighbours and the spell that had been cast. Melissa was gone. Finally. Out of their lives forever.

"And where were you standing when you saw the woman?"

With a sigh, Blake pointed out the doorway. "In the hall outside the kitchen."

"And what else did you see when Melissa opened

the door?" the detective went on. "Did she recognise the woman? Say anything?"

"Probably, but I didn't hear because her back was to me. She opened the door, bent over, walked out, and the door slammed shut. That was it. Look, can we go? I want to get to the hospital so I'm there when Mum wakes up." Blake looked from Hanahan to his worn out father.

"Blake…" Michael murmured. "Stop saying it, please. There's no way she's your mother. She's gone. She died three years ago." He rubbed his eyes and ran a hand through his hair. "Where's Melissa going?"

"To the morgue," Hanahan replied. "It's in another part of St Josephs." He watched Michael carefully for any sign that he'd done something to his wife. But so far, he just seemed exhausted and shocked. Not a coldblooded murderer. "Tell me, why was your wife in the hospital the other day?"

Michael looked up wearily. "What?"

The detective saw Blake fidget from one foot to the other, and he repeated himself, never taking his eyes off Blake. "Why was your wife in the hospital the other day?"

Blake noticed the detective's stare and looked away.

A sigh heaved out of Michael. "She took a tumble down the stairs. Sprained an ankle, fractured her collarbone or something."

"And how'd she do that?" Hanahan's eyes flickered back and forth between father and son.

"Toppled over in her stilettoes," Michael mumbled.

"I wasn't here. The boys were."

"Boys?"

"My friends," Blake spat. "What? I'm not allowed to have any?"

"Defensive, aren't you?" Hanahan pushed on. "Why don't you tell me what happened, since you were here. And you can give me a list of your friends' names while you're at it."

Blake's brows slid down in teenage anger. "Why?"

"So, I can see if they corroborate the story."

"Mmm," Blake mumbled and looked down at the floor. "We were in the attic when she came up. When she walked out the door she stumbled on her stupid high heels and then Snowball ran around her legs and she tripped. That's how she fell down the stairs."

"And what is Snowball?" Hanahan asked, making notes in his pad.

"What do you mean, what is Snowball?" Blake asked in return.

Arching a brow, Hanahan looked into Blake's eyes. "Cat or dog?"

"It's a white Persian cat," Michael replied. "Doesn't really like us, so tends to hide a lot unless Melissa's..." He let the sentence go.

"Unless Melissa's?" Hanahan pressed.

"Here," Blake finished, scowling at the detective. "It hates us, causes damage wherever it goes, but loved Melissa because she let it eat her food from her plate, drink tea from her cup, and licked her lips which was just gross and disgusting. It hides when

Melissa's not around and comes out when she's here. It's a stupid cat and does stupid things."

Snowball chose that moment to race down the stairs and out the door, screeching all the way.

Everyone in the room followed him with their eyes then went back to how they had been.

"See what I mean?" Blake returned with an arched brow of his own.

"Didn't get along with your stepmother?" Hanahan noted Blake's demeanour and body language, and wondered if the kid had anything to do with his stepmother's demise.

"Of course not," Blake sneered. "She hated me. I hated her."

"Blake, stop," Michael cut in.

"She wanted me gone at boarding school and thought it was okay to slap me."

"Blake, enough." Michael heaved out of his seat and faced his son. "I am telling you now; do not say another word or you will incriminate yourself for something you have not done. Now, shut up." Michael turned from a wide-eyed frozen Blake to a mildly surprised detective. "Blake did not kill my wife, detective. Neither did I. And considering she has not been autopsied, you have absolutely nothing to go on or base any accusations on. Besides which, we have security cameras installed which will show Melissa answering the door and then collapsing. And no," Michael put up a warning finger when Hanahan opened his mouth, "you will not get the actual footage, just a copy of it. So, if you want it, come along." He led them across the hall into his office and flicked on the light, then his computer. He pulled out a blank disc from his drawer, found the footage he was after, and recorded it onto the disc. "There, you see?" He sucked in a shaky breath. "Melissa was fine when she answered the door."

"If the other woman looks so much like your other wife, would she had thought it was your wife and been shocked enough to have, say, a heart attack?" the detective asked. The whole situation was riling his ire. It made no sense unless something wasn't true. There was no way a man's first wife, who had reportedly died three years ago, could come back to stand on her front doorstep, knock on the door, and then…what? From the outside footage, this woman had just turned up and banged on the door. The kid had come downstairs and looked through the window. The woman had turned her head to look at him and then the kid moved away. Melissa had flung open the door and stood in shock. And while he wasn't a lip reader, he'd bet a hundred bucks she'd spoken the first wife's name. Then she lurched forward and collapsed. Nothing untoward about it. "What was your wife's name?"

"What?" Michael was back in a daze having seen two wives come face to face. "Melissa."

"I meant your *first* wife."

"Adalind," Blake replied. "Adalind Williamson." He'd been just as curious about what was on the footage and was relieved it didn't show him doing anything he shouldn't have.

Hanahan made the note and flipped his pad shut. "We will need to talk more, Mr Williamson. Especially after the DNA test on this new woman, and the autopsy on your wife. Until we know who she is, and whether it *is* your wife come back from the dead, and, of course, what your other wife actually died from, there's not much else to do tonight. But I will be talking to witnesses tomorrow. Especially the woman who turned up." Turning to Blake, he added, "Your friends' names and addresses. Now." He handed over his pad and pen.

Grumbling, Blake supplied the details, hoping his friends didn't mention how he'd cut off Melissa's hair, or their trip to the storage locker.

Hanahan finally noticed the bandage on Blake's hand. "What happened there?"

"Cut myself," was all Blake said.

"When?"

Wincing, Blake said, "A few days ago."

"Day of your stepmother's so-called fall?" Hanahan pushed.

"That's enough for now, detective. You can leave." Michael snapped to attention and took charge of the situation.

Hanahan glanced at him and nodded. "That's our cue to leave. Thanks for the security footage. We'll be seeing you both real soon."

CHAPTER THREE

Once the door was shut, Blake grabbed his dad's arm. "We have to go to the hospital. Mum's there. She'll need us when she wakes up."

Michael, in turn, grabbed his son by both arms and shook him. "Stop saying she's your mother. She's not. That woman is *not* your mother. She *can't* be. There is *no possible physical way* she can be." His tone softened as his son's eyes watered with unshed tears. "Blake, that's not your mother. There's no way it can be. It's just not possible."

"Why not?" Blake cried, trying to desperately cling to what little hope he had left. With Melissa out of their lives making things a hundred times better, his mother could be alive and waiting for them in the hospital.

"Because…" Michael pulled his son close and wrapped his arms around him. "I saw her body three years ago, Blake. There is absolutely no way she's alive. There's absolutely no way she could be your mother."

"But she looks just like her, and she turned up here, where she used to live. She *knew* where to come. *Home.*" Blake pulled out of his father's arms. "She's Mum. She's come home."

"Oh, Blake, no." Michael shook his head at his bewildered son. "No. It's not her. There's no way she's your mother."

With trembling lips and overflowing eyes, Blake let the tears do as they would. "Argh!" The wail came out of him and exhaustion took him to his knees. His body bent, his head touched the floor, and he continued to wail. Shuddering, gasping, shaking. Three years of grief poured out of his fourteen-year-old body.

"Oh, Blake. Oh, my son." Michael fell beside him on his knees, trying to comfort his son the best way he could. He'd never taken the time to fully understand how his son had felt. When he'd lost his wife he'd needed to keep it together for Blake, and spent many a sleepless night by his son's bedside listening to him cry himself to sleep. So, he'd shoved his own grief down. The grief of losing the only woman he'd ever truly loved. The woman he'd shared so much of his life with, was gone. The woman who'd given him a son, was gone. And while he'd tried to make things better, the assumption that Blake needed a new mother was a stupid one. He hadn't recognised that his son needed time to grieve. Time to comprehend and digest that his mother was never coming back. Time to just cope and deal with the life-changing fact. No, he'd assumed, and stupidly so, that his son needed a replacement, a substitute, another woman to take the place of his mother. And so, he'd found Melissa delightfully adequate. But in hindsight, that was more for his male needs and not his son's emotional ones. Melissa had never wanted Blake for a stepson. Didn't care for him to be around. After two years, that was more than obvious.

Michael got to his feet and pulled his wailing son to his. "Come on, Blake, let's get you upstairs, it's late." Helping his son to his room, he laid him on the bed and covered him over, then sat beside him. "I am so sorry, Blake. I didn't know how to fix your pain then, and I clearly don't know how to fix your pain now. Marrying Melissa wasn't the solution I thought it would be. Look how that turned out. But that woman tonight, she isn't your mother. And I don't know how to make this better."

Blake heard his father's words and stopped crying long enough to roll over and look at his father. "What if she *is* Mum? What if the DNA test says she is?" He so desperately wanted it to be so.

"What will you do when the test says she isn't?" Michael asked in return, brushing his son's hair out of his face. "What then? Just because she looks like your mum, doesn't mean she is."

"Then who is she?" Blake wiped his face, but the tears kept falling. "Who is she?"

"I don't know, Blake." Michael's voice was soft. "I just don't know. We'll find out after the DNA test. Okay? In the meantime, we both need to get some rest. I know it will be hard to sleep, but at least try. Okay?" He smoothed the blankets over his son. "And tomorrow, we'll try and start getting things sorted out."

With a silent nod, Blake pulled the blanket under his chin and curled into a ball. After his father had shut the door, he waited five minutes before going into his closet and retrieving the bag of Melissa's things from the roof cavity. He placed it next to the closet door and picked up the files and diaries, placing them into the Ziploc bags. He didn't want to read any more. Had read all he needed. Melissa had killed his mother and that's all there was to it. And she'd had her comeuppance in grand style, dying by the hand of the woman she'd killed. He didn't need to know the details of how she'd seduced his father to get him into bed and propose. The cold hard facts were, Melissa was obsessed with his father and wanted him and his mother out of the way. And she'd gotten her wish. Partly. Get the wife out of the way and Michael was free and clear to marry.

But when and how was she going to get rid of me? he thought. *If I'd been in the car that night, I'd be dead too. She stalked us to kill us both, but only got Mum. The one person who really stood in the way of Melissa Dubrey getting Michael Williamson. And now she's dead. Got her just desserts. Finally.*

Leaving the bags by the closet door, Blake got back into bed and lay staring at the mirror opposite, remembering all the stories his mother had told him. With renewed hope that his mother had finally come back to him, Blake fell into a troubled sleep.

After leaving Blake's room, Michael had walked

into his. He stood in the middle of it, staring at everything around him. His things. Melissa's things. The femininity of the décor, the placement of the furniture. So different to how it had been when Adalind was there.

"Oh, Adalind," came out of him in a sigh. "You can't be alive. You just can't be. It can't be you. It just can't be." Trying to control his emotions, he breathed in. "And now I've lost another wife. Melissa's gone too." Remembering all the nights she had made him happy, a sick feeling washed over him. How was it possible for his dead first wife to come back and his second wife to drop dead right in front of her?

How in God's name was that possible? It just couldn't be. There must be some reasonable explanation for it all. Maybe Melissa had a blood clot and the shock of seeing a woman who looked so much like his dead wife dislodged it and it travelled to her heart and killed her? After her fall, something else could have been wrong. Maybe she had a heart attack; maybe she was scared to death. What the bloody…

Knowing he couldn't sleep in a room that had been occupied by two deceased wives, he walked downstairs to the lounge room, got himself a stiff drink from the cabinet, fell into the easy chair, and drank the whole bottle.

*****

The pounding on the door woke him and he opened his blurry eyes to bright sunlight. "Argh." Covering them, he breathed in and heard a second pounding. "Argh, all right," he yelled. His own voice was loud in his ears. Wiping his face, he heaved to his feet, staggered to the side window, and looked through. "Argh." He opened to door to Detective Hanahan. "What do you want now? They wouldn't have done the autopsy."

"True," Hanahan told him, taking in Michael's dishevelled and alcohol emitting appearance. "But we have some questions I need answers to. Can we come in?" He pushed through the doorway followed by two constables.

"You clearly don't wait to be invited." Michael's sarcasm was evident

"Not in a case like this." Hanahan watched Michael close the door and slowly wander back into the lounge room. He saw the empty whiskey bottle, its wrapper on the floor next to it. "Have a drink or ten last night?"

Michael slumped into his chair. "What do you expect? My wife drops dead in front of a woman who looks exactly like my first wife. You'd drink too." The pounding was becoming predominant and he stretched his neck to work out the kinks from sleeping in a chair.

Hanahan conceded. "Yes, I guess I would. But then I've got four ex-wives, so it would be a mess." In his fifties, Harold Edward Hanahan also had seven children by those four ex-wives. "How about we get you into the kitchen for some coffee instead. And maybe some painkillers."

Grateful, Michael allowed the detective to help him up and into the kitchen where he sat him down. He watched him put the kettle on and get two cups of coffee ready, plus, after raiding the fridge, make toast with Marmite spread. For the both of them.

Walking a cup of coffee and a plate of toast to the table, Hanahan placed them in front of Michael. "Get that into you. It should help the hangover. Got any paracetamol?"

"Ah…" Michael thought through his fog-filled mind. "First aid cabinet in the corner."

Hanahan rifled through the cabinet and grabbed the packet of pills before collecting his own coffee and toast. He sat at the table and slid a slab of pills towards Michael. "Take a few of those. Hope you don't mind if I help myself? It's been a long night." He popped four pills into his mouth and washed them down with a big swig of coffee, not even bothered by how hot it was.

Michael swallowed his and eyed Hanahan. "You're being overly helpful, detective. What is it that you want?"

Hanahan took a bite of toast and swallowed. "I read your wife's accident and autopsy reports last night. I'm sorry."

Michael's toast paused halfway to his mouth as memories of his wife's dead and crushed body came flooding back. His arm fell and the toast clattered onto the plate. He heaved a sigh. "Thank you. So am I. Defending criminals pales in comparison to identifying the remains of a loved one."

"Yes, it would." Hanahan chose his words carefully while studying the husband's body language. "They never did find who was responsible. From the report, your son was usually with your wife on Thursday nights. I'm glad he wasn't. It would have been devastating to lose both of them."

Michael swallowed the lump in his throat, his head barely nodding in response.

"I also noticed from other records, that you married Melissa Dubrey within a year or so…that was quick." He left the comment hanging in the air.

Michael barely noticed through the pounding in his head that was yet to subside. "I wanted a mother for Blake. I thought that was best. And she made me happy again."

"I guess we never can tell when we'll fall in love again. Even if it is so soon after a death or divorce." Hell, he'd fallen in love and married wife number three within six months of divorcing wife number two.

"No. I guess we can't," Michael mumbled, and finally ate a bite of toast.

"Did you know Melissa at the time of your wife's death? Had you met then?"

"Um…" Michael thought about it. "No. I don't think so."

"You don't think so?" That comment made the hairs on Hanahan's neck stand to attention and astonishment kicked in. So did suspicion. "You don't remember if you'd met Melissa around the time of your wife's death?"

CHAPTER FOUR

The lawyer in Michael came out. "No, I don't, detective. I know when I met Melissa; it was two months after getting back to work after my wife died. But, just recently, while clearing out the attic of all our junk, Blake came across four boxes of paperwork from my office. One box had paperwork with Melissa's name on it from the year leading up to Adalind's death. I don't know why, unless she worked for my law firm. But I haven't had a chance to dig into that yet and find out if it's even true. Or even if it's the same Melissa Dubrey that I met and married."

"You know of another one?" Hanahan asked. "So, you could have crossed paths and not even known? Not recognised her?"

"From the paperwork, she did the schlep work as a legal assistant. Our paths would not have crossed, so I would not have known her. I knew she was a beauty pageant queen and she'd told me she'd taken a part-time job to supplement her pageants. I met her in the business district. She never told me she worked for my law firm."

"Seems she didn't tell you a lot, Mr Williamson. Does she have any enemies, besides your son? Any friends we can speak to. Any family you know of?"

"No." Michael shook his head. "I don't know. She's only twenty-six, didn't mention family. Doesn't mention friends, really. We don't have guests over for dinner. We got married in the registry office in town. Her family didn't show up."

"Did yours?"

Michael glanced up sharply and studied Hanahan's battle-weary face. "My parents are elderly and living in another state, so do my brothers. I told them over the phone. They wished me good luck. Blake was at school. We did it during the day."

"Did your son know you were getting married?" *No wonder the kid has issues,* he thought.

"No. I told him after. He yelled and screamed and threw a tantrum for days. Can't say I blame him, now. I guess I didn't really know my wife at all."

"Your first or your second?"

"My second, detective," Michael said sharply and finished his coffee.

"Do you think your first wife's accident was actually an accident?" Hanahan pushed on. "There was water found in the tank, the car stalled because of it."

"And that could have been a prank," Michael replied.

"Someone stripped the four-wheel drive that ran into your wife of its plates and VIN. We couldn't trace it to anyone. Someone smashed into your wife then ran off, leaving the car there to be found. The person who owns that car is a murderer."

"Or it's a plain old accident and the person got scared and ran away. It happens, detective. Doesn't mean it was on purpose. It was an accident."

"No, it wasn't." Blake stood in the doorway to the kitchen holding all the Ziploc bags containing Melissa's thing. He'd been listening on the stairs and knew it was time to reveal Melissa for the killer she was.

"Blake," Michael said wearily. "We've been over this."

"And you didn't know your wife." Blake walked in and stood before them. Holding up his right hand, he said, "Melissa's clothes that she wore the night she killed my mother." He slapped the bags on the table in front of the astonished detective. "The keys to the car are in there also and these," he held up his left hand, "are two files of photos and detailed documents about us. She stalked our family for a year before killing Mum. She took photos of us, made notes on our daily schedules, had someone following us or followed us herself, and she wrote all about it in her diaries." He dropped the bags on the table. "I only got up to diary number six. She details exactly how she killed Mum. What she wore, and what she did leading up to it. She stalked us, and killed Mum by ramming that four-wheel drive into her." He choked on his words, his father and Hanahan staring at him in amazement. Shock was still setting in for Michael, and curiosity was getting the better of the detective.

Blake held out his hand. In it was a small Ziploc

bag containing his mother's amethyst necklace that he'd found in the trench coat pocket. "She wrote that she snatched the necklace from Mum's neck because she was sure you'd given it to her. See…" He pointed to it. "It still has blood on the chain and some of Mum's hair."

Hanahan moved to Blake's side, gazing down at the small packet. "How do you know all of this, and where did you get…this…?" He waved a hand over the bags, looking at Michael who sat stunned.

"Melissa's storage unit," Blake wearily told him. "The day she fell down the stairs she'd told me, and I quote, *I will get rid of you, Blake Williamson, just like I got rid of your mother. That's right, I'll get rid of both of you.* It made me suspicious. Why would you say something like that unless you actually *had* killed someone? So, before Dad brought her home from the hospital, I went through her things and found a key hidden in a jewel box up top of the closet. I recognised it because we had a storage locker at the same place years ago. Me and the boys went there yesterday morning before the skate park. She had boxes and boxes of stuff and we found all of this in one of them. I read six diaries yesterday, up until she killed Mum." Blake looked from Hanahan to his father. "She detailed every little bit of it. Including how she held Mum's nose so she'd choke on the blood to make sure she was dead. How Mum actually muttered *help me…*" Hot tears poured down his face. "But she didn't," he stuttered. "*That bitch* killed my mother instead and ripped her necklace off her dead neck." His hand gripped around the small bag that held the necklace. "No one could find it afterwards. You said it must have gone missing in the crash or rescue. No one could find it. Not the cops, not the hospital, no one. That's because Melissa had taken it. And the car…" His eyes went to Hanahan's. "That belonged to an ex-boyfriend. She says so in the diary."

Hanahan stared hard at the kid. *Poor bastard,* he thought. *To go through all of this and then find out all of that. Jesus.* "Blake," he kept his voice soft. "I'm going to need to take your mum's necklace so we can have it tested. Make sure it's your mum's blood and hair. Test for fingerprints, etc."

"You'll find mine." Blake loosened his grip and pointed to the plastic bag containing her things. "Melissa wore those gloves."

"I'm also going to need that key." Hanahan turned to Michael. "And permission to search that storage locker."

Michael stared dazedly at him. "I don't know about the key, but you can search whatever you want." He slumped into his seat, unable to comprehend everything he'd just heard.

Hanahan nodded. "Thank you." Picking up the bags of clothes, diaries and folders, he handed them to the constables. "Blake. I need your mum's necklace for testing and as evidence." Holding out his hand, he waited.

Blake looked from the detective and his outstretched hand to his own and the necklace.

"You'll get it back when it's all over. I promise."

Nodding, knowing he was right, and that he hadn't had it for three years now, Blake handed it over.

"I also need that key." Hanahan saw Blake's second nod and watched him pull it out of his short's pocket.

"It's the storage facility on Wadsworth Lane behind the skate park. Unit 354."

Hanahan took the key. "I know the place. Have some stuff there myself."

"I want a full report." Michael's voice was stronger. "And photocopies of every single diary and report. I want to see for myself what she did. What she…" He choked and gripped the edge of the table. "I want to know every little thing she did."

Hanahan's heart went out to him. "I'll copy them personally and get them to you. If all of it's true, then we've solved the crime of your wife's death."

"And if Mum's still alive and in the hospital?" Blake asked.

"Then we'll solve that mystery too," Hanahan replied. "We'll leave you be now. The results of the DNA and autopsy won't be back until later today or even tomorrow." With a nod, he made his way down the hall and opened the door to run smack bang into Blake's friends. "Ah, just the eyewitnesses I need to see. Skedaddle back to your own homes boys; I'm coming 'round to talk to you." Seeing their frightened expressions, he chuckled as they ran off in four different directions. He closed the door behind him and the constables. *Poor bastard. Wouldn't want to be in his shoes right now. It's hard enough with my ex-wives all still alive, but to have two dead wives. Jesus.*

Inside, Blake slid an arm around his father and helped him to the lounge room, sitting them both on the sofa. "Dad?"

Michael's eyes were glazed over, his mouth barely moving up and down even though no words came from it.

"Dad, we need to find out what's going on. We need to find out if that's really Mum." Blake desperately wanted it to be her, but the light was dawning. Melissa, his stepmother, his father's wife, had killed his mother. And in that case, who was the woman in the hospital? If it *was* his mother, somehow miraculously back from the dead, then what was going to happen now? All he knew, was he still desperately wanted his mother back and wanted to get to the hospital to see the woman he believed was her. "Dad?"

"Argh." Michael's body jerked. "What do we do? What…oh…God…" His head fell into his hands and he sobbed.

Blake had never seen his father like that, but had been that way himself, so all he could do was comfort him.

*****

Two hours later, the boys turned up on his doorstep.

Leaving his father sleeping on the sofa, Blake took his friends into the kitchen for something to eat and drink. "Well?"

"That detective asked us all the same questions. What happened that day in the attic? What did she say? How did she fall? What happened when we went to the storage facility," Callum told him as the boys had conversed when they'd arrived at Blake's before knocking.

Blake swallowed a mouthful of soda. "Asked me the same thing. Thought I'd done it, which is why he wanted to speak to you lot."

"Done what?" Jarrod asked. "Killed her?"

"That, and pushed her down the stairs," Blake replied, in desperate need of a chocolate bar or another of Mrs Baker's chocolate cakes. "We have the security cameras, so he clearly saw that I didn't kill her. And Snowball ran out of here like a bat out of hell, so who cares and good riddance."

"How did she die?" Adam watched his friend carefully.

Blake shrugged. "She just dropped dead. Won't know anything till the autopsy." At this point, he just didn't care. He never had about Melissa. Didn't want her for a stepmother. Didn't want her in their lives. And now his wish had come true. She wasn't.

"You give the cops Melissa's stuff? What we found in her storage locker," Jason said.

"Yep. Figured, since the detective was asking Dad about Mum's accident, that it would be a good time to hand it over and prove what a fraud Melissa was. She killed my mum. She detailed it in her diary."

"She did?" Callum screwed his face up. "Gross."

"Yep, she did." Blake sat on a bench stool and glanced at all of his friends. "Every little detail."

"And now you have what you want." Jarrod was disappointed on so many levels. "Melissa gone and out of your life."

"Good riddance to bad rubbish," Blake spat. "She killed my mother." He went on to tell them exactly what had happened, including seeing the couple next door on the porch when they found Melissa and his mother. "And then they were gone."

"So, what happens with that now?" Callum finished his soda and set the can on the bench.

Blake shrugged a shoulder. "I got what I wanted. I don't care where they go now."

"But what if there are consequences?" Jarrod asked, overwhelmed with sadness for his friend, and disappointment at never being able to see Melissa again.

"What other consequences could there be?" Blake asked in return. "They said when she comes back a life would end. One for another. My mother came back and Melissa's gone. I got what I wanted. Mum's back and Melissa's dead. That was the consequence. End of discussion."

For the next few hours, Blake and his father rested, occasionally answering the door to neighbours who dropped by to offer food and comforting words, but after some serious thinking, he pushed his dad into calling the hospital that night to find out the condition of the woman. They found she was resting comfortably, but drifting in and out of consciousness, and they would know more in the morning.

Blake and his father had their dinner, picked at their food in silence, and retired to bed early. Again, Michael's bed was his easy chair in the lounge room.

CHAPTER FIVE

Monday morning, Detective Hanahan was on their doorstep bright and early.

Blake answered the door to him and heaved a weary sigh. "What do you want now?"

"Is your dad here?" Hanahan motioned to come in.

Reluctantly, Blake opened the door further. "Dad, that detective's here."

Michael came slowly downstairs, having showered and dressed. "What now, detective?"

"The autopsy report is in, and I thought we could go down to the morgue to find out what your wife died of. And while we're there, go and check on that DNA test of the other woman, and check on her too."

Blake excitedly looked at his father. "Can we? I want to go and see her."

"Blake." Michael was dead tired and not sure he even wanted to know the answers. To any of it.

"Please," Blake pleaded. "We need to know if she is or isn't Mum."

Knowing he was right, Michael relented. "We'll meet you down there, detective," he told Hanahan.

"Morgue first?"

"Morgue first," Hanahan replied and walked back to his car. He moved slowly, giving them time to gather their things and get out to their car. After sliding behind the wheel of his, he adjusted himself and buckled in, starting the engine as they locked their door. He drove off and soon arrived at the hospital where he headed for the morgue.

Michael and Blake met him there twenty minutes later after finding their way to the hospital and then the morgue.

"Mr Williamson, please identify the body of your wife," Hanahan said as they stood in the showing area. He motioned for the attendant to pull back the cloth covering her.

Michael slowly breathed in and said, mechanically, "That's her. That's Melissa."

"Okay, let's get to the report." Hanahan moved into the examiner's office and introduced them. "Detective Hanahan, Michael Williamson, husband of the deceased. His son, Blake Williamson. What did she die of, doc?"

Medical Examiner Hawkes picked up the file and handed it over. "My official conclusion is a DVT in the heart."

"DVT?" Hanahan asked, his eyes skimming the file.

"Deep vein thrombosis. More than likely caused by the fall recently. It would have occurred and travelled to her heart. Which is why it happened so quickly."

"So, not a heart attack, stroke, aneurysm?" Hanahan went on.

"No, detective." Hawkes smiled grimly. "She was in otherwise good health and I checked her file from the other week when she was in. She was fine."

"How would she have gotten a DVT?" Michael asked. "I thought they'd put her on meds for that just in case."

"Meds don't always work, unfortunately," Hawkes told him.

"Okay, thanks doc. I'm sure Mr Williamson will make plans in the next few days concerning his wife's body." Hanahan glanced from Hawkes to Michael. "He just needs to gather himself. Now, let's go check on the patient." He led the way up to ward 3A on the third floor and inquired at the desk about the DNA test and the patient.

"Dr Frida is in with her now," the nurse said, and pointed across the hall.

Hanahan walked over, flung open the door, and confronted doctor and patient. "Well doc, how is she and is she the kid's mother?" He swung his left hand up, his thumb pointing over his shoulder at Blake.

"And you are?" the tall woman in the white doctor's coat asked.

"Detective Hanahan," he replied. "I need to know who she is and what she knows."

Irritated by the interruption, Dr Frida glanced from Hanahan to Michael and Blake. "She hasn't said anything so far. I've been asking her questions while examining her, but she doesn't speak." Reading the chart, she rattled off some stats. "Vitals are fine, blood pressure, etc, motor skills are a little slow, bloods are fine so far. We're having it tested for diseases. Don't think she's mute or deaf, just…slow…"

"And that's caused by?" Hanahan watched Blake step toward the woman and the woman turn her head. She had been staring straight ahead, as if she hadn't seen or heard them, but when Blake stepped closer, she moved.

"Mum…" Blake whispered. "Is that you?"

"Blake," Michael murmured, unable to look at the woman, yet unable to look away. "We don't know—"

"Speaking of…" Hanahan turned back to the doctor. "Got that DNA test?"

Frida flicked through the patient's file. "I do. They show a ninety-eight percent match to each other. They are mother and son."

"No." Michael stumbled back in shock. "There's no way. She can't be. No."

Hanahan helped him into a chair before focussing on the doctor. "You sure 'bout that doc? Especially since I have the autopsy report that the boy's mother died three years ago."

"What?" Frida looked up from her chart. "That's not possible. The samples definitely say they are mother and son."

"Mum." Blake moved toward the woman and stretched out his hand. "Mum." His fingers curled into her hair and pushed it back from her forehead. "Mummy. You're home. You've come home."

The woman stared blankly at the boy, not

comprehending a word. But she felt it. Felt the love radiating from his eyes, felt the warmth from his touch. Knew that he was someone special. Someone she knew.

The nerves didn't connect.

"That can't be. It just can't be," Michael sobbed, covering his face with his hands. "It can't be. She died three years ago. I saw her body in the morgue. She was cut up and…and…argh…" Tears flowed forth. *What is going on?*

"Yes," Hanahan murmured. "What *is* going on?" He had two dead wives, but one back from the dead on his hands, and something was rotten in Denmark. There had to be more to this story than what they knew, what was in the reports, files and tests. This woman was Blake's biological mother, yet she'd died three years ago in a car crash caused by Melissa Dubrey in the process of elimination. All to get the man, Michael Williamson. Was there more to him than met the eye? On paper, he was a fine upstanding citizen. He'd never been in trouble with the law and always upheld it. His record as a lawyer and law firm partner was outstanding, and, until three years ago, nothing unusual had happened to him. But now, his wife was back from the dead. *Man. I really feel sorry for the poor bastard.*

"Look, clearly something happened three years ago that needs to be re-opened and looked at again. And this time, I'll do it personally and do a thorough job. I *will* get to the bottom of this," he told Michael and rested a hand on his shoulder.

"But, in the meantime, you're gonna have to decide what happens to your wife." He pointed to the woman in the bed. "Because she is *clearly your wife.* She's biologically Blake's mum. Which makes her Adalind Williamson. Your first wife."

Michael raised his head and stared at his son who sat on the bed gently caressing the woman's face. "It looks like her, but how can it *be* her?"

"I don't know. But I plan on finding out," Hanahan told him, wondering where the hell he was going to start. "You're the lawyer, any ideas?"

"Ha!" Michael gasped. "I deal in truth, law and science. How the hell am I supposed to deal with, or explain, this?"

"Mmm, good point," Hanahan conceded. "Guess I'll go back to that night then."

Dr Frida scribbled something in Adalind's chart and checked the machines.

"Doc?" Hanahan noticed her watching the patient. "What's wrong?"

"Mmm? Nothing," Frida said. "But it is most bizarre."

"What is?"

"She's responding."

"To what?" Hanahan didn't understand where Frida was going.

"To her son."

"Why would that be a big deal?" Hanahan asked.

A nurse came in with a folder and handed it over to the doctor.

"Thank you." Frida read through the file, nodded, and handed it to the detective. "Because she's more than likely been in a comatose or vegetative state, potentially for years. She definitely was on Saturday night when she was brought in. Hasn't responded to anyone or anything, but here she is, responding to her son."

"How do you know what kind of state she's been in?" Hanahan sped read the file.

"When we did the exam of her we took bloods, x-rays, scans. Did the full body. We found multiple breaks, fractures, old wounds. All were relatively healed and would coincide with three years ago. The head injuries she sustained would have caused the vegetative state she's still in. You need to start with hospitals, long-term care facilities, maybe even mental hospitals. If she didn't die in that accident, then it was due to something else happening. And it wasn't good."

Hanahan shut the file. "Thanks, doc. How long does she need to stay here and where would be the best place for her?"

"Physically, she's in reasonably good condition. And the best place would be with her family." Frida glanced from Michael to Blake. "You took fingerprints the other day, the DNA test proves she's Blake's mother. What more proof do you need of her identity?"

"A lot." Michael slowly stood. "I can't...I don't know how...ah..."

Hanahan grabbed his arm to steady him. "It's okay. We'll sort this out. You're a lawyer. I'm a cop. We'll get through this. Right now, you need to put your lawyer cap on and get with the program. Your first wife may have never died, and your second one died of a DVT. All we need to do is find out *who* it actually was that night in your car, and what actually happened to your *real* wife. I suggest you get some carers in and set up a room for her. You've got a wife to look after, Mr Williamson." Hanahan saw Blake's smiling face. "And you've got a son to help that happen. So, get your lawyer cap on and start sorting things out on your end, and I'll get them sorted out on mine. Doc, thanks for the files." He nodded at the doctor and left them to deal with the situation.

"Okay, Mr Williamson," Dr Frida said. "What do you want to do?"

Michael knew he had to get his brain in gear and decided to set aside all emotion and work it like a case he was taking to trial. Taking a deep breath, he followed it with another and focussed his brain. "How long does she need to stay here?"

"A day or two," Frida told him. "We do have a temporary care facility across the road. Patients go there when they're ready to leave hospital, but can't be taken home yet because of equipment needs, etc."

"Put her in there," Michael said. "It will give us a chance to get the house ready and all of the legalities sorted. I hope."

CHAPTER SIX

A week later, after turning the sitting room into a temporary bedroom, a rushed job of redecorating the house at Blake's urging to get rid of all things Melissa, organising carers, filling the fridge with all the things they hadn't eaten in two years, and late nights of figuring out all the legalities, they finally brought Adalind home.

"Mum, this is home. Do you remember?" Blake helped her through the door and they stood in the entrance. "Dad's office is to the left, the lounge room to the right." He pointed and moved her down the hall. "The bathroom is there, if you need it, with the laundry. The basement is downstairs with our bikes and stuff. Here's the kitchen and dining. And here's your new bedroom." He helped her into the room. "It used to be the sitting room, but now it's your room. All for you." They had moved some of the furniture to the attic and brought in a medical bed and pretty pastel coloured linen. "We've got a TV for you to watch, and you can look out over the back patio and garden." He walked her to the French doors and out onto the back patio. "It's summer, and the flowers you planted are all in bloom and beautiful and just smell them." Breathing in, he studied his mother to see if there were any signs of life. She could walk, that was a definite. She could move her arms and head, but the spark came and went from her eyes. One moment it looked as if she recognised Blake and knew who he was, and then she didn't. And there was no spark now. He knew it would be a hard slog, caring for her and trying to get her back to where she once was. Although the specialists from the hospital had said don't hold your breath, Blake was confident that with the love of her son and husband, his mother could and would come back to them. It would just be a hard slog.

"How about we sit you down and you can breathe in the warm summer's day and maybe remember when you planted the flowers." He settled her into a chair and fluffed the pillow behind her back.

"Blake," Michael called from the sitting room.

Keeping an eye on his mother, Blake went in to talk to his father. "What?"

"The carer comes at eight tonight and stays until eight in the morning. Then we have another come for a few hours during the day to help out." He let out a whoosh of air. "I'm not sure I can do this. But Hanahan assured me she is your mother. So, that means she's my wife and I have to deal with *that* the best way I know how. Which isn't very well." He crossed his arms and watched his wife. Her head moved left and tilted up, as if she was looking at something. "The legalities this week have been a nightmare to deal with. The insurance company wants her life insurance back. I argued with them over the fact she has indeed been injured and suffered a great deal of trauma, so they had to pay out on their policy, but it's still up in the air. My salary is paying off the mortgage on this house, and if I take more time off we'll be living on a reduced income. So, as much as I don't want to burden *you* with this, we need to come up with a plan for it." He looked his son square in the eye. "We take out a loan, another mortgage, or we sell off one of the properties in your trust. If caring for your mother is what you want to do, we need to be able to afford it, and right now, within a few months, we won't be able to. Especially while the insurance company's holding out and causing me grief."

Blake absorbed all of his father's words and made the choice that was most logical to him. "Sell one of the properties. Hell, sell them both and put the money into an account to pay for Mum's needs. The doctor said that if she responded to me in the hospital, then it was possible that being around me all the time might make her remember. Or at least better." He saw his father exhausted expression. "We have to at least *try* for Mum. Something happened to her three years ago and we have to make up for it. Giving it a red hot go for the same amount of time is the least we can do. Sell a house, pay off our debts and put the rest aside for Mum's care, so if you have to take time off work, you can."

Michael grabbed his son in a bear hug. "What do we do about Christmas? Do we still celebrate it? I don't even know what to do about Melissa's gifts. Or Melissa?"

"Have you buried her yet?"

Swallowing the lump in his throat, Michael nodded. "Yesterday," he managed without crying. "But I really don't know how I'm gonna deal with all of this."

"Like a lawyer dealing with a court case," Blake replied. "Look, it's Christmas. I know we haven't put up decorations. But we can. It might help Mum remember something." He saw the emotions flit over his father's face. "It's okay. I'll do it. We'll sit Mum in each room and I'll decorate around her, and maybe she'll remember Christmas again."

Michael breathed out and shook his head. "I don't know how you're being so adult about this, Blake. Especially since you're the kid and I'm the adult, and I'm the one who should be taking care of everything."

"You are." Blake put his arm around his father shoulders. "You're taking care of all the important stuff. The legal stuff, the money, Mum's cares and needs. I'll take care of Mum and helping her to remember."

"And what about school?"

Blake pulled a face. "It's not even Christmas yet. I have all of January off, and if I have to take the year off to look after Mum, then so be it. You can hire me a tutor."

"Blake, I don't like the idea of that," Michael started before his son interrupted.

"I've already made up my mind. I've lost three years with Mum. I'm not losing another minute. I'd rather be homeschooled for a year or two than lose more time."

Michael knew he was beaten, and considering how exhausted he was, he didn't want to argue with his son who was so happy his mother was back. The last couple of weeks had taken him emotionally and psychologically to his knees, and he hadn't been that way since his wife died. Well, since he *thought* his wife had died. But here she was, back in his, *their* house, sitting on the porch the way she always did. And he'd had to deal with the death of Melissa, the arrival of Adalind, finding out Melissa had killed Adalind, or whoever was in that car, and dealing with being told his wife was back from the dead. All of the medical expenses and legal problems that came with it had been an absolute nightmare. But, luckily, his partners at the law firm had come through for him and helped him out. His cases were spread out amongst the staff, and he'd received help dealing with wills, insurance, policies and medicals. Adalind had been declared dead, now she wasn't, and that had to be legally reversed.

"Argh." Rubbing his hands over his face, all he wanted to do was collapse into a comatose state and let someone else deal with it. But he was the head of the family and couldn't dump it all on Blake's fourteen-year-old shoulders. No. He had to do it all himself. Thank God for being a partner in a law firm. His assistant was helping with everything else. "Okay. We will celebrate Christmas and I'll get one of the properties sold off to pay for everything."

Blake hugged his father. "Don't worry about the decs, the boys'll help put them up. We can do it today if they're free. I hope Mum likes them."

They looked out at Adalind who sat peacefully in the warm summer air and then spied a dirty grey white animal sniffing the ground and making its way toward the new stranger in the house.

"Is that...?" Blake frowned. They hadn't seen Snowball in over a week, not since bolting out the door when the cops were there.

"A dirty Snowball," Michael lamented. "Now we'll have to clean the damn thing and you know how it hated to be washed."

"Melissa used that grooming service in town. Take it there, or get rid of it. It hated us, why keep it now Melissa's gone?"

"We can't just dump it at the pound."

"Why not?" Blake watched Snowball sniff around his mother and his mother look down. Snowball jumped onto his mother's lap and settled on his haunches staring up at her.

Blake moved to shoo him away, but Michael stopped him. "Wait."

They watched Adalind slowly raise her hand and slide it down Snowball's body. Snowball meowed and sniffed at Adalind.

She raised her hand and stroked again. Slowly,

monotonously. And Snowball liked it, purring and settling into her lap. He started licking himself while being petted.

"Bloody hell!" Blake whispered, not quite sure what he was seeing. "Snowball? Likes Mum?"

"Looks like it." Michael shook his head in amazement. "And your mum is responding. She's moving, mentally connecting how to pat it. That's a good sign. The doctors said there was a slight chance she would be able to come back and remember things. She just needed the right care."

"Well, if Snowball can do that for Mum, then we'd better get him cleaned up and fed. I take it he'd know Melissa's not here."

"More than likely. He knows there's a stranger in the house, and apparently, cats have a sixth sense when it comes to sick or dying people. They're also very good for helping the elderly and mentally disabled stay calm and help improve motor skills, I think I read."

"Naw, bum. Guess we'd better keep him then," Blake muttered, watching his mother stroking the he-devil they'd dealt with for two years. *Wonder if he'll be nicer to us now.* He quietly walked over to his mother and laid a hand on her shoulder.

She turned her head to look at it, then looked up at him.

"Mum, this is Snowball." He pointed to the grey dirty mess on her lap and Snowball purred and rolled onto his back. "Crikey!" Blake exclaimed. "You're lovin' yourself sick, ain't ya, Snowball."

Adalind moved her head to look at the cat. Her lips twitched at the corners and her mouth formed the word snow, but nothing came out.

Blake saw it and repeated, "Snowball."

Adalind mouthed *snow…ball,* but nothing came out.

Blake's face lit up. If his mother could form words, then she could hear them. He leaned down so his face was beside hers. "Mum, look at me."

Adalind turned her head.

"Say…snow…ball…"

She mouthed the word, *snowball,* but nothing came out.

"Snow…ball…" Blake repeated.

"Snow…" It was low, barely a mumble, or even recognisable.

"That's it, Mum. Snow…ball…"

"Snow…" She formed the word ball, but it was still low, barely a whisper.

But Blake heard it and his grin grew bigger. "Yes, Mum. This is Snowball, our cat. He's usually white, but he's been missing for a week. We'll need to get him fed and cleaned up."

"Here." Michael held out Snowball's food bowl heaped with a can of his favourite, chicken and beef.

Blake took the bowl, sat on the chair next to his mother, and held the bowl out for the cat, who shifted positions on Adalind's lap to greedily inhale every single morsel in that bowl. "Geez, Snowball, guess you haven't eaten since you were here last. That's what you get for running away. Oh, and by the way…" He watched the cat lick the remains in the bowl and then his lips before nestling in his new mother's lap. "You need a bath."

Snowball opened one green eye, meowed, and then went to sleep.

Blake sat the bowl on the patio table and saw his mother petting the purry ball of dirty fluff. Maybe Snowball was going to be worth having around after all.

The knock at the door sent an astonished Michael down the hall to answer it. "Ah, detective."

"Mr Williamson. I want your permission to excavate your wife's grave and test the body. We need to find out exactly who is in the grave, and if it was *she* who died that night." He thrust a clipboard with papers into Michael's face.

"My wife? Melissa?" Michael's astonishment changed to confusion.

"Adalind's grave," Hanahan corrected. "I know you buried Mrs Williamson number two yesterday. I'm sorry, but we need to sort this mystery out once and for all."

Michael took the clipboard and signed the necessary documents. "Do whatever you have to detective. You have my permission to search whatever you want."

CHAPTER SEVEN

Later that day, Blake and his friends were decorating the lounge room while his mother sat on the sofa with a freshly washed Snowball. They'd called in the groomer who made a house call, and washed and blow dried Snowball in the laundry. Now he sat purring happily on his new mother's lap.

"String it up higher," Blake told Jarrod as they hung the lights across the bay window. "It needs to be just right." After hooking them up, he stepped down from the ladder and plugged them in. "There, how's that, Mum?" He looked over his shoulder to see a small smile on her face. She was stroking Snowball and seemed at peace.

Grabbing an old short piece of tinsel, Blake walked over and draped it over the cat. "Maybe we should decorate Snowball." He moved it back and forth across Snowball's head, making his ears twitch, and finally, making him wake up, alert to the intruder upon his nap.

He spied the brightly coloured tinsel and grabbed for it as it moved, rolling onto his back so he could attack it with both paws.

"He's definitely a lot friendlier," Callum commented. "Not hissing and growling all the time." They'd been amazed when Blake told them the story of everything that happened Saturday night after the skate park, and they'd helped get the house ready for his mother.

"Definitely a lot nicer." Blake saw his mother's smile grow and put the tinsel into her hand. "You wanna do it, Mum? Tease Snowball." He held her hand up while she got used to the motions and then let go.

Adalind dangled the tinsel above Snowball's face, smiling at his antics, his paws reaching up to grab it, rolling over and meowing. Her hand moved up and down slowly, getting used to the motions.

Blake's heart soared. Within hours of being home, his mother was smiling and moving. It was a good day all round.

"Are we doing the whole house?" Adam asked, glad that his best friend finally got what he'd wanted. He had his mother back.

"The downstairs at least. And maybe hang tinsel up the stairs or something." Blake sorted through the boxes to make sure they'd finished with the tree decorations and then packed them to be stored in the attic until it was time to take the decorations down. It was barely a week before Christmas, but he was just glad he had his mother back.

"Okay, so what's next?" Jarrod asked, adjusting the stockings on the mantel. "Is that this room done?"

Blake looked at everything they'd done. The tree in the corner, the lights and tinsel hanging from the window, the lights and stockings on the mantel, a few Santa decorations on tables. "Yep, that's it. We've got the kitchen next and Mum's room." He turned to his mother to see her gently scratching a purring Snowball's head. "Come on, Mum, let's go decorate the kitchen and maybe have a drink or something to eat." He slid one arm around her back, the other around her front. "Can you get up? You can bring Snowball with you."

Adalind slowly wrapped her arms around the cat, cradled him like a baby, and got to her feet with her son's help.

Blake led her to the kitchen and sat her down at the dining table. "Let's get this place decorated and then we'll move on to your room, hey."

They quickly hung tinsel and lights which they turned on. "There we go, how's that?" Blake saw his mother gazing at the lights, a small spark in her eyes. "Do you remember all the Christmases we had here, Mum?" He slid his hand through her hair and tucked it behind her ear. "Do you remember?" He desperately wished she did, and that they could have conversations like they used to, but he knew it would take time, and while they had that, he was impatient. Glancing down at Snowball, he pulled at the old piece of tinsel tangled around him and tied it to his collar in a bow. "There you go Snowball, Merry Christmas."

Snowball meowed his appreciation and licked himself.

"Would you like something to eat, Mum? A drink?" Blake got everyone sodas from the fridge and poured his mother's into a plastic two handled cup.

They'd been told by the outpatient centre that she had general motor skills, eating, drinking, walking, but needed help learning how to do everything else. With time and therapy, there was always the possibility of her getting better.

"Here you go, Mum." He placed the cup in her hands and waited while she raised it to her mouth.

Automatic reflex took over and she swallowed, then shakily set the cup on the table.

"That's good, Mum. I love you." He kissed her on the cheek. "Let's go decorate your room, huh." He helped her up and walked her into the sitting room. "Right, I want lots of tinsel and lights so she can see them." Blake directed the boys on where to hang the decorations and soon the room was filled with colourful Christmas decorations.

"There you go, Mum, Merry Christmas." Blake settled beside her on the bed and put an arm around her shoulders. "It's Christmas, and things will get better. I promise."

A small sigh left her and her hand continued rubbing Snowball's stomach as he lay across her lap. It was the only thing so far that made a connection in her brain, that kick-started it into gear and kept the neuron's going. "Snow…ball…"

It was low, but Blake heard it. "Yes, Mum, that's Snowball. I'm Blake, and it's Christmas. Merry Christmas."

"Mer…ry…Christ…mas…" Adalind barely managed although it was somewhat garbled.

Blake's smile lit up his face. "Yes, Mum. Merry Christmas."

"Bl…a…ke…" she said, staring at her son with vacant eyes.

His smile disappeared as tears sprang to his eyes. "Mum…Mummy…" Those tears flowed and he leant his face against hers. "Mummy, come back."

"Bl…a…ke…"

He hugged her and wiped his tears away. "Yes, Mum. I'm Blake. It's me. I'm Blake. I'm your son." Smoothing back her hair, he kept repeating himself. "I'm Blake, I'm your son."

The boys quietly slipped out of the room, taking the boxes with them. They deposited them in the attic and prepared to leave, happy for their friend that he had his mother back, but also saddened by the fact something so horrible had happened to her it was going to be some time before she got better. If ever. And *that* would take another toll on Blake. They kept a long strand of tinsel out and wrapped it around the bannister from the first floor to the ground floor stairs as they came down, meeting Michael in the entrance hall as he came home. He'd been gone for a few hours sorting out other things. "Hey, Mr W."

"Hello, boys, Blake not with you?" Michael placed his briefcase on the floor inside his office door. "Or is he with his mum?" He couldn't bring himself to call her his wife. It was still too bizarre to comprehend.

That his first wife wasn't dead, even though he'd seen her body in the morgue three years ago. Seen what the accident had done to her. Buried her and then remarried. Now his second wife was dead. All of it was just too much to comprehend and digest.

"In the sitting room," Jarrod said. "It's getting late, we should go."

"Want dinner first?" Michael led the way to his wife's room. "You've done a lot to help Blake this last week, moving furniture and helping to clean up. And I see all the decorations." He stopped in the hallway to watch his son with his arms around his mother on the bed. He was quietly talking to her as they both patted the cat. "Wow, that's a shock." The sight caught him unawares, and his guard fell down. His wife with his son. She was still alive and looking the same as she had three years ago. But there was something else. She looked as if she had a century's worth of weight on her. Mentally, that was. Aged in the face, older, burdened by something. And he still didn't know what had happened. *I hope Hanahan can sort this out*, he thought. *We all need to know what happened in the last three years.*

"Blake," he called quietly. "Do you want dinner?"

Blake wearily looked up. "Can we have KFC? I need chicken. And potato gravy. And chips, and ice cream for dessert." He was so glad they had junk food back in the house. His body had been craving salt, sugar and chocolate.

"I'm not sure your mother would be able to eat chicken, but I guess chips and potato gravy. Okay,

I'll go and get it. Dinner's in half an hour. Make sure the table's set." He left them and was back a half hour later laying it all out on the table. "Do you want to give your mum some mash and chips?"

"Yeah, I'll help her." Blake sat his mother down and pushed her chair all the way in then sat beside her. Dealing out a large spoon of mashed potato and gravy, and a handful of chips, he helped her get started, dunking the chip into the potato gravy then putting it to her mouth. The outpatient centre had told them to give her mashed food, or food without bones and seeds, and to show her how to eat to get her started. After that, muscle memory kicked in and she could do it herself. A bit like a toddler learning to eat for the first time.

The boys dug into their food, felling a little uneasy about seeing Mrs Williamson like that, but knowing it wasn't her fault. They knew Blake was being attentive at every turn, and applauded him for doing so.

Meanwhile, Michael sat silently at the head of the table watching his wife slowly eat her food. This was all new to him. Having her back from the dead, while dealing with Melissa's death, and knowing Melissa had killed her all to get him. Yet, she wasn't dead.

Clearly not, since she was sitting at his table. *Their* table. Just the way she used to. Except for being different. And he wasn't yet ready to call her his wife, even though she was, and even though sorting out the legalities meant she was, and that meant his marriage to Melissa wasn't legal, which, in hindsight, was probably a good thing. But with everything he had to deal with, he just wasn't ready for any of it.

After dinner, the boys helped wash up and went home. The carer came at eight to help out overnight, and get Adalind showered and ready for bed. But Blake wanted to continue her therapy and had his dad hang her mirror in the sitting room so she could look at it every day.

"Remember this, Mum?" He stood her in front of it. "It's the mirror you used to stand me in front of and tell stories about. We used to go on adventures in it. Do you remember?" Watching her reflection, he saw her face was passive. They were the same height now, had the same green eyes and brown hair. He recounted some of the stories she'd told him and watched sparks light up her eyes. Snowball meowed and wound his way around her legs and she noticed, looking down to her feet, bending and picking him up into her arms. She buried her face in his fur and Snowball peacefully rested his head in her neck.

Adalind stared into the mirror, seeing the boy beside her. She knew he was someone important, knew he was someone who loved her, but she just couldn't connect to who it was. She heard his words. Blake, mum, son. But just couldn't connect to what it meant. She knew her heart felt warmth and wondered what it was. What the *word* for it was, but again, just couldn't connect. Or to where she was, or what she was doing there. But what she *did* know, was that she was safe, loved, and at peace.

CHAPTER EIGHT

"And here's my birthday album." Blake laid the first one on his mother's lap and opened it to the first page. It showed him as a baby being brought home from the hospital. "This is you and Dad bringing me home when you had me. We lived in a different place then." He pointed out the different times and birthdays throughout the book. "And this is my tenth birthday. Do you remember?" Watching for a sign in her eyes, he noticed she was more at ease after being there for a few days.

Snowball, as usual, was by her side purring away as she scratched him.

She looked down at the album. "Tenth…"

"That's right, Mum. My tenth birthday party. And here's you and Dad, and you and me and Dad, and me and my friends. We've been friends ever since we moved here when I was little. I was two or three, and now I'm fourteen." He closed the album and picked up the next. "And here's my eleventh birthday party. We went to the theme park." He told her the story behind the day. How he'd begged to go and they'd arranged it for him and his friends. He bypassed his twelfth and thirteenth birthdays and turned to his fourteenth. He'd finally printed off the pictures from his party and put them in the album, completely eliminating Melissa from any of them and just having him and his dad, plus his friends. A bit of Photoshop magic on his dad's computer, that was. Just a pity he couldn't do that to his two previous party pictures as well, although, he could maybe scan the pictures they did have and try and print out new ones. "And here I am at my last birthday. Just a few months ago I turned fourteen, can you believe it. And I had a growth spurt. I'm as tall as you now." He rested his head on her shoulder and pointed out the pictures. "That's me, Blake, your son. Here, at our house."

"Bl…a…ke," Adalind murmured.

"That's right, Mum, I'm Blake," he replied and put her finger on the photos. "Blake, your son. I'm fourteen."

"Four…teen…"

"That's right. I'm fourteen and this was my birthday party, and look, here are other photos you might remember." He picked up another album and showed her pictures of her and Michael at law school, graduation, starting work at the same law firm, their first date, all the pictures in between and their wedding. "That's right, Mum, you and Dad got married fifteen years ago and then had me." They were propped up on her bed, the French doors open, the warm summer breeze drifting in, bringing with it the scent of all the flowers she'd planted in those ten years. Blake had brought down all of the albums he had, plus her art books and notebooks, hoping they would bring back her memories, or at least spark something.

"Fif…teen…" Adalind murmured.

"Yes, Mum. Fifteen years ago you and Dad got married. Michael and Adalind Williamson."

"Ad…a…lind…" Her mouth formed the word and her voice said it.

"Yes, Mum, that's you. That's your name." Blake's hopes soared more and more that every day she was connecting. It may have only been in spits and spurts, but it was better than what they'd been. And Snowball seemed to be helping her motor skills. She knew how to pick him up and hold him, and how to pat him and scratch his stomach. Plus, she was trying to say more words. He'd been researching online about brain-damaged people and trying to find treatments that could help her; new drug trials or therapies that might make her brain fix itself. He lived in hope, and that hope also went toward his father sorting out the life insurance and selling a house to pay for the treatment because he knew it would help greatly.

Seeing her eyes drift shut, he stroked her forehead till she slept, then carefully climbed off the bed and left the albums nearby in case she wanted to see them when she woke. It was three in the afternoon and he wanted a nap himself. After grabbing a drink from the kitchen, he was walking across the hall when there was a knock at the door. He saw the boys peering through the side window and hurried down the hall to let them in.

"What are you doing out now? It's late, and *wow* it's hot." The heat hit him like a wave in the face and he quickly shut the door behind them.

"I called the boys because of what's going on next door," Adam said. "Do you know?"

"Know what?" Blake gulped down his drink. "Want one?" He led them back to the kitchen and got them sodas. "Know what?"

"That there's a for sale sign up next door," Callum jumped in. "The neighbours must be gone."

Blake shook his head. "I heard something outside this morning. But I've been with Mum all day. We've been going over the albums hoping to jog her memory." He glanced into the sitting room. She was still sleeping and Snowball was curled by her side.

"That means the old kooks are gone," Jason added. "If they were even there to begin with. Did we imagine that, or what?"

"Dunno. But considering Blake's mum came back, it's hard to say anymore," Adam said, and knocked back his drink. "What they said would happen, happened. But are we even sure it's because of them, or just some weird setting the universe straight thing? Clearly, Mrs W wasn't dead, and has miraculously come back, and Melissa died of what, a DVT caused by the fall. Isn't that just stuff happening in real life?"

"His mum coming back from the dead is

extremely weird and not normal," Jarrod told him. "Who even *does* that in real life? It's usually something you see in some TV drama or movie."

"But it happened," Blake cut in. "And whether or not the old kooks next door actually existed, and what happened that day actually happened, I don't know. What *I do know* is, Mum's back and Melissa's gone. Not even Snowball's fussed with it, or missing her. In fact, I don't think he cares that Melissa's not around. He attached himself to Mum and he's been by her side since they both came home." They all looked across the hall to see Snowball stretching backwards over her legs. "He's lovin' himself sick with Mum. And maybe that's a good thing. So, for now, I'm not worried about the neighbours. If they're gone, they're gone. If they didn't exist and were only a part of my imagination, then so be it. I've got Mum to look after."

After talking a while longer, devouring another of Mrs Baker's cakes, and drinking another soda, the boys left and Blake climbed back up beside his mother. He needed a nap, and what better place to take one.

*****

Christmas was a quiet affair in the Williamson household. On Christmas Eve, they sat in the lounge room watching the Christmas carols on TV and singing along. Well, Blake was, and he tried to get his parents to join in.

Adalind sat transfixed at the TV. The lights and sounds and music triggered neurons and she nodded her head slightly to the music.

On Christmas Day, Blake opened his presents as he always did, scoring a new laptop computer, plus games for his WII.

Michael had found Melissa's present for Snowball, a brand-new Swarovski crystal collar that Blake put on him. It had a name tag in the shape of a snowball, and a bell. It fascinated Adalind who touched the bell to make it tinkle and played with it all day.

Michael also found Melissa's presents for him, and not being able to bear the emotions that came with them, threw them in the bin. Even though they'd cleared out her things last week, he'd found them in a cupboard that was rarely looked in. He'd also come across his presents for her, and returned those he could, and threw out those he couldn't.

He hadn't bought anything for Adalind. Why would he? But after asking Adam's mother for help, he'd given her money to go and buy Adalind clothes and toiletries. He'd remembered her favourite perfume, which was still being made, and had that bought as well. Blake sprayed it on her morning and night after her shower and hoped it triggered memories.

Michael could smell it now; a mixture of citrus and spice.

They watched Christmas movies and ate turkey for the rest of the day.

*****

By New Year's Eve, Michael finally had the insurance policy sorted out. The company had given in to the pressure and gone over their policy with a fine-tooth comb. While it wanted the money back because Adalind was not dead, it did still have to pay out because she had been severely injured. So, in the end, they deducted the death clause from the policy which left the assault and injury clause, and Michael paid back what was owed. That still left half a million for her care. And since he hadn't sold the house yet, they needed it.

Also, Detective Hanahan stopped by.

"Detective, come in." Michael invited him into the lounge room where they had been watching TV. "Any news on how the hell this happened? I haven't heard anything in weeks."

"And it's been a busy two weeks." Hanahan nodded to Blake who was beside his mother, and noticed Snowball curled up in her lap. "That's interesting."

Blake grinned. "We think so."

"Take a seat and tell us what you've got." Michael took his place in his easy chair.

Hanahan took the other. "Well, once I went to my boss with the details, she gave me twenty cops and four other detectives. We've been working night and day to find out what happened."

Michael was impressed. "Good to know it wasn't taken lightly. What did you find out?" He hadn't heard anything since the last time he'd seen Hanahan.

"First of all, I want to give you these and ask you what you want me to do with all of your wife's…" He glanced at Adalind. "*Melissa's*…things when this is over." He handed over the box he was carrying. "It's the photocopies of her diaries and files."

Michael took it and held it with both hands, trying to figure out how he felt. Sighing, he finally said, "I don't want her things. Keep them as evidence for however long you need. Throw out what you don't."

Hanahan nodded. "I'll let them know." His eyes moved to Blake and his mum who was scratching Snowball's head. "How is she doing?"

"Better," Blake replied, gazing adoringly up at his mother. "She can repeat words, and knows how to feed herself and do stuff."

"That's good. Well, I have a very long and complicated story for you. This may or may not make things easier."

"You've found out what happened?" Michael asked, and put the box on the floor beside his chair. "What happened that night?"

"Well, to get to that, I have to go back further." Hanahan settled into his chair. "We might want to have something to drink first, as it's a long story."

"Of course, where are my manners? Blake." Michael waved his son toward the kitchen.

Blake rolled his eyes and got up, going into the kitchen for the drink. He came back and handed a large cola with ice to Hanahan.

"Thanks." Hanahan drank half and set it on the small side table. "We exhumed your wife's grave two weeks ago and had extensive DNA tests done on the body inside. We found it to be a familial match to your wife." He looked at Adalind. "But clearly, not your wife. More like her twin."

"My wife didn't have a twin." Michael frowned. "I think I told you—"

"You told the paramedics that night," Blake reminded him.

Michael thought about it. "Right, yes. Go on."

Hanahan started again. "After finding out the results, the best thing to do was go straight to the source themselves. Your wife's parents. I flew interstate and spoke at length with them. They finally conceded that yes, your wife was a twin. But because there was something wrong with the baby, they gave it up. They never breathed a word of it. Ever."

"Jesus," Michael muttered. "I never knew."

"That meant Mum never knew either." Blake rested his head on her shoulder and she tilted hers to rest on his.

Hanahan saw this, and said, "She's definitely responding to you. So, anyway, we followed up with the hospital and welfare home who reported that your wife's twin was mentally disabled. We traced her through her life to a home for the mentally disabled and found she had a room. We found a shrine to your wife, and, in passing, you and your son." His eyes flicked to Blake. "Your mother's twin seemed to know exactly who she was and what she did. And she didn't like it one bit. Apparently, she had been acting out for a year at that time, and was on medication. But, since she had permission for days out, we're pretty sure she was also stalking your wife. Just like Melissa."

"Jesus Christ." Michael scratched his head in disbelief and rubbed a hand over his face. "We never knew. Any of it. So, what happened next, or do I already know?"

"It's not hard to guess," Hanahan replied. "While we can't trace the twin's whereabouts that night, we do know she wasn't in her room, and had been reported missing. We went back through all of the CCTV footage we have from all of the shops in the area, and do have some small sightings of her. It seems the home she was in isn't far from the store or the soccer ground your son was practising at that night. From what we can put together, there was an ambulance called out to the 7/11 after closing where they found the body of an unconscious and badly beaten woman. She was taken to the hospital for several weeks and identified as being from the home your wife's twin was living in. The clothes she was wearing had tags for easy identification. Once she could leave the hospital, they reclaimed her as the twin sister, and that's where your wife has been ever since."

"I don't get it," Blake jumped in.

"From what we can gather, your mum's twin was following her, and when your mum stopped at the 7/11 she must have jumped her somehow, got her outside in the alley, undressed her, dressed in her clothes, took her bag and ID etc. Your aunt is the one who got into the car and left. Your aunt is the one Melissa followed and ploughed her car into. Your aunt is the one *she* killed and *you* buried." Hanahan looked at Michael. "That's why you believed it was her, but why she's sitting here in your lounge room."

His head turned and saw her staring right at him. It unnerved him because it was the exact same stare he'd seen in the last photographs of her mentally disabled twin. She had the exact same expression right down to the evil in her eyes. A chill fled down his spine, making him shake.

"So…my wife was found beaten in the alley and taken to hospital, but because of the clothing she had been dressed in, she was identified as her sister and taken back to the home where she's been the whole time. The last three years." Michael was incredulous. "Why the hell…? How the hell…? How did we not know? Not find out?" He shook his head in shock and amazement.

"All I can say is, everyone didn't do a very good job." Hanahan finished off the last of his drink. "The hospital your wife was taken to, the morgue and their tests, the home for the mentally unstable; they all ballsed up at some point. And the cops on the cases never linked them up."

"And because everyone didn't do their jobs properly, I went without a wife for three years. Blake went without a mother for three years, and she sat in a home for the mentally disabled for three years." Michael watched Hanahan nod and shook his head at the injustice of it all. "Oh, I smell a mega lawsuit coming on."

Hanahan sighed, defeat plummeting through him. "If that's what you decide, that's up to you. I can certainly see how this has affected you."

"How did Mum get here?" Blake asked. "How did she manage to get here that night, three weeks ago?"

"I have no idea." Hanahan gave a shake of his head. "Maybe her memories were coming back. Maybe something compelled her to find her way home. Muscle memory, whatever it was. But your mum has come back to you."

"Yeah." Blake smiled up at her. "I'm glad she has."

"Well, that's me done." Hanahan hefted himself to his feet. "If there's anything else I can help with, you have my number."

"Yes, thank you, detective. I'll walk you out." Michael walked into the entrance hall and opened the door.

Thunder rumbled in the distance as Hanahan stepped onto the porch. "Looks like we're in for another summer storm." He turned to look at Michael. "Let's hope you don't end up with another dead wife on your doorstep."

Michael frowned. "Not funny, detective."

"No, guess it wouldn't be, *for you*." Hanahan nodded. "Mr Williamson."

"Detective."

CHAPTER NINE

That evening, as the thunder rumbled and cracked and split the sky open in two, a hand thrust up through the ground and into the wet windy air. It was perfectly manicured in blood-red, and it looked just as good as the day it was done.

Clawing at the sodden ground, a second hand made its way up and out, and it too was perfectly manicured.

Reaching, the arms clawed and pushed the sodden soil aside until it could pull the rest of itself up from its grave at the Knightsbridge Cemetery. It had been there for three weeks in a fairly nice coffin, but now it had a mission.

Crawling from its grave, the body jerked into a standing position and got its balance. It knew where it had to go. Knew what it had to do. And regardless of the fact it had been dead for three weeks, it knew how to get there.

Jerkily, with stunted steps in the rain, the body made its way to the front gate and turned left.

*****

"This is the attic," Blake said to his mum. "Me and the boys cleared it out weeks ago. Dad paid us fifty bucks each for it, but he and I also got rid of a lot of stuff we didn't want or need anymore."

"Att...ic..." Adalind murmured and moved her head to the right. "Att...ic..."

"That's right, Mum." He led her over to the couch and sat her down. Snowball jumped up next to her and sat on his haunches.

"Me and the boys cleared this space out to do our dance routines. We thought we would be the next One Direction. Do you remember them?"

Adalind stared blankly at the wall opposite.

"Guess not." Blake glanced around at the still fairly empty space, but now with spare furniture from the sitting room, and saw the hole had been plastered over. "I used to look at the photo albums when they were up here and I'd cry a lot." He looked back at his mother who had her left arm around Snowball, scratching his chest. He sighed and sadness washed over him. *If only she'd do that to me...* "We never did get around to using this space, did we? Maybe we could have turned it into a bedroom and bathroom for me and kept mine as a guest room or something. I dunno. You and Dad never ended up having more kids, so there was no need for another bed and bath."

*****

The body stumbled and jerked down the street. The stilettoes didn't help; neither did the animal print mini dress, and the blonde Marilyn Monroe bob was washed out. But, it was determined to get to where it was going. It turned down a street and kept on going.

*****

"And this is the first floor landing. Over there is my bedroom and bathroom, and here is your and Dad's room." Blake walked her into the room. "It's been redecorated a couple of times in the last three years, but once you're able, you can put it back the way it was when you were here last."

Adalind moved her head. Her eyes took it all in, but it didn't really connect. "Bed…room…"

"That's it, Mum. Your and Dad's bedroom. Come on, I'll show you to his office."

*****

The body jerked across the road, broke a heel, and stumbled over the median strip. It fell, and lay there, its dead brain connecting to its dead body. Its arms jerked up and clawed, and pushed the body from the ground. The legs folded underneath and forced it to stand. Its face had been smashed into the tar of the road, and the skin was peeled back from the right eye socket down to the chin where it hung loose in a flap. But that didn't stop it. It was almost home.

With jerking motions, it finished crossing the road and limped down Huntington Way.

*****

"And here we are, back on the ground floor." Blake stepped off the bottom stair, his arm around his mother, her arms around Snowball whom she'd picked up in the bedroom, and who purred like the queen of Sheba at being carried around.

"As you know, that's the lounge to our left, the kitchen and sitting room is back that way." He pointed over his shoulder. "And this is Dad's office." Walking into the room they saw the Beatles memorabilia on the wall opposite. "Hey, you hung it up."

Startled, Michael looked up from behind his desk. "Huh? Oh, hey, yeah, um, I figured, why not." He kept an eye on them as Blake showed his mother around and pointed out awards, trophies and pictures.

"And there's you and Dad at *King, Cavill and Williamson*. That was when he made partner. And there's you and Dad when you worked there."

Thunder cracked above them, rattling the windows, and making the house shudder. Lightning bolted across the sky, lighting up every window and room in the house before diminishing. The lights flickered and dimmed.

Knock. Knock. Knock.

Blake looked over his shoulder at the door

Michael frowned and looked at the clock. "Who

could that be on a night like this? It's nearly midnight." The clock started striking down.

"Partygoers?" Blake suggested, helping his mother turn around.

Knock. Knock. Knock.

Blake's heart hammered with memories and his head spun towards his father. His eyes saw his father look out the side window and flick the outside light switch off and on. Saw his father shrug and reach for the doorknob. "Dad, no," Blake yelled and took off across the room and into the entrance as the door was pulled open. Out of the corner of his eye, Blake saw the corpse of Melissa Dubrey standing, lopsided, on the porch. He flew at his father, pushing him out of the way, landing with a thud on the entrance floor against the side table, and with his right foot, kicked the open door shut.

But it didn't close.

A freshly manicured hand stopped it. The freshly manicured blood-red nails, one by one, came around the edge of the door and the hand pushed it open.

"No," Blake yelled again. "No." He kicked the door as the rain and wind howled into the entrance hall and in the crack of lightning they saw the body of Melissa looking down at them.

She had one heel broken, scrapes and scratches, her face half hanging off, her blonde Marilyn Monroe hair limp and wet.

She reached out to them. Her rotting eyes leered down at them, and her protruding teeth and gums moved as her jaw did.

Adalind's neurons kicked into gear. She knew she had to protect the child, and in turn, the man.

Snowball screeched, flew out of her arms, and into the entrance where it ripped at Melissa's legs before bolting down the hall and into the sitting room to hide in the far corner behind the cupboard. That provided enough time for Adalind to make her way into the entrance to face off with Melissa.

"Mum, no!" Blake's voice rose hysterically. He didn't want to lose his mother again.

"What the hell," Michael breathed, unsure of what he was seeing.

Blake frantically looked around for something to stop Melissa with, and saw the umbrella tips at the bottom of the umbrella stand. It was perfect. Wrenching out an umbrella, he turned and saw his mother holding Melissa's arms, as if they were fighting, or she was trying to stop her. "Mum, no." He watched his mother's right hand let go of Melissa's arm and thrust itself into Melissa's chest.

"Mum, no." Blake rushed to his feet, held up the umbrella, and charged the spike into Melissa's temple.

The body screeched, flailed and jerked haphazardly, and dissolved into dust which shocked them all.

"Dad." Blake spun around to see if his father was all right.

Michael climbed to his feet and gazed down at the pile of dust. "What the hell? Was that Melissa?"

"Don't know, but at least you're safe." Blake hugged him fiercely, then turned back to his mother. "Mum, you okay?" He took her into his arms as the clock struck its final toll.

"Blake…" Adalind said. Her eyes moved up to her husband who stood behind their son. "Mi…chael…"

Michael sobbed, and suddenly everything else melted away. He grabbed his wife and son into his arms. "Adalind." And kissing her cheek, he wept.

EPILOGUE

Unable to explain what had happened on New Year's Eve, the Williamson family chose to put it out of their mind. They had too many other important things to deal with, like Adalind's recovery.

It was a long process, and Blake had been right. They owed her at least three years' worth of care after she'd been gone that long.

After selling the house easily in the New Year, they had sought the best treatment and doctors, and success became a common occurrence. With mild electroshock therapy, Adalind's neurons kicked in and extensive speech therapy and daily muscle memory training saw her treatment make great strides. By the end of the year, she was able to speak and put sentences together, albeit slowly, to get herself food and drink, and give Snowball a bath. By the end of the second year, she could read and write to the equivalent of a high schooler, and in the third year, Blake was able to spend his final year of school back with his friends and graduate with top honours in maths and science with his parents standing to ovation. They were married again and happy together, kissing and hugging as they always had. And regardless of what had happened that night in his attic when he was fourteen years old to make his wish come true, he would forever be grateful that he had a second chance with his mother. His parents were back together, happy and married, and because of everything he'd been through, he'd decided to go into medicine and maybe become a neuroscientist or researcher so he could cure his mother completely, and anyone else like her.

THE BONES OF WRATH: MONSTERS

CROC-O-JAWS

"Come on, Dad, can't you drive any faster? We wanna get to Lake Kirriwaka," Billy complained from the backseat of the family's four-wheel drive.

They were going camping for a week and were towing their fully decked out caravan behind them.

"We'll get there when we get there and not a minute before," Ben Daniels told his twelve-year-old son. "I'm not rushing and putting our lives in danger just because you're impatient." He clicked on the blinker and veered into the exit lane for Lake Kirriwaka. "It's only another fifty ks to go."

"Fifty!" Nick, Billy's fifteen-year-old brother got his own complaint in. "Geez, we're never gonna get there." He elbowed his brother to get off him and hit the window button for air. "Jesus, Billy, you stink. Mum, Billy farted."

"Did not," Billy whined, trying to hide his giggles.

"Ew, Billy," Molly, their eight-year-old sister, cried, shaking her head out of the other back window. "Mum!"

"Billy, stop passing gas," Terri Daniels told her

middle child. "I don't know what it is you're eating, but it makes you horridly gross. Stop it." She peered over her shoulder at her three children and saw their border collie Razzer in the back of the four-wheel drive shy away from Billy and stick his nose over Nick's shoulder and out the window for air. "And don't even think about blaming it on the dog. We know it was you."

"No, it wasn't, it was Razzer." Billy smirked, loving the fact he could blame his gaseous problems on the dog who couldn't talk back.

"You stink, Billy. Razzer smells better than you, so we know it was you." Molly slid her window up half way and smoothed out her pigtails. Her flaming red hair curled in large loops down to her shoulders, and her bright flashing green eyes highlighted the light spattering of freckles across her face. Molly was the only one in the family to have red hair. A throwback from their great-grandparent her mother had said, so she relished being different to her brunette family. She also had two missing front teeth which showed when she smiled, and she was smiling while retying the bright green ribbons in her doll's flaming red hair, tied in two pigtails like her own. Her dolly was a mini version of her.

"Razzer eats dog food and stinks. I eat human food and *do not* stink," Billy informed everyone, elbowed Nick back for the blow to the ribs he'd taken earlier, and then went on to inform the whole family about his non-existent issues for the next half hour.

"While you lot have been talking about your horrid gas resources…" Ben cast a glance at his wife and grinned. "We've arrived at Lake Kirriwaka."

The kids craned their necks out of the back windows to take in the picturesque country town in outback Australia. The town was named after the lake, but the drinking supply was provided by a natural spring and aqueduct two kilometres away which also supplied the water for the cattle and crops. The town was spread across those two kilometres making it a short drive to the lake.

Ben pulled up to the petrol station and alighted to fill the tank, only to be greeted by the town's resident tour guide, who also happened to own the station.

"Let me fill that up for ya, mate," the man said. "Where ya's from?" He shoved the pump into the tank and casually leaned on the car.

"Melbourne," Ben told him. "We heard about the lake and decided to come for a holiday to see it for ourselves. As blue as blue can be, it's supposed to be. And as clean as the air we breathe."

"Yep, well, that's what it says on the brochures we put out. I'm Mudgee, by the way." He extended a chocolate brown hand to shake Ben's.

Ben eyed Mudgee up and down as he shook his hand, taking in the dark curls, brown eyes and brown skin. "I take it you're from here. How long?"

"All my life." Mudgee nodded to the kids who eagerly leaned out the window. "Hello, youngins. I'm Mudgee, aboriginal born and bred here in Lake Kirriwaka." He tweaked Razzer under the chin.

"And who's this fella?"

"That's Razzer," Billy informed him, eyeing the man's appearance. "Got anything to tell us about the lake? We're camping there."

Mudgee's eyes landed on Billy's. "Ya are, are ya? Ya'd better be careful then, tourists have been known to go missing from the lake at certain times of the year. Especially if they park too close to the edge. And don't go swimming alone," he warned. "Or the Croc-o-Jaws will getch'ya." The pump came to a clanking stop and he put it back in its holder.

"The what-o-what?" Billy asked, leaning halfway out the window and shoving his brother and Razzer aside.

"The Croc-o-Jaws," Mudgee repeated, his black eyes flicking back and forth from Billy to his dad. "The tale goes, that when this country had dozens of rivers and lakes, a giant shark swam inland. All the way of the furthest point it could go. And that, was Lake Kirriwaka." He spread his arms wide. "It swam here, and it is said that to survive it bred with a crocodile and had multiple babies." Mudgee hopped from one foot to the other, doing a little dance around in circles. "Time has not erased the Croc-o-Jaws, it has descended down through time just like the lake has transcended with it." He stopped and peered down the road towards the lake. "The tale has it, that it hid deep down in the lake bed because the lake bed is an old volcanic shelf thousands of feet deep. Deeper than the oceans." Mudgee spun around to Billy. "And it is said that after a series of earth tremors, the volcano let go of its secrets, and one of those was the Croc-o-Jaws, giving it life all over again. And so people have gone missing, and so have cows and sheep that wandered down to the lake." He tweaked Razzer's chin again, his head next to Billy's. "So better not let this one off on his own. Ya may not get him back." Grinning, he turned to Ben. "That'll be a hundred fifty."

Ben handed over the money, a twinkle in his eyes as he looked from a grinning Mudgee to his son. "Well, that's quite a story. We'll have to keep our eyes open for this Croc-o-Jaws, won't we, Billy?" He ruffled his son's unruly hair and thanked Mudgee before getting in the car. Making sure his sons were buckled up, he left the station and headed down the road for the lake, leaving Mudgee frowning in his wake.

"That was *so* made up." Billy rolled his eyes and crossed his arms. "I can't believe *how bad* that story was. Croc-o-Jaws, half shark, half crocodile. Can they even mate with each other?" Even though he was saying it, he was secretly hoping something *did* happen, and something *was* out there.

"Clearly it was something made up for the tourists," Terri said, watching the campsite come into view. "Think of it as a funny adventure tale."

After pulling alongside the other vans at the campsite, they got out to set up theirs with water and power.

"I'm going to look at the lake," Billy declared and raced off with not a care in the world.

"Billy, be careful," Ben yelled, exasperated by his son. "Nick, go with him and keep him out of trouble."

"Ugh, *why do I have to do it?*" Nick's head fell back in disgust. "I'm not his keeper. It doesn't matter if I'm there or not, he *always* finds a way of getting into trouble."

"But at least you'll be there to pull him out of it," his mum told him. "Now go." She watched her eldest drag his feet down to the water's edge where Billy was craning his neck to see everything. A sigh left her and she looked from her boys to her daughter. "How come you're the good one in the family?" She affectionately tickled Molly's cheek.

"Coz I'm a girl," Molly replied emphatically. "And boys have more testosterone. They're predisposed to getting into trouble." She sat down on a camper chair and started brushing her doll's hair.

Terri raised a brow at her husband, wondering how and where their daughter had learned such things.

Ben grinned back and pulled out the caravan's annex. "Think we'll need the sleeping bags for the boys?"

"Depends on whether they want to sleep on the ground, or on a mattress in bed." Terri slapped her arm and spied a dead mosquito. "It will also depend on whether they want to be eaten alive."

Down at the lake, Billy held his hands above his eyes to shade them from the sun. He scanned every inch of the lake that he could see to his left, then turned his head to the right. His brother came into view. "Get out of the way."

"What *are* you doing?" Nick asked. With his hands on his hips, he tried looking authoritative, but it didn't work.

"Ugh," Billy groaned. "Looking for the so-called Croc-o-Jaws. Get outta my way." He stepped to the side to scan the lake, but couldn't see anything other than lake. "Do you remember if the guy from the petrol station said it came out at night, or during the day?"

"What does it matter?" Nick stared out across the water. "It was a load of bunkum anyway. He was just having a lend of you like Mum said. All made up to give the tourists a thrill."

"But what if it *is* true?" Billy's gaze flitted over the lake. At five kilometres in diameter, it had somehow formed several rocky tree-covered islands, probably from old lava built up over time before the volcano had flooded with water. The water itself looked as blue as Superman's costume, and it had an ethereal feel. Almost…ancient, desolate, untouchable. Haunted.

A chill seeped into Billy's bones and he shuddered. "For all we know, it's completely true. Who knows what ancient relics came up via the old rivers to live in the lake. Look at Loch Ness. Bunyips in billabongs."

"*They* don't exist either," Nick cracked. "*All of it's* bunkum. *Bunyips* don't exist, *Nessie* doesn't exist. The so-called Croc-o-Jaws doesn't exist. All made up by the local towns to get the tourists in and their money in their pockets. That's all it is. A tourist trap. And you've fallen into it. I'm heading back, come on." He started walking for their campsite, but when he noticed his brother wasn't with him, he turned back. "Come on, jerk for brains. Mum'll have my guts for garters if I don't bring you back."

Reluctantly, Billy fell into step beside his brother. "Why don't you want it to be real, Nicky?"

"Ugh, don't call me that. I hate it when Mum and Dad call me that, so don't call me that." Nick shoved his hands in his jeans pockets and lowered his head. "Because it doesn't exist, Billy. It's not real. Why would I need it to be?" He glanced at his brother and extracted one hand from his pocket to ruffle his hair. "Why do *you* need it to be?"

Billy pulled his head away, both offended and chuffed that his brother thought enough of him to show affection. "I dunno." A shrug of his shoulder. "It would be cool, is all."

They got back to the van where their mother was asking after Razzer. "Did he go with you? He was here a minute ago."

"Razzer!" Billy yelled, spinning around to look for their dog.

Razzer's ears picked up the sound of his name being called, but he stood steadfast at the lake's edge. He had wandered down after the boys, sensing something was wrong. Sniffing the air, hearing the sounds, he barked at the water, saw the gentle rippling about twenty metres from shore, knowing it was not the wind making it. Knowing there was something out there, *in* there, waiting, just beneath the surface.

"Razzer." Billy raced to his side. "Bad boy. Don't run away like that again. What if something happens to you? We wouldn't be able to find you." He tugged the dog's collar, but couldn't budge him.

Razzer growled from deep in his throat. His eyes pinpointed on the rippling water like two lasers.

Billy glanced towards the spot and saw the ripples. He saw the bubbles pop to the surface. And that chill from before came down his spine. He felt the fear crawl up to his throat, but wedged it down. With both hands, he tugged on Razzer's collar, and keeping his eyes on the water, pulled the dog back to the campsite.

*****

After a restless night where Billy had slept inside on the bunk with Razzer by his side, and their faces at the window for any signs of life, the family left the van and drove into town for a look around and to buy some souvenirs and supplies. At the town's gift shop, they found an assortment of Croc-o-Jaws memorabilia. T-shirts, keyrings, posters, you name it they had it with a crudely drawn half shark half crocodile cartoon figure on it, with *Lake Kirriwaka, home of the fabled Croc-o-Jaws*, printed on them.

Billy stood staring at the posters on the wall, imagining the beast walking out of the water in front of him. *How high would it be? How long?*

Would its breath smell of fish? Did it even eat fish? Mudgee had said tourists, cows and sheep had gone missing, and even dogs. So no, it probably didn't eat fish.

"Bah!" Nick grabbed his brother's shoulders, making Billy jump. "Ha ha, made you jump." Getting a scowl for his trouble, he glanced at the posters. "You can't seriously still be thinking about it? It doesn't exist for goodness sakes." He leaned closer. "Look at how badly it's drawn. Horrendous. Besides which, I seriously doubt a shark could breed with a croc."

"Who says it can't?"

The boys spun around to come face to face with the owner, an aboriginal man dressed in khaki shorts and shirt with a name tag that read *Temby*.

"Who says it can't?" Temby repeated, hands on hips, and a grin on his lips.

Nick shrugged. "Evolution, genetics, DNA."

"But other animals have bred with other species. So why not sharks and crocs?" Temby went on. "I did the drawings myself."

Nick rolled his eyes at the childish pictures. "Breeds have been bred by idiot people who think it's funny to breed Chihuahuas with German Shepherds, for example. It's not. Just because tigers and lions are closely related, doesn't mean they should breed. Same with horses, donkeys and zebras. Just because they can, doesn't mean they should or could. In the case of a shark and a crocodile, they definitely shouldn't *and* wouldn't, as one would eat the other before the deed anyway, so the deed is never done?" Nick waited for Temby's reply.

But the man just stroked his chin and narrowed his eyes. "You're a very informed youngster, clearly know a little somethin' 'bout animals. But just because it shouldn't, doesn't mean it won't. And just because you think it's genetically and physically incapable, doesn't mean it can't or won't happen."

"Have you seen it?" Nick cut in, eyeing Temby suspiciously. "Have you actually *seen it* to say *it does* exist?" He pointed to the posters. "Or to get a description such as this? Or is it something you just made up?"

Temby was offended. "Just what do you think I am, mister. A liar? I've seen it for myself, right there at the lake. Saw it eat a whole cow, it did." His eyes grew wide and he became animated. "Saw it fling that cow up in the air, open its jaw and swallow it whole. Snapping its jaws shut just like that." He clapped his hands together in front of Nick's face.

Nick flinched and a frown darkened his face. He didn't believe one word for one minute, but could tell his brother did from the way he was clinging to him and hovering behind. "Prove it."

"What?" Temby stepped back. "Prove what?"

"Prove that it exists. Show it to us," Nick defied him.

"Okay, mister." Temby nodded. "Come on the lake ride this afternoon and we'll see if it shows itself to you."

*****

After lunching at the local restaurant, the family met Temby down at the lake's dock for an afternoon boat ride. The other campers were lined up, and they filed one by one onto the cruiser.

"Ladies and gents, please take your seats. Keep your hands and heads inside the boat at all times, and do not stick anything in the water. You never know what might pop up and bite it off." He chuckled and steered the boat into deeper water.

Nick rolled his eyes and glanced at his brother. The day before Billy had been rearing to go, ready to track down the infamous Croc-o-Jaws, but today, especially now, he was deathly white and clinging to Razzer who was tied up. Their dad was beside them closest to the outside of the boat, while their mother had Molly on the seat in front of them.

"And if you look to your right, ladies and gents, you'll see the rocky outcrops that have formed over thousands of years out of molten lava and the current of water." He moved the boat closer so they could see the bird life making the outcrops their home. "We have some local wildlife living here. They find it safer than living on the mainland because wild animals can't eat them, and because of that, we have a thriving bird life here at Lake Kirriwaka." He drove on, taking them around the outcrops to the other side of the lake. "The water has a distinctive blue colour because of the calcite crystals which give off the shade you see before you when the sun bounces off. But if you were to hold it in your hand, you would see it is not blue at all, but clear."

The boat hit something under the water and lurched.

Razzer barked and strained on his lead, standing on Billy's legs to get to the side of the boat.

"It's all right everyone, we have plenty of rocks and underwater bits and bobs around these islands. We probably just hit a fallen tree. Let's get a little bit further away." He steered the boat away from the outcrops and kept powering on, trying to keep the tourists calm.

But Billy knew. Knew it was the Croc-o-Jaws, and knew it would not end well. Hanging on to Razzer for dear life, he bit down on his tongue.

Nick heard small sounds coming from his brother and looked at him. Saw the fear, the terror, the white skin, the wide eyes, and slid his arm around him. "He's just trying to stir you up. Don't let him," he whispered.

The boat lurched again, sending small waves of panic through the rest of the tourists.

"Don't worry ladies and gents, sometimes the trees float. I'll get a wiggle on, shall I?" He slowly pushed the accelerator handle forward and the boat sped up.

Another lurch.

"What *are* we hitting?" one man asked, flustered at the disturbance. His bright red Hawaiian shirt flared in the afternoon sun, and he removed his white Panama hat and fanned himself. "Can we go faster? It's so hot out here. And stop hitting trees."

"Yes, mate." Temby pushed the speed up.

"Ew, what's that?" Molly pointed past her mother to the half-rotten half-eaten carcass of a cow floating just off their side of the boat. "Ew, gross."

The other passengers agreed and urged Temby to go faster. Finding a dead cow in the lake to be quite offensive, they demanded their money back when they reached the dock.

Waiting while the other passengers alighted and Temby tied the boat, Billy cast a glance over the lake, seeing ripples and bubbles slowly move past them. He stared, trying to see under the water, and saw a dark hulking figure cruise by. Shivering in the late afternoon sun, he allowed his dad to move him off the boat and back to their van where they had dinner and settled in for the night.

But Billy wasn't to be put off. He knew something was out there. He knew something had hit their boat, and eaten that cow, and floated by when they'd docked; knew that whatever it was, it was something bigger than all of them.

Before bed, Razzer needed the toilet and Nick was volunteered.

"Why do *I* have to take him? I'm ready for bed." He groaned, dressed in his shorts and t-shirt. "Besides, isn't it Billy's turn?"

"I did it last night." Billy turned from the window beside his bed. "I don't want to go out there."

"Chicken," Nick grumbled and slid into his shoes. "Come on, Razz." He grabbed the lead, and led the dog out into the night to do his business.

But Razzer was too busy staring at the lake to do anything. A low growl emanated from his throat and he strained on his leash.

"Razzer, stop it. Just do your business and let's get back in. It's cold." He shivered despite himself and rubbed his arms.

And Razzer took that moment to bolt from his owner's grasp and race down to the lake's edge, growling and barking into the night.

"Razzer, for God's sake," Nick yelled and threw his head back in disgust. "Get back here you little jerk."

"What's going on?" Ben stuck his head out of the van.

"Razzer's run off," Nick whined. "I need a torch."

His dad retrieved one and handed it over. "Make sure he does his business."

"Ugh." Nick trudged off towards the lake, passing other campers.

"Feisty thing, isn't he?" The man in the Hawaiian shirt from that afternoon's boat ride grinned. "Careful, he might get eaten by the Croc-o-Jaws."

"Har har," Nick grumbled and kept walking until he reached Razzer. Picking up the lead, he tugged. "Come on, you jerk for brains. Quit your yammerin'."

"What's going on?" Billy ran up to them with Molly right behind.

"Razzer's barking at something." Nick pulled the dog back a few paces, but it didn't stop him barking. "Shut up, Razzer. There's nothing there."

And if by a miracle, Razzer stopped barking, whined instead, and backed up of his own accord.

"Phwoar, Billy, stop farting." Nick screwed his nose up and waved and hand in front of his face to clear the air.

"That's not me." Billy froze in fear. "Definitely not me."

"It's not Razzer, either," Molly piped up. "It's something else." She held her nose and buried it in her dolly's mop of hair.

Razzer whined and backed up against Nick's legs, making him turn to the dog. "Razzer, what—?" His torch, and the faint light from the campsite, lit up the creature before them as all three Daniels children looked up into the crocodile-like snout, legs and tail, and the shark-like head and body.

"Bah…bah…it's ah…bah…ah…" Billy mumbled in fear as the stench of the Croc-o-Jaws wafted around them.

The growl was deep and throaty, the jaws wide and full of teeth, and finally the Daniels children found their voices.

"Holy Jesus bloody hell," Nick yelled.

"Croc, Croc-o-Jaws," Billy screamed.

Molly's shriek pierced the air, and the rest of the campers raced down to the lake with lamps and torches.

The Croc-o-Jaws opened wide, ready to bring its teeth down on the tasty morsels before it. But before it could, the boys dived in different directions and their father raced past, scooping Molly into his arms.

"Dolly." Molly's arms reached out for her fallen doll as Ben raced back to the campsite.

"What in blazes is going on?" Hawaiian shirt guy stood staring into the night with his torch, managing to get a head scratch in before the Croc-o-Jaws clamped down on him and swallowed him whole.

The rest of the campers scurried in all directions, screaming in terror at the abomination before them, disbelieving what they had just seen.

The Croc-o-Jaws retreated into the water and Nick took the opportunity to flee back to the van, scooping up his sister's doll from the ground as he passed, pulling Razzer with him, shoving his brother ahead of him as his father bundled their sister into the back of the four-wheel drive and their mother gunned the engine.

"Hurry up," Terri screamed and hit the accelerator. The caravan forgotten, she'd only managed to grab her handbag and her husband's work bag and fling them in the car before the unholy beast ate the other camper.

An unearthly growl ripped through the night and the Croc-o-Jaws smashed into several vans, theirs included.

Terri slowed for the boys to jump into the backseat.

Nick threw Razzer in and then his brother, before jumping on the sideboard. "Hit it," he screamed, looking over his shoulder to see other campers doing the same.

"My clothes," Molly whimpered from her father's

lap, staring out the back window at their destroyed caravan and clutching her rescued dolly.

"We'll buy you some more, Bubba," Ben comforted his daughter. "That's why we said don't pack your good stuff."

The Croc-o-Jaws chomped down on another tourist, eliciting screams from the woman's children who were next. The husband tried fighting it, but he became the next victim.

Disgusted, Nick slid into the car and slammed the door.

Squashed in the back seat, Razzer in the front, they sped towards the town followed by those who had got away. Lake Kirriwaka the town was silent; dark except for a few lights from the petrol station and pub. Not even the police station was alight.

The small cavalcade of cars slowed as they passed through, the tourists breathing a sigh of relief that the beast hadn't followed.

Glancing in the rear-view mirror for any sign of it, Terri noted the scared expressions on her children's faces.

"Look out," Ben yelled, his hand reaching toward his wife.

Looking back at the road, Terri screeched to a halt. Around her, other campers did the same.

In the middle of the road in front of them stood the people of the town, but they were no longer people. Their noses had grown into snouts and their limbs into the legs of a crocodile, their heads and bodies into those of a sharks. Their eyes were piercing white, their teeth long and sharp, and they could tell that because their mouths were open. They were the descendants of the Croc-o-Jaws.

A low growl made the Daniels family turn their heads to the right to see the snout of the Croc-o-Jaws beside the car.

Their mouths opened in silent screams.

GODJIRA

"This is so cool," Dustin Hooper cried out, grasping at the window frame of the monorail train. It was taking them around the perimeter of the newly opened theme park, *Senshijidaino Tochi*, Japanese for *prehistoric land*, on a small island off Japan. A billionaire had set up the island to be his adventure playground, with rides, stores, an entertainment hub, and animals and plants from the four corners of the globe. Dustin and his family had been lucky enough to win tickets to the opening week.

"Don't lean out so far," Martha, his mother, warned. "We don't want you falling out." The monorail had no solid windows so the passengers could get up close and personal with the variety of wildlife. The train shook lightly and everyone looked around in surprise.

"What was that?" an American girl of about twenty called out. She was blonde and dressed in tiny denim cut-off shorts and a tight red tank top that showed off her ample curves. Her friends reiterated her words.

"Ah, that was nothing," the young Japanese tour guide proclaimed in perfect English. "The island we are currently travelling on is a prehistoric volcano that has lain dormant for centuries. Mr Yukugawa would not have been allowed to build on the island if it was not. It all adds to the mystery of the island. The prehistoric with the present. Old meets new. Tyrannosaurus Rex meets Disneyland. There is nothing to worry about. It is all part of the fun." The guide brushed her straight black hair out of her face and looked at the twenty or so tourists in the train car. "You will feel a tremor or two, it is normal. The ground also trembles from the movement of the monorail you are on, all of the amusement rides, and whenever the animals decide to go for a run. And look, there is a herd of wildebeest going for a run now." She pointed, and the passengers looked to their left at the racing beasts as they played and frolicked in the green fields.

Moving on, the train made its way around the back of the island where a lush green tropical oasis resided. Colourful birds flew from lush tree top to lush tree top, while others casually strolled around as if they owned the place. It all made the atmosphere heady and exciting.

"Oh, how gorgeous," Martha gasped, snapping a photo of the macaws perched in a nearby tree. "Darling, look." She grabbed her husband's arm and saw him look up from his phone. "Oh, can't you shut that damn thing off for once? You're always on it. This is our holiday."

Mathew Hooper was the youngest court judge in Australia to ever sit on the crown bench, and unfortunately, that meant he took his business on holiday. He reddened and tucked his phone away. "Sorry, luv, work's always calling, you know that." Sliding an arm across the back of their double bench seat, he tapped his fingers on his wife's left shoulder.

"You also told me you'd leave that work at home." Martha arched an annoyed brow. "This is the one holiday we get to take this year, so leave it home." She went back to watching the birds.

Dustin, in the seat in front of his parents, exchanged a glance with his twin brother, Lincoln. At thirteen, both were on the cusp of puberty and manhood, and both were worried that their parents' marriage was on the rocks. They'd heard arguments and raised voices in the last few months, and that's why Dustin had entered the competition. In the hope they'd win so they could spend time together. And they had, so here they were, but his parents were still fighting. Sighing, he turned his head back to the left to watch the animals roaming in their compounds.

It was a beautiful summer's day with not a cloud in the sky, but that didn't stop another tremor from rocking the monorail.

Dustin grabbed the windowsill while his brother grabbed the seat in front.

"Just a little speed bump, ladies and gentlemen. We have switched tracks as we are making a detour around the animal medical centre. There's no need to stop there, so we will bypass it. Up next we will be passing your hotel, so if any of you need to disembark, just pull on the cord above you running down the ceiling on the side." She indicated to the rod above their heads. "For those who are staying, we will continue on back to the front gate for you to enjoy the rides and amusements."

The monorail slowed until it came to a stop outside of the island's hotel. It had five levels divided into five parts that resembled a star. And it was the star of the island, aptly named *Itsutsu Hoshi No Hoshi,* which is Japanese for *five pointed star.*

The Hoopers stayed in their seats while half the passengers disembarked and other tourists got on board. Once they were settled, the train left the hotel and continued around the island, past animals, the hothouse for all of the exotic plants the owner had brought in, the waterslide, and roller coaster, before reaching the front where the entrance led them to the main purpose of the island.

Enjoyment.

The main entrance led straight down the main street with shops of every kind on either side. Exotic candy, which they had already indulged in and bought big bags of, Japanese clothing and accessories, which they had filled up a case with, a Japanese music store, toy stores, and old-style tea houses and modern restaurants led to the main auditorium where the cinema, theatre and museum were. Roller coasters, ghost trains, dodgem cars, waterslides and all manner of Japanese rides were set up behind the stores, and golf buggies transported people around.

Dustin and Lincoln opened their eyes wide to take it all in as they strolled with their parents down the main street toward the auditorium.

"Cool." Dustin ran to one shop and saw stuffed animals, birds, elephants, lions, and tigers; basically the whole animal kingdom. "Can we get some?" His hands were flat against the shop's window, his face squashed against the glass.

"Why have they got dinosaurs?" Lincoln asked, staring at the stuffed dinosaurs on the shelf behind the rest of the animals. "There are no dinosaurs on this island. It's not Jurassic Park."

Dustin shrugged. "Who cares? Can we have one?" He turned to his parents with pleading eyes. They were big, round and blue, and he knew they couldn't resist when he pulled his little boy look.

Martha knew that expression well and sighed. "You can buy it yourself. You did get money to spend on this holiday." Glancing at her husband, she saw his nose back in his phone. "Mathew." she complained.

"What? Oh, huh, sorry." He glanced up sheepishly and shoved his phone in his pocket. "What? Oh, what were you saying?"

Frowning at her husband, she reached an arm out for her boys. "Let's go. If you've got any money left over you can buy a toy. Just pick wisely." She led them inside and they ran to the stuffed animals in the window.

"Cool, a tiger." Lincoln swooped on the first one he saw and grabbed it by the tail. Swinging it around in one hand, he dug into the pile of stuffed toys with the other, looking for something else to buy.

Dustin was staring at the dinosaurs on the shelf above the rest. "God, that's ugly. That's not a normal dinosaur, is it? You know what it is, Linc?"

Lincoln looked up and watched his brother pull down the ugly dinosaur. Black, scaly, with beady eyes, short arms, a long tail, and standing on two back legs. It looked like an uglier version of a T-Rex. "That is one ugly dino. You even sure it's a dinosaur? It doesn't look like anything I've ever seen." He walked over to the shelf and eyed the rest of the stuffed dinosaurs. "That is so ugly."

"Boys, you want anything else? Don't forget to spread your money across the week so you have some to spend in other stores," their mother reminded them as she rummaged through a table of homewares, looking for something to buy.

"Yes, Mum," the boys replied in unison and ran over to look at some 3D models of the animals in the park. There was even a Lego version of the park and the island.

The boys were so busy looking at everything they didn't notice some of the models fall off the shelves until they broke at their feet. Startled, they turned and saw the other shoppers grabbing for counters and tables to steady themselves as an earthquake rippled through the island. They saw their parents clinging to each other and looking around frantically as the store rocked on its foundation.

Merchandise fell from shelves, shelves fell from walls, and all clattered to the floor. The boys dived for the corner of the shop, hoping they wouldn't be hit. They covered their heads until it was over.

Outside, screams were overshadowed by the soothing voice coming over the loudspeakers. "Ladies and gentlemen, please remain calm. That was just a minor earth tremor, and if you are unhurt, you are okay. We will be stopping the rides to check for safety issues, but in the meantime, please eat, drink and be merry."

"I didn't sign up for earthquakes," Martha told her husband as they straightened themselves and looked for their sons. "Boys, come on."

The twins dashed over to their parents and they headed for the register to pay for their goods.

"Boys, I know we won this holiday, but I really don't feel safe here," Martha said as they stood in line. "We've been here three and a half days and that's not the first earthquake we've had. I don't like it; I think we should leave today."

"But we haven't seen everything yet," Dustin whined. "We have the robocopter and the spaceballs to go in so we can get close and personal with the animals. And we haven't been to the hothouse yet. All we've done is the rides, the auditorium, and now the monorail. We haven't even seen the aqua dome and aquarium."

"I don't care. This is freaking me out," their mother told them as they moved up the line. "So if you want anything else, get it now so we don't have to come back, and we'll leave on the boat this evening."

"Aw, Mum." Lincoln joined in the whining. "We don't want to go yet. Why can't we stay the week?"

"I just told you. These tremors are freaking me out and I don't want to stay, they're getting bigger and longer. Now go and get whatever else you want. Quickly, we're almost at the register."

The boys scurried off, grabbing at toys and models they'd had their eyes on, but were saving their money for. If they were leaving now, there was no point leaving the toys behind.

"Don't you think you're overreacting just a little?" Mathew murmured in his wife's ear. "Japan is known for tremors, and being on an island with tonnes of amusement rides just makes them seem stronger. Haven't you noticed every time the rollercoaster goes around it makes the earth shake?"

"Maybe if you didn't have your nose in your phone all the time you would have noticed what's actually going on," Martha replied, not bothering to look at her husband. They reached the head of the line and she handed over her items. "Boys, come on, time to pay."

The boys scurried over and Lincoln placed his items on the counter.

The two salesgirls were working in tandem. One scanned the item and passed it to her colleague who packed it. They took Martha's money and handed over the bag before moving onto Lincoln's toys.

"Do you really need all of those, boys? You've got so much at home." Martha put her purse away and uneasily stared out the door to the street. There had been no more tremors, but it still freaked her out.

"If we're leaving and never coming back, then yes." Lincoln handed over his money and took the bag of toys. He stepped aside for his brother and noticed the dinosaur Dustin was putting on the counter along with the models and Lego sets. "You aren't buying that ugly thing, are you? It's not even a real dinosaur *and* it's god-awful."

The two shop assistants glanced fearfully at each other and remained silent.

Lincoln and Dustin noticed the exchange.

"I like him," Dustin replied, poking at the black plastic scales and dorsal fins. "He's kinda like T-Rex, only uglier and fatter." He looked at the assistant as she scanned the price tag. "What's its name?"

"Ah, what?" the young girl muttered, surprised that he'd asked. She quickly handed it to her co-worker who shoved it in the bag.

"Its name. What is it?" Dustin repeated and handed over his money.

"Ah…" She nervously glanced past him into the street. "He does not have name. He is imaginary animal. Please, leave now. Here is your receipt." She shoved it into his hand and ushered him aside to serve the last customer. "Please, quickly, we need to leave."

Intrigued by the girl's response, and unnerved

by the tremors, Martha moved her children out of the store and to the right.

"Where are we going?" Dustin asked. "Are we having lunch?"

"We're heading back to the monorail so we can go back to the hotel and pack. I want to leave today. I told you before I don't want to be here."

"But Mum, there's nothing to worry about," Lincoln said. "And I want to eat at the sushi train. It's so cool."

They wound their way through the crowd as they walked back down the main street.

"We ate there yesterday, and we have sushi trains back home," Martha said, one hand firmly on her son's shoulder, one firmly on her bag strap. "I have a really bad feeling about this and I want to get off the island as soon as possible."

They made it to the end of the street and stopped for a succession of golf carts transporting people to the auditorium or amusement rides.

The ground shook, the sound of a freight train roared into their ears, and the tremor took them to their knees and cowering against the corner of the closest store.

Tourists screamed and pointed, shouting about *volcano, fire, earthquake.* Store walls crumpled, glass windows shattered, rooves tumbled down on top of customers and travellers as everyone else who wasn't on the ground or injured ran pell-mell in all directions. The ground shook with the ferocity of a bomb, and Martha and Mathew lay on top of their sons on the ground to protect them.

"We need to get out of here. We have to get back to the hotel and the boat. We have to get off the island," Martha yelled above the cacophony of noise.

People stumbled to the ground; others were pushed over in the rush to get away. Some were crushed by falling walls or killed by breaking glass.

Looking over their shoulders, the Hooper family saw molten rock and lava being spat into the air, somewhere behind the auditorium building.

"The volcanic pit in the middle of the island," Dustin said. "It will take a while to get to the edge. If we can get a boat, we'll be fine."

With the ground rocking and rolling, and the air filled with gas, fire, smoke and screams, the Hoopers looked at one another and knew it was the only way. They had to get back to the hotel as the dock was on that side of the island. Managing to climb to their feet, Mathew and Martha hauled their sons up and thrust themselves forward, dodging people, buggies, falling walls and debris. The shaking worsened and they stumbled, falling to the ground.

An almighty devil sound came from behind them and they turned to see the unearthly creature in the distance rise behind the broken-down auditorium. Black, scaly; evil incarnate, it opened its mouth and let out an unearthly roar.

"Ah, what the hell is that?" Lincoln screamed, scrambling backwards, his eyes wide, his mouth wider.

"Don't know, but it's time we left." Mathew

hauled his son to his feet and grabbed his wife who had a hold of Dustin. He glanced past her to see the roller coaster off to the side of the entrance gate sway on its foundation. He heard the screams of the trapped riders, and saw the four car coaster leave its tumbling track and come careening straight for them. "Move!" he yelled, and raced his family toward the entrance arch as it came tumbling down. The coaster flew behind them within a whisker's breadth, ruffling their hair with its wind, and choking their throats with the smell of oil and petrol. The first car smashed into the ground and bucked wildly, setting the remaining three cars free to thrust, smash and heave into the buildings and rides on the other side of the street.

They waited a moment to catch their breath before looking up. The entrance arch lay only a metre away in a crumpled mess, and the town lay behind them in an equally crumpled state.

The beast let rip with another sound and shot lasers from its eyes, setting the surrounding bushland on fire. It had risen from the depths of ancient gods and monsters, growing on the molten lava hidden hundreds of kilometres beneath the surface until that day. The day it would finally make its re-entrance into the world it once ruled.

Looking back, the Hoopers stood up and ran, climbing over the rubble to get to the monorail to take them back to the hotel and safety.

And everyone else that was still uninjured had the same idea.

They ran across the tracks and were sent to the right, all the way down to the first car. Each car sat twenty, but three times that many got in. Managing to get in the first car, the Hoopers daren't sigh in relief just yet. Along with everyone else in that car, they held their collective breath and stood staring out the window at the towering beast in the distance, burning everything in its path with its laser vision. And when that wasn't enough, it breathed fire instead.

Lincoln whimpered and backed up against his dad who put an arm around him.

Dustin frowned and pulled his stuffed dinosaur toy from his shopping bag. Through all they had just been through, they'd hung on to their shopping. *It's him,* he breathed, staring from the toy to the creature in the distance. *It's him.*

A loud metal-on-metal groaning was heard and everyone tilted their heads up. Through the Perspex roof, they saw the waterslide tube collapsing toward them. Everyone screamed and ducked, and the train operator put on speed.

The tubes tumbled through the forest and hurtled at them, and with only a cat's whisker to spare, it missed them to come crashing down on the track behind them. Unfortunately, the monorail car that was following wasn't so lucky. It was obliterated underneath the tubing and the car behind smashed full force into it, making it fly up and tumble turn over the wreckage to land on the track upside down.

"Oh, my God," Martha murmured, her hand flying to her mouth. "Those poor people."

"Don't look," Mathew directed his family, shielding them from the carnage. "Just keep your eyes on that beast."

Within five minutes, they had left the wreckage behind and arrived back at the hotel to find one of the wings had collapsed.

"Quickly, quickly, please go through the hotel and down to the dock. You will be taken to safety." The hotel staff was waving people on while keeping an eye on the beast in the distance.

"We need to get to our room," Mathew told his family and veered them off to their part of the hotel, bypassing cracked walls and fallen plaster. They reached their room. "Get your passports, papers, and electricals. Quickly."

They scurried around, slamming cases shut and zipping up backpacks and briefcases. The boys jammed their toys into one suitcase as the other held all the clothes they'd bought, and Martha had insisted they stay packed at all times in case of a quick getaway. They were done in five minutes.

Dustin stared out the window as a tremor shook the hotel. The beast was still heading away from them, burning everything in its sight, but he knew it could turn and head for them at any moment.

"Dustin, come on," Mathew yelled and they raced back the way they had come, through throngs of people doing the same, back into the lobby, down the main hallway with hundreds of other holidaymakers, screaming, crying, and out the back terrace. Staff directed them down the stairs, through the main area, and down to the docks where smaller vessels had come to help rescue the trapped tourists on the island.

"Quickly, quickly, no pushing. There is enough for all." Staff directed them to a yacht, which they boarded. They hurried to the back as it quickly filled up with passengers.

The cruise liner that had brought them was loading wounded on board as it had a hospital.

The Hoopers scanned their surroundings. Coast guard, yachts, boats, the police. All were there en masse trying to help. Jets flew overhead trying to scope out the beast in the middle of the island. This just irritated it and the beast shot them down with its laser vision. Screams drifted through the crowds and the yacht pulled away from the dock. Those not on board were directed to the next, or onto the cruise ship. There was a mad rush of the crowd, pushing, pulling to get onto the next boat. People fell off the dock and needed rescuing, or were knocked down and trampled, while others were hurt in the tug of war amongst the tourists.

As the yacht sailed away, Martha finally heaved a sigh of relief. They had managed to escape intact, and none of them was physically hurt. She glanced at her sons and saw Dustin holding his god-awful dinosaur, staring from it to the beast on the island. So did she. Seeing the resemblance and remembering what the shop assistant had said, *"He does not have name, he is imaginary animal.*" If they didn't know what it was, or that it was imaginary, how did she know it was a he, and how was there a stuffed version of it selling in the gift store that looked exactly like it?

Jet fighters flew past and dropped bombs on the beast, but they only angered it. It turned, shot down one of the planes with its laser vision, but missed the other that circled overhead and dropped another bomb before flying back the way it had come.

The beast followed, setting its lasers on the plane and taking out the top three floors of the hotel, and the cruise liner. The hotel and ship both burst into flames, explosions ripped through, and the beast lumbered towards them.

"Oh, my God." Martha covered her mouth with both hands, watching the cruise ship implode and break in half. The hotel crumpled under its own wreckage.

"Bloody hell." Mathew pulled his wife into his arms and she pulled the boys closer.

"Oh, Mathew."

"It's okay, luv. We're safe," he said, never taking his eyes from the island that grew smaller and smaller on the horizon.

Dustin's frown was deep. *How could this creature not exist, but be turned into a stuffed animal that even the store assistants didn't want to talk about? And what is it? Where did it come from? How did it breathe fire and have laser vision?* In the distance, he saw the animal bend over and a glow start to emanate from its body. Blue lasers shot out from its dorsal fins and scales, and it thrashed around, twisting and turning until everything around it was cut down with precision. Once the blue died down, red glowed from it, and opening its mouth, it breathed fire across the island, burning what was not cut down.

Everything was ablaze. The hotel, the cruise ship, the forests. Helicopters buzzed over them, jet planes joined them, heading for the island. They all watched in horror as they valiantly tried to shoot it down with every missile they had, only to be shot down in its wake.

Dustin wearily slumped on a bench seat and stared from the island to his toy. His ears pricked up at a conversation in Japanese, and while he didn't understand much, he could pick up a few words from his foreign language class at school.

Beast, creature, devil, god, zilla, no…jira… godjira? *Is that what they called it? Godjira? But what is it? Where does it come from? How can it shoot lasers and breathe fire? It isn't a dragon, is it? Part dragon, part dinosaur?* He picked up a few more words, volcano, lava, made of…

Made of lava? No, that can't be…

The conversation abruptly ended when the men saw the stuffed toy in Dustin's hands. "Godjira." A man pointed. "Godjira devil. Godjira." He waved his hand toward the island then back at the toy. "Godjira, Godjira."

Not understanding what he meant with his hand

movement, Dustin was glad when the men moved on. As the island grew smaller on the horizon, he wandered over to the railing and stood watching the burning speck of an island. Did he really want a reminder of hell on Earth? A hell he and his family had barely survived when thousands hadn't. Did he really want to be reminded of the horror every time he looked at the stuffed toy on his shelf? They had the rest of their toys and usual touristy ornaments they'd bought. They'd taken a thousand pictures of them doing stuff, had been on most of the rides and eaten in the restaurants, had been through the museum, cinema and auditorium that now lay desecrated by evil. Just like the hotel, the monorail, the cruise ship, the amusement park, and all of the stores on the main street. Just like the hothouse would be, the robocopter and spaceballs would be, and the aqua dome and aquarium would be empty of water. *Those poor animals. What about the animals and the ones in the medical centre? Would they be dead along with the people that didn't make it?*

Glancing at the tiny speck of fire in the distance, he let the stuffed toy fall from his hand into the churning dark waters of the sea.

KING OF THE CASTLE

"Get out of my way. I want to see." Rose Thorn pushed her younger brother aside and flattened her face against the plane's window. Down below, like a tiny emerald speck in a vast royal blue ocean, lay the magical *Vessor Island*, home of the historically renowned Professor Vessor, her great-great-grandfather. The island had been in the family for generations, and today she and her brother would be finally getting to see the place that had produced a thousand cures for everything from minor skin rashes, to cancer and hepatitis. It was all thanks to her great-great-grandfather's knowledge passed down to her great-grandfather, then her grandmother, and now to her father. Rose, and her brother Ricky, would get to see the island it all came from. The island that was their legacy.

"Get your own window view." Ricky shoved her back and peered out the window. At twelve, he was three years younger than his sister, but possessed the same fiery red-brown hair and green eyes. Inherited, so their father said, from their great-

great-grandfather. They had only seen black and white photos of the legendary professor, so couldn't tell if he was a redhead or not, but they did possess his spirit for adventure, as did their father.

Mandrake Thorn was a world-renowned professor in his own right. A botanist, marine biologist, and all-round adventurer, he had encouraged his children to seek adventure in every corner of the world. Now they were exploring even more by joining him for a week on the family's island. A fifty foot yacht was his home, and it was parked at the dock near where they were coming to land.

"This is your captain. Please buckle up for descent. It might get bumpy."

Rose and Ricky buckled in and prepared for the landing. They had flown by seaplane to meet up with their father after spending the term at boarding school.

The plane skipped lightly across the waves and settled down into a light hum as it motored into the cove and parked next to the yacht at the dock.

They jumped out of their seats, grabbed their backpacks and barrelled out of the door to be greeted by their father.

"Dad." They dived at him, hugging him fiercely as they hadn't seen him in months.

"Hey, kiddos." Drake Thorn slid an arm around each child, lifted them, and spun around. "How was your plane ride? Have fun?"

"Yes," they replied, kissing their father on the cheek before being released.

"Have you found any new creatures?" Rose was a budding zoologist in her own right. "Do we have a new species on our hands?"

"Have you found another cure, yet?" Ricky slung his backpack over his shoulder and grabbed his suitcase that one of his father's workers had placed beside them.

Drake laughed and ruffled his son's hair. "Trust you to want to cure the world, *but*…we might be on the cusp of something new. Come on, let's go and I'll show you to your cabins first." He led them on board the yacht and showed them where they would be sleeping.

"What now? Can we see, can we see?" Ricky excitedly bounced from one foot to the other. "Can we see where great-great-grandfather worked?"

"Sure, let's get you something to eat and then I'll take you to the famous laboratory." Drake took them to the dining room where they had a quick lunch before hiking into the forest. The island was an estimated twenty-five kilometres in diameter, and the majority hadn't been touched in decades. Theseus Vessor had settled in the most richly abundant part of the island. The north side. It was safe from strong winds and most storms, and held a plethora of wild plants, natural herbs, trees and wildlife. Scarlet macaws flitted from tree to tree as did a wide variety of other bird life.

Rose gasped in delight as a brightly coloured butterfly fluttered in front of her in the densely packed forest. With the sun shining down through the canopy of trees and branches to create ethereal surroundings, it touched on the beauty of the life growing under it.

Blue and yellow parrots flew past Ricky's head and he turned to see them swoop around and fly back, passing them a second time.

Drake stopped and gazed around them. "It *is* quite magical, isn't it?"

"It's beautiful," Rose said, taking in the sights and sounds of a place that made hothouses and botanical parks pale in comparison.

"Come on, it's this way. Not far now." Drake put an arm around each of his children, and kept them moving along the wooden path that led them over small hills and around a mountain, to come face to face with the most beautiful place they had ever seen.

A natural pool was cratered in the shell of a volcano with a natural waterfall pouring into it, surrounded by high mountains and lush green forest with bright coloured flowers, bushes and trees to the left, and a two-storey building to their right.

"Is that Great-Great-Grandad's?" Ricky was eager to get to exploring.

"Sort of." Drake led them down the path to their right. "The building had broken down a little in the decades since he was here, and every generation that's come since has tried to either restore or rebuild. Most of it's been rebuilt, so not so original." He smiled at his son. "But we've tried to make it better each time. It has lots of rooms upstairs, and room downstairs for growing all the plants necessary.

My great-grandfather didn't want to destroy the island by using all that it had, so he grew what was needed from one or two plants. Come, I'll show you."

They climbed the wooden stairs to the top floor veranda and entered through louvred doors that led to a huge square room full of chairs and lounges to sit and talk. The whole abode was built in a plantation style and painted white to be seen from the air. It was settled into the side of the mountain without doing too much damage to the environment.

"Through that door is the kitchen and that one is a bathroom." Drake pointed to two doors in front of them. "And to the left and right down the hallways are labs for research and working. Let's go downstairs." They walked back outside, nodding to some of the workers passing through, down the stairs, and through a door on the ground floor, where they saw technicians wearing white lab coats performing scans and tests on different plant species.

"We have to be careful with the tests we do. We're cataloguing the new species we find and are running tests to see what they could be compatible with. But we also don't want to destroy the species just for the sake *of* those tests."

They watched a technician carefully extract the sap from a flower stem with an eyedropper and dot it on a small glass plate which he carried to a microscope and set under the magnifier. The technician took a few moments to adjust the lens and then made notes on a clipboard. This went on for several minutes until Drake ushered his children out into the sunshine. "I'm not entirely sure what you kids will find to do. You might get bored watching plants being tested, but you could go on the next hike for plants and animal life. And oh," he clicked his fingers, "we did find a few of my great-grandfather's journals in a box in a cupboard when we were fixing up the place." He saw his children grin at one another. "I personally don't have the time to go through them. His handwriting is quite spidery and faded on the paper, but who knows, maybe you'll find a treasure map amongst them."

"Cool, when can we see them?" Ricky cried. "And when can we go exploring?"

Drake grinned at his son's enthusiasm. "The boxes are on the yacht, and I'll find someone to take you exploring tomorrow. Deal?" He held his hands out to his children who had definitely inherited their sense of adventure from him.

"Deal." Rose and Ricky shook his hands.

"Right, the boxes are on the desk in the office, so you guys head off. I have some work to do here. I'll see you at dinner." Watching his kids race off, he yelled out, "and stick to the path."

Grinning at their exuberance, he turned to go back into the laboratory just as the ground shook slightly. Dust fell from the rafters onto his head and he brushed it off. Another shake. Not significant, but enough to be noticed. It had been happening a lot since he'd been there, four months now, at different times each day. Sometimes the tremors seemed close, at other times, far away. But every time it was noticed. A falling of dust, a rattle of glass, a tinkle of instruments. He knew they were on an inactive volcanic island, but the seismometer machines never registered an earthquake, or volcanic surges. So, if it wasn't an earthquake or volcanic interruptions, what the hell was making the ground shake?

His gaze travelled over the natural pool, up the mountain range that divided the island in two and rested on the peak, almost expecting something to appear to explain the tremors. It wasn't the first time he'd looked at it. He'd done it ever since he'd been there, every day that the ground trembled, and it *had* trembled every day. Sighing, he hoped his children had stuck to the path and made it back to the yacht safely. He knew them well; any little thing could lead them astray, and the sense of adventure in them just wouldn't *and* couldn't say no.

*****

Rose and Ricky raced back to the yacht, up the stairs onto the top deck, through the door, and down the hallway where they found the office and the four ancient boxes hiding the treasure within.

Rose carefully pulled the flaps of one box back and they peered in. "Whoa."

Ricky reached in, pulled out an old black leather journal, and carefully opened it to the first page. "Theseus Vessor's journal #5 1858. Whoa, that's old. How'd it last so long?" He flipped through the pages to find equations. "It looks like maths."

"It probably lasted that long because they were in a laboratory. Maybe the cold kept it intact." Rose lifted a second journal and opened it. "Theseus Vessor's journal #6 1858." She quickly checked all of them in the box and found them to be from the same year, and all looked to be specifically about detailing the plant life that he'd found. "Not much here, just about plants. Let's check out the next one." She pulled the second box over and opened it. "Whoa." Holding up a small skull, she figured it was some sort of monkey from the shape and structure. She set it aside and opened another journal. "Theseus Vessor's journal #1 1859." Turning the pages, she noted it was a detailed list of animal species. Her paternal great-great-grandfather had even drawn pictures of each species. Many were birds, some rodents and similar familial species, such as beaver-type animals, and small kangaroos or wallabies, bugs, beetles and arachnids. She checked the other journals in the boxes and found similar drawings.

"Look at this." Ricky had unrolled a parchment on the desk. "It's the island. How did he chart the island without an aeroplane?"

"The old-fashioned way." Rose grinned. "By using longitude and latitude, time to sail around the island, to knots versus miles, and probably explored a lot of it. He was here for over thirty years."

"Yeah, but not all at once." Ricky gently ran his fingers over the faded green of the forests and they landed on a familiar face. "Hey, this looks like an ape. Look, here are its eyes, nose and mouth." He pointed to the black dots on the other side of the island.

Rose glanced at it. "It does look like a skull, but that could just be coincidence. Let's see what else is in the box." She pulled out more parchments and journals. Rolling the flimsy paper out, they saw more detailed sketches of the island, mountain ranges, pools, trees and rocks. Their great-great-grandfather had mapped it all. Rose laid the last parchment on the table and stared at the drawing on it. So did Ricky. They breathed in, their eyes widened, and their mouths turned into o shapes.

"Whoa. That can't be real," Ricky barely managed. "It looks so huge."

"It *can't* be that big," Rose added, taking in the scale of the creature compared to the mountain range beside it. "Surely he made it up. It's not possible. It *can't* be real." Her finger traced the ape-like figure from top to bottom. "It can't possibly be as large as the mountains. That would be impossible."

"Why would Great-Great-Grandfather lie about it?" Ricky flipped through the journals and came across another picture. "Look. Let's see what it says." Peering closely, he managed to make out the professor's scrawl. "*Large ape-like creature, many times larger than normal, ten, maybe twenty times. As large as the mountain range dividing the island.*" He turned the page and kept reading. "*I have been here for five years and explored what I thought was every inch, but I had not come across this beast until now. Perhaps he had been hiding. Perhaps he had been growing. He had to have come from somewhere. This island is built from molten lava. The trees, plants and wildlife had to come from somewhere. Was there another here before me who brought all I see? Had travellers come by sea in the hope of finding new countries, new islands, new territories to land and cultivate a life on? How did this beast come to be here? It was not spewed from the earth beneath my feet. None of it was. So, how did it come to be? And how is it so tall? Is that what's been causing the tremors? This giant beast, walking, running, playing. It is so large it could easily shake the ground. I am yet to engage with it. Scared to in case it decides I am a play-thing, or worse, lunch. So, I will leave it for now and stay on my side of the island. If it has been here longer than me, it has never come to my side. Never breached the mountain top, never come to see what all the noise was about. And for that, I thank God."* Ricky's eyes turned to his sister. "Whoa, a massive ape creature on this very island. Cool, we've got to find it."

Rose rolled her eyes. "You do realise that was over a hundred and fifty years ago. It's long dead, just like our great-great-grandfather."

"Yes, but our great-grandfather, our grandmother, *and* our father have all come here for months, if not years, at a time. How come it never got mentioned? I wonder if Dad would know."

"Know what?" Drake came through the door to

see what his children were up to. "Dinnertime. We have roast chicken especially for you."

Rose had quickly rolled up the parchment and pushed it aside. "Cool. I love my roast chook. We were just wondering if the rest of the Vessor Thorn bloodline wrote journals and drew pictures while they were here on the island. We've heard the stories, but never read anything." She turned to her father and leaned against the desk. "Do *you* keep journals?"

Drake's smile widened at his daughter, who was so much like her grandmother, his mother. "I have been, and as far as I know, any papers and personal letters are in England at the manor. Kept for prosperity, apparently." Drake's mother and father had moved to Australia from England and had Drake there. So, while his children were second generation Australian, and Australia was part of the commonwealth, the Vessor Thorn bloodline was still predominantly English, with a couple of stately homes and a few titles to their name. Hence the ability to own their own island. And Theseus Vessor's selling of the cures had helped boost the family fortune significantly. Even if it had come a century after his findings. It was Drake's mother who had followed in her father's and grandfather's footsteps and finished off the testing of the plants to find the final equations for the cures. And she taught Drake to follow in her footsteps. Now his kids were following in his. "Let's go and have some dinner. We'll catch up on what you've been doing at school the last few months."

After a filling dinner with ice cream for dessert, the kids headed to bed early, sneaking into the office to grab the parchments and journals before racing back to their rooms. Once the lights were out, Ricky sneaked into Rose's cabin via the adjoining door. She had already spread the papers out on the bed, and was tracing her finger down a red line on the map of the island.

"I think this is the route the professor took. Straight over the mountain and down the other side. We should be able to see everything from up there."

"Can we go tomorrow?" Ricky asked, pausing from reading more of the journal to ask the question. "We'll need permission."

"And probably a guide," Rose mused, finding what looked to be a path up the mountain. "We can climb the same way. It should be okay."

"Let's ask Dad in the morning then." A yawn escaped Ricky. "I'm tired and going to bed. Night." He took the journal with him.

"Night." Rose gathered the papers and gently set them on the small desk before tucking herself into bed.

*****

As they ate a hearty breakfast the next morning, they hounded their father to let them go exploring.

He knew they would want to, so had directed two of his staff to go with them with supplies in case they wanted food and water, or needed help.

They high-fived one another, then raced back to their rooms to dress appropriately and grab the map for directions. Setting off with their guides, they made their way back to the laboratory, and, after checking the map, walked past the building, around the crater, and toward the waterfall that gently fell into the pool.

"I think it's here," Rose said. "Some kind of path either beside or behind the waterfall." They pushed aside the vines and plants and found a naturally ingrained staircase leading up. They climbed, finding it hard going, but three hours later they emerged from the greenery to stand atop the mountain, seeing the beautiful spectacle before them.

"Oh, it's beautiful," Rose murmured, taking in the distant mountains and hills, the green plains and ponds of water. This side of the mountain seemed much higher than the side they'd just come up, and Rose ran back and forth, gauging the distance, looking down at the laboratory then looking at the rolling plains. "It's two to three times the height on this side, and if it took us three hours to get up, it will take us just as long to get down then twice as long to get back up. We'd be climbing all day."

"We could go down halfway," Ricky suggested. "See what's down there and then come back up. Maybe next time we could bring camping gear and a tent and stay the night."

Behind their backs, the two guides exchanged worried looks.

"I do not think that would be safe," one guide said. "Many wild creatures ready to eat you. Come, let's walk a little way down instead, just to that flat rock down there." He pointed down to a large chunk of rock jutting out of the mountainside. "We can stop to eat and enjoy the view."

An hour later, they made it to the rock to discover the beautiful wildflowers growing from the outcrop.

Rose pulled her camera out of her bag and took pictures from every angle, and not just of the flowers. Scanning the plains below, she snapped photos of everything, hoping to put together some sort of photographic map of the area. A movement caught her eye and she zoomed in. "Is that…?"

Ricky shielded his eyes and looked in the general direction. "What?"

Rose pulled back and glanced at her brother, mouthing the word *ape*, before looking back into the viewfinder. Waiting for the image to clear, she followed the movement, but was disturbed by rocks falling at her feet and landing against her legs. "What's going on?" She looked down then back towards the mountain wall.

"Just some loose rocks," one of the guides said, stealing a glance at his companion. "Do you want to eat?"

"No, not yet—" Rose was cut off by the rumbling of the mountain. "What's—?"

The guides scrambled to safety off the side of the rock leaving Rose and Ricky behind.

"Is that an earthquake?" Ricky yelled to his sister.

"I don't know, but I think we need to get off this thing like our guides did." Taking a step toward them, they had no chance to go any further.

With a trembling wail, the jutting rock gave way beneath their feet as did the rocks around it, and tumbled straight down into the vast cave system that fed the water from the pool and waterfall to the other side of the island.

"Ah…" tore out of their throats as their hands flailed for rocks or branches or vines to cling to. But there was nothing, and down, down, down they fell into the freezing water.

Their guides got on the satellite phone. "*Mayday, mayday,* the mountainside has collapsed and the children have fallen with it. *Mayday, mayday.*"

Word at the laboratory got back to Drake who immediately put a search and rescue team in place. They had heard the rumbling, felt the tremors, but hadn't realised it was the children in mortal danger. "Get me the radar and sonar maps of the island. The ones that show what's under the mountain."

*****

Rose and Ricky clung to each other as the freezing water rushed them along the ancient lava tube to God knows where. They tried to stay afloat, but the low ceilings made for head injuries, and their hands feebly reached for outcrops or something to cling to.

There was nothing.

*****

Drake scanned the radar maps. "The aqueducts lead under the mountain and eventually spit out at Three Ponds. So, that's where they'll end up coming out. Get the plane and helicopter ready."

*****

Winding and whirling, Rose and Ricky hung on, taking great gulps of air when they could, until they could take no more because the tunnel dipped down. They clawed at the ceiling, but found no air. They clawed at one another, but found no one was there, and finally, just when they were out of breath, they were spat out and landed in the shallow pool at Three Ponds. Unconscious, their bodies floated to the edge.

The animals Rose had seen through her camera jumped at the intrusion. They had no reason to fear another beast coming, but this beast was different to the ones they played with on the island. The creatures made their way to the pond, suspiciously eyeing the humans. Not that they knew they were human. One of the beasts poked at one of the creatures with its finger. It didn't move. He glanced at his brother who shrugged. He poked again and then gently pulled the creature from the water and turned it over. They had no idea what a girl was. He grabbed at the creature's chest and it coughed. They jumped back and waited.

Rose coughed, curling into a ball as she wretched water from her lungs. "Ugh." After sucking in breath, she vomited water and lay still, dazed from the head wound. "Ugh."

The beast poked her back.

"Ugh, Ricky." Rolling over she came face to face with the beast. And blinked.

The beast blinked and moved its face closer to hers.

Rose blinked and registered what it was. She screamed and scurried backwards, only for her left hand to land on something furry. Too scared to look away from the creature before her, she knew she had to see what she was touching. Slowly turning her head to her left, she found her hand looking tiny and white against the monstrous black silver fur-covered foot. "Foot?" Her head shot up to see another creature. "Argh," she screamed and scuttled backwards. Her eyes flitted from ape to ape that towered over her. They weren't the normal sized silver backed apes. They were the size of a two-storey house.

The apes bent down to peer at the white creature that had screamed. They glanced at one another then back at the girl.

Rose just sat petrified, her teeth chattering as she tried to control her fear.

"Rose, don't move," Ricky quietly called. "I don't think they'll hurt us."

Hearing the words, the apes turned to the boy creature that lay at the edge of the pool. Their heads moved back and forth between the two and neither human took their eyes off the two apes that stood between them and freedom.

The apes turned back to Rose and the first one poked her in the chest, opening its mouth into a smile. He poked her again and made a grunting sound.

The second ape sat on his haunches and smacked his stomach, emitting sounds similar to chimps at playtime.

"I think they're friendly," Ricky was slowly slithering his way toward his sister.

The ape poked Rose, and this time she found the courage to gently touch its finger.

The ape pulled back, shocked by the touch. He looked at his brother and tried again. He poked Rose, but left his finger in front of her and she laid her hand on his, clenching her jaw shut to keep from screaming, clenching her insides to keep from wetting herself.

The ape leaned closer and sniffed the human, marvelled at how tiny her hand was to his, and how little she was to him. A grumble came from it and its lips turned to a smile.

The second ape noticed Ricky, who stopped. He eyed the creature and Ricky eyed him back. And because the ape was more curious than scared, it moved over and poked the human.

Ricky reached out and laid his hand on the ape who smiled, imitating his brother. It made a deep guttural sound then sharply looked up at the intrusive noise above.

The seaplane and chopper flew overhead looking for them.

"I found them," the captain of the plane radioed through. "Down near the ponds with, holy Jesus, are they apes? They're ten times the normal size."

The apes let rip with guttural sounds of war and pummelled their chests as the plane circled the area and the chopper turned back.

"Keep them distracted and get them away from the kids," Drake said from the chopper. "I'll circle and pick them up. Where in God's name did apes come from?"

"Roger that." The pilot circled the plane to distract the apes and it worked. They ran towards it, jumping, clawing at it to take down the flying beast. That gave Drake the opportunity to fly in and hover near the pond to pick up the kids. He flung back the door and yelled, "Get in," waving for the children to get up and get in, all while keeping an eye on the beasts.

The children managed to scramble to their feet and rush for the chopper, being pulled in by their father who slammed the door behind them.

"What in blazes?" he spat. "Are they apes? Get us out of here, they've noticed us." He tapped his pilot on the shoulder and strapped his kids in. "Are you two okay? You're not hurt? They didn't hurt you?"

"No, we're fine. I think they wanted to play," Ricky told his dad. "They didn't hurt us. They were as surprised as we were."

The apes had noticed the chopper and were pounding back to it.

The pilot yanked the lever and rose higher, veering to the right just in time to avoid a hand as the apes swung into the air in a dive.

Looking out the left window, Drake, Rose and Ricky saw a new creature rise from the horizon.

"Veer right, veer right," Drake yelled into the radio on his helmet. "Veer right and get away from the island. Head for the boat."

The creature was possibly fifty times the size of the apes below.

It swung its right arm towards the plane and missed by the breadth of a cat's whisker.

The air from the swing pummelled the plane, creating turbulence, but the pilot regained control and kept on flying away from the ape.

"Jesus Christ." Drake wrapped his arms around his children. "What in God's...?"

"The professor found them," Rose said. "It's in his journals. He found an ape as big as the mountain."

"What?" Drake stared at his daughter. "I never saw that."

"You didn't go through Great-Great-Grandfather's belongings," Ricky told his dad. "We did."

"No, I didn't. As I said, the writing was difficult and I didn't have time to decipher it."

Hearing the screeching cry of the ape behind them, they flew on and landed on the helipad of the yacht anchored at least a kilometre out to sea. Once it was safe to alight, Drake and the children went to the upper deck to look back at the island. The seaplane buzzed them and landed in the water alongside. They saw the great ape stand upon the mountain range dividing the island and pummel his chest. He was joined by another beast, only slightly smaller than he. And the two smaller apes climbed up on their father's shoulders to imitate him, pummelling their chests and screeching.

"Well, now you know where your two playmates came from." Drake grinned. "They've got a mummy and daddy."

ARACH NO PHOBIA

"Okay kids, don't go too far," Janet Codsworth yelled out to her twelve-year-old twins. "We don't want you falling down a well or something. And take a satellite phone and some water in case something *does* happen." She knew her children and knew exactly what they were like. Rambunctious, non-stop, inquisitive knowledge machines. They wanted to learn everything, see everything, *touch* everything, and had no off filter when it came to educating themselves on life. They basically ate encyclopaedias for breakfast, lunch and dinner.

"Yes, Mum." Mike and Bobby traded a glance and smirked. She had no idea *what* they got up to when they got up to it. They may have only been twelve, not yet teenagers, which wouldn't happen for another seven months, three weeks, two days and fifteen hours, but they had a zest for learning that got them into trouble often.

Not that it was their fault. Their parents, Janet and Peter Codsworth, were high ranking scientists with some of the highest IQs in the world, and they'd handed down their intelligence to their twin sons, the blond, blue-eyed Michael Charles Codsworth and Robert Hannaford Codsworth, named after grandfathers and great-grandfathers. The boys had IQs of 130, not far behind their parents', hence the thirst for learning and education.

Mike and Bobby rummaged around in the supplies tent and grabbed bottles of water and sandwiches from the canteen. Their parents had taken them on an expedition deep into the heartland of the Amazon rainforest with one hundred people and fifty tents. Besides supplies and canteen tents were laboratories, the latrine, offices, and, of course, bedrooms. The twins got one of their own next to their parents'. It wasn't their first expedition, and wouldn't be their last, and they certainly had fun learning about life instead of sitting in a classroom reading about it. They got to live it while the other kids did not, and they didn't feel sorry for them one little bit.

Grinning at one another, they set off with their backpacks to explore the forest around them. They had a guide, an Amazonian native who appeared out of nowhere, leading them out of camp. Surprised, they exchanged a glance and slowly followed, hoping to get away on their own without a guide or anyone else.

"Um, guess we can't do what we want now," Bobby whispered to his brother as they walked along.

"No, you can't," Redford, their English-speaking companion said.

"Ah," the boys screamed and spun around.

"Where'd you come from?" Mike sputtered.

Redford grinned. "From behind you. You know you can't go anywhere without me or a guide, or both. You'd get lost." At forty-two, he was a world-renowned travel guide with such extensive knowledge of South America and its language that he was highly sought after for expeditions, and it earned him millions. He removed his old-fashioned pith helmet and mopped his sweaty balding head with his hanky. "It's hot out today, boys. Hope you've got your sunscreen on and have plenty of water."

"Um, yeah." The boys frowned and turned back to the front, but managed another glance at one another, trying to telepathically communicate that they were not happy with the double intrusion.

"So, anything in particular you want to see? The birds, the trees, the flowers?" Redford asked, trailing behind the boys. "The river is close by, but the wildlife might eat you."

The boys looked over their shoulders and scowled. "Not funny, Redford."

Redford chuckled. "Wasn't trying to be. Just trying to keep you safe."

"Yeah, well, we don't need you to keep us safe." Mike pretended bravery a lot, but he really was full of hot air, always defying his parents' authority, but never backing it up. He was all bravado and no substance.

"So, you can keep yourselves safe?" Redford hid a smile. He knew all about the Codsworth family, having read up on them before the expedition as he did all of his clients. The twins were smart, but not savvy, and not knowledgeable about the ins and outs of the South American rainforests.

"Of course we can," Bobby boasted. "We've read every safety manual, read all about the dangers of the forests we are currently residing in, and know first aid proficiently." Puffing out his chest, he added, "I could even perform surgery if I had to."

"Surgery?" Redford pretended to be astounded as he played along. "You mean like, a tracheotomy, or an appendectomy? Or even brain surgery? And what if someone broke a leg? Could you set it?"

"Of course," Bobby's boasting continued. "I've read all of the surgery manuals and could outdo any top-notch specialists in the world."

They trudged along behind their native guide, hearing the birds in the trees, and the gentle buzzing of insects. The foliage was thick, lush and green, and home to an assortment of bugs and spiders.

"What about spider bites, or snake bites?" Redford went on. "Know what to do if you get bitten?"

"Of course we do." Bobby was tired of the game and just wished they'd been left alone to go where they wanted.

"Like the giant Goliath Birdeater in front of you?" Redford grabbed them by their shirts, bringing them to a halt.

The spider lazily slid down its silken cord from one frond to another, balefully eyeing the humans before it.

"Crikey!" Mike exclaimed, his eyes wide to take

it all in. "Look at the size of that mother."

"And you know it's a mother, how?" Redford asked, waiting while their guide slowly slid his machete under the frond.

With a sharp flick, the guide flung the frond to their right and the spider went flying. With a grunt, he waved them on with his machete.

Redford nodded his appreciation and motioned the boys forward. "And that is why you need to stop *boasting* about what you supposedly know, and *show* that you know it by putting it into practice." He loosened his grip on their shirts and kept an eye out for other spiders and creeping crawlies.

"Yeah, yeah," Bobby muttered, disappointed they hadn't been able to examine the spider and play with it. Spiders didn't worry them; they had a large collection of arachnids back home, all pinned to boards under glass. That only happened *after* they played with them, tortured them, and killed them, of course. They also performed spider autopsies to see what their insides looked like. Hideous, to say the least, but then, so was their idea of fun which could probably be considered as psychopathic by some. They loved to kill animals and inspect them. As the sons of scientists and professors, they had spent their twelve years growing up in labs, museums and on expeditions. They were scared of nothing, while everything was scared of them. And they knew it.

"Okay, we shouldn't go too far from camp. The sun's getting low in the sky and we should start getting back." Redford stared intently through the canopy of green. "Besides which…" He looked at the twins, but they were gone. "Boys?" Spinning around, he looked in every direction. "Boys, where are you?" Oh, Jesus. If he lost them their parents would have his guts for garters. "Boys, where are you?" He felt the tap on his shoulder and turned to see the guide pointing to the side of the path they had been taking. "They went that way? Come on." He urged their guide forward and followed, calling out for the boys. "Michael, Robert, we need to get home." Pushing aside branches, he muttered, "Where are you, you little brats?"

Mike and Bobby giggled. They heard the yells for them, but didn't stop. The moment they'd had their chance, they'd dashed off the path and raced through the foliage, stopping only long enough to gauge where they were by noting the sun in the sky. They were west of their camp.

"Let's go that way," Bobby urged, pointing south. "We'll be parallel with the river and maybe find an alligator or two." Shoving his brother ahead of him, he heard the calls grow louder. "Quick."

They hurried along, the calls growing distant, and looked out for arachnids, insects, rats and other native animals they could dissect.

"Michael, Robert. I see you." Redford saw the vague dashes of colour from the boys' shirts as he peered through the trees and bushes. "Come back. This isn't funny and your parents will be angry." Seeing the colour move, he and the guide took off after it.

Side-stepping, the twins veered left, then right to avoid detection.

"This is fun," Mike whispered, stomping on a creepy crawly as they made their way through. "Why can't we do this more often?"

"Because we have babysitters," Bobby muttered. He spied a massive spider on a tree and slowly pulled his pocketknife from his pants pocket. Never taking his eyes from the arachnid, he unfurled the knife, held it by the point, brought his hand up to his ear, and expertly threw the knife at the tree. It hit the spider dead centre in the body. "Yes," he crowed and his brother slapped him on the back.

"Spot on, old chap." Mike put on his best upper crust British accent. "The execution was brilliant; what will we do with it?"

They approached the tree and saw the blue haemolymph drip from the spider's back.

"Bloody good show," Mike said, watching his brother remove a plastic Ziploc bag from his backpack. "Taking it back to camp?"

"Yep." Bobby opened the bag and held it under the spider. "Pull out the knife for me. And be careful. I want it in one piece."

"The knife or the spider?" Mike joked and grasped the back onyx handle of the knife. It had been a twelfth birthday present from their father and they'd received one each with their initials in silver on the handles. He rocked it back and forth until it came loose from the tree and placed it in the bag. With his left hand, he held the bag together at the hilt of the knife and slid the knife from the bag so the spider came off as it went. Once the spider was off, he wiped the blade clean on the tree while Bobby sealed the bag and put it in his backpack.

"Cool, give it back," Bobby told his brother and took it. Closing the blade, he kept it handy in case they found anything else.

"Michael…Robert…"

Gasping at the closeness of the calls, they hustled through the dense foliage, but stopped when they heard a crack.

"What was that?" Mike whispered and gazed around, hoping some wild animal had made the sound.

"Probably a tree. Did you step on one?" Bobby kept his eye out for animals too, wanting something else to kill.

"No. I don't think so." Mike slowly moved forward and heard the crack from under his foot.

"Michael…Robert…" Redford called, following the guide through the forest. The guide stopped and stared at a tree, muttering something in his native tongue.

"What is it?" Redford stopped beside him and looked to where the guide was pointing, hearing the native words for tree, hole and spider. "Oh no." He noted the gauge in the tree from a wound and the blue blood. "Damn it."

Mike looked down at his feet. "It came from there. Must be the same covered branches. Careful."

Bobby slowly inched toward his brother. "It's

solid ground, what are you worried for?"

A frown crossed Mike's brows. "Don't know, just a feeling." He noticed his brother moving toward him. "Don't come any closer. Get away. We don't wanna put more weight on it."

"Weight on what?" Bobby watched Mike's expressions and laughed. "Dude, we're on solid ground. What are you carrying on for?" The ground crunched beneath his feet and he looked down. "It's just a pile of branches and stuff. Look." He jumped up and down on the spot. "See, nothing. Solid ground."

"Dude, stop jumping." Mike grabbed his brother's arms. "Let's just get out of here before something happens."

"Scaredy cat," Bobby mocked, jumping up and down some more. "Scaredy cat, scaredy cat, scaredy—" Crack. "Argh."

The boys sank through the ground to their ankles.

"What was that?" Redford glanced in the direction of the sound.

"Bobby, I told you not to do that," Mike snapped. "We need to go back the way we came and be careful." He pointed to the side and sent his brother moving slowly, foot by foot, back the way they'd come. "Be careful," he repeated. One wrong move could send them God knows where. He didn't know what they were standing on, an old well cover as their mother joked, or even a treasure cave, but he definitely did not want to fall through it even though his sense of adventure told him to enjoy himself doing it.

"Easy," he told his brother. "Easy."

"All right already," Bobby snapped, sick and tired of the boring way their day had ended. If only it was more exciting. Making his way forward, he heard another crack, and another, another, all louder than the previous ones. "Mike…"

"Bobby." Mike's voice cracked like the wood beneath their feet. "Run."

The boys launched from one foot to the other only for the ground to open up and swallow them whole.

"Argh…"

"Boys?" Redford and the guide heard the scream and raced off in the general direction. They found the knife first, having been thrown clear from Bobby's hand when he fell. And just as Redford was about to move to pick it up, the guide grabbed him by the arm and pointed to the gaping hole in the ground that was partially obscured by fallen branches and leaves.

"Jesus," Redford muttered, poking the ground with his foot to see how much solid ground they had before the edge of the hole. Inching closer, he cleared the debris and peered into the black mouth of the tunnel to hell. "Boys? Michael, Robert? Are you hurt? Can you hear me? Can you talk to me? Boys?" He waited, but heard nothing. "Crap! Ah…" He glanced at the guide and spoke in native tongue. "You stay here, I'll go for help. Help." The guide nodded and Redford took off for camp, noting the position of the trees and the path, making his way back to camp within twenty minutes. "Get search lights, get rope, get the pulley system," he yelled to the workers. "Get fire and the first-aid kit. And get the stretchers."

"What's going on?" Janet and Peter exited their tent to see what the yelling was about. "Where are the boys?"

"Down a hole," Redford replied, grabbing supplies and loading them into bags as the workers brought them over.

"What do you mean, down a hole?" Janet asked. "What *are* you talking about?"

"Your children ran off at the first convenient moment and have managed to fall down a hole. Mineshaft, alligator burrow, well, not sure until we get back there and get them out." Redford directed for a trolley to be filled with everything else. "It's about twenty minutes away and the sun is setting. Are you coming with us?" He pushed off with the cart and a dozen workers.

The Codsworths glanced at each other and followed.

Mike and Bobby had fallen ten metres into a hole, and not just any hole. A nest. Of the thing… they loved most…

Mike's cheek was tickled and his hand brushed it away. "Mmm, Bobby, stop it." Hitting their heads when they had fallen, they'd lain unconscious for fifteen minutes. But something was trying to wake them up. It touched Mike again. "Bobby, stop it." His hand swiped at it, but Bobby jerked on his right.

"Mmm, what are you doing?" Bobby muttered, scratching at the tickle on his arm. "You're tickling me."

"No, I'm not, you're tickling me," Mike muttered. His senses were slowly coming back to him. "Mmm, Bobby."

Bobby yawned, covering his mouth, which was just as well considering what was dangling about a foot above his face. "Is it time to get up?"

"Probably. We been asleep?"

"Yeah." Bobby sighed. "Must've had a nap. My head hurts." He moved his right hand to the back of his head and felt warm furry bodies beneath it. His fingers felt furry long legs. "Ugh, Mike. I don't think we're alone."

"What do you mean?" Something scuttled over Mike's arm and he brushed at it. "Just kill it."

Bobby slowly opened his eyes. What little light there was filtered down into the hole, and was enough for him to see the massive eight-legged shape in front of his face. "Mike," he said slowly, becoming aware of the other bodies as his eyes roamed the space around them. "We have visitors."

"What?" Stretching, Mike's arms brushed their furry friends and he froze. "Bobby, are they what I think they are?"

Keeping an eye on the one above him, Bobby slowly moved his head closer to his brother so they were side by side. "Yep."

*****

The search team made it back as the sun was setting, and under Redford's instructions, set up the pulley system, spotlights and rope. He peered into the hole. "Boys, can you hear me?"

Janet and Peter rushed forward, barely being stopped by Redford and their guide. Ground crumbled beneath them and sent it flying down into the hole.

"Careful," Redford snapped. "Or we'll have to rescue you two as well."

"Boys, can you hear me?" Janet called down. "We're here to get you out. Hang in there. We'll be down in a minute." She snatched at the harness in Redford's hand, but he pulled it away.

"You may be high IQ scientists and professors, but you have *no idea* what's down there, *or* how to go about getting them out. *I do.* At least about getting down. As for what's down there, no idea." He strapped himself into the harness.

"I'll have you know they're my sons and I want to—" Peter was cut off.

"What! Get yourself trapped down a goddamn hole like your two idiot sons did." Redford shook his head and clamped on a carabineer. "You lot may have high IQs, but you're quite stupid when it comes to your own safety. Your kids are in this mess because they didn't do as they were told. And who taught them to be wild spirits?" He pointed at the stunned parents. "You two do whatever you want, go wherever you want, we don't care. Kill innocent spiders by knifing them to a tree, we don't care." He waved his hands around in emphasis. "You clearly *don't* care, which is why your boys are now in trouble, possibly badly injured, or worse, dead." He turned to speak with the guide.

*****

The boys had heard their mother's voice and knew rescue was close at hand, but that meant less time in the cave.

Slowly opening his eyes, Mike glanced around in the dim light. "You wouldn't happen to have a torch handy, would you?"

Bobby pulled one from his khakis' pocket and flicked it on the one above his head.

The arachnid scuttled away in the sudden burst of light, as did the others around them. Bobby swung the torch back and forth, and the zigzagging beam sent the huge adult hand-sized spiders racing for the dark safety of the inner cave. It had been their home for centuries, since their ancestors had come and settled and bred and mutated and mated with the local species to create a brand-new species; a species no one had ever seen, never heard of, never come across. Until now. When a human, make that two humans, had stumbled upon the cave in the ground in the heartland of the Amazon rainforest. But just as humans had never seen them, they had never seen humans. And the two beings slowly sitting up and swinging a weird tube back and forth intrigued them, and scared them. Unsure of whether to be on the attack or stand down, they watched the humans in silence while the queen approached.

Mike and Bobby stared in utter fascination. They'd seen large spiders before, unusual and foreign ones, but not quite like this. Noticing that the spiders stayed away from the torch beam, they took that opportunity to slowly rise to their feet and brush themselves off. They'd never had such an amazing find, and wouldn't it be so cool if their names were featured in science magazines worldwide as the twins, and first humans, to find a new species of arachnid?

Bobby moved the torch in wider arcs. "Look at them." His voice was barely a whisper. "It's like they're standing to attention. Weird."

All of the spiders were indeed standing to attention.

He swung the torch up and around the hole, taking note of the cave-like structure, the variants in spiders' spots, stripes, some with, some without, some with both. Some black, some brown, some white. "Albino," he breathed. "We found albino spiders, Mike, look."

Mike looked up to see the white-legged creatures. They were larger than his hand, probably nearly as big as his head, and he let his gaze roam the cave until it fell on the one spider that would be the jewel in the crown. "Bobby."

Bobby turned his gaze from the ceiling to his brother, making note of the thousands of spiders nesting in the cave, to see what his brother was staring at. "Holy mother of God," he whispered.

The queen was an albino, the size of a one storey house, and had black stripes on her very furry and very long legs.

"Now we know where the albinism comes from. Look at their eyes. They're red," Bobby whispered, absolutely fascinated by the sight.

"That might be where *they* come from," Mike replied. "But how is *she* an albino, and where did *she* come from? And where's the daddy?"

They noticed movement from the spiders that seemed to gather around the queen as some form of protection, or shield.

"Fascinating," Bobby murmured, mesmerised by the thousands of furry creatures.

"Bobby, she's starting to produce silk. She's looking to make a meal of us," Mike whispered, knowing exactly what spiders did to capture their prey.

"Here, take this and swing it back and forth." Bobby shoved the torch into his brother's hand, and never taking his eyes off the prize, slid his pack from his back and unzipped it. Digging inside, he found the two things he was after. Letting the bag fall, he held up a lighter and a can of bug repellent. "That bitch wants us for food, let her come and get us." Bobby smirked, flicked the lighter on, and fired up the can.

The smaller spiders went up in flames, and the queen made a run for it, just as the boys knew she would. But it was her they wanted to dissect the most, her they wouldn't be leaving without.

OH, YET I DID

"So, what are we doing now?" Sophie Watkins whined from the back seat of the family's four-wheel drive.

"Hunting for Sasquatch," her big brother, Ben, told her.

"A what watch?" Sophie slid her plastic star-shaped sunglasses down her cute button nose and arched a brow at her brother. She may have only been eight, but she'd seen enough models and celebrities to know how to imitate them.

"Not a what watch." Ben frowned in irritation. He hated the fact they'd brought his little sister along on the trip when he'd just wanted his male cousins along. "It's a big foot, abominable snowman, a yeti, a big hairy beast."

"But why are we looking for it?" Sophie shuddered delicately, and slid her glasses back into place. "I thought this was a family holiday." She stared out the window at the passing shrubs and desert soil. "We're in the middle of nowhere. Where are we?"

"Yarrumburra," Kath Watkins replied from the

front passenger seat. "It's renowned for yeti sightings and we're here to research it."

"Why?" Sophie yawned and patted her mouth with her hand. "It all sounds rather boring."

"Only *you'd* think that. *You're a girl,*" Alex Watkins, their cousin, said from the other side of Ben. "If you didn't want to do this, you could have stayed home with our grandparents." The kids' dads were brothers, and his parents were following in their car with *his* three older brothers. "Besides our mums, you're the only girl."

"And she wasn't staying home," Kath told him. "She'll be with me and Sally all the time helping to log the research. Won't you, Soph?"

"I suppose." Sophie screwed up her nose. "But it all sounds *sooo* boring. Just as well I brought my games and iPod along."

"How boring are you?" Ben remarked. "Not even interested in the find of the century. Oh, well, more money for us."

There was a million dollar reward going for the capture of the Yarrumburra Menace, put up by the local mayor's office. There had been sightings and disturbances all around town. Rubbish bins had been gone through and tossed around. Dogs and cats had gone missing, stores were broken into, and all they found every time was a patch of fur. No fingerprints, or shoe prints, only fur. The townspeople were too afraid to step out of their homes after dark, and begged the local police and mayor to call someone in, anyone who could catch the person or animal responsible for the crime spree. Not knowing what to do, the police had sent the fur off to the city forensics lab for analysis. When they couldn't figure out what it belonged to, they contacted animal specialists, Kath and Terry Watkins, the leaders in their field of zoology. After analysing the fur, they came to the conclusion it was not synthetic, was not from any human, or any animal they had ever seen, and informed the mayor that they'd be interested in coming to town and searching for the creature.

The mayor had been all for it, if it meant getting rid of the perpetrator and getting the town's residents off his back.

The Watkins made it to Yarrumburra's city limits and followed directions to the mayor's office off the side of the town hall.

After pulling up, they all alighted and glanced around the main street. It was quiet, with only a few people wandering around doing their usual shopping.

"Not very busy, is it?" Sally Watkins, wife of Adam, joined her sister-in-law. "They don't need to hide away during the day. The crimes don't happen until after dark."

"Better go in and find out what's going on," Adam said, and followed his brother into the mayor's office. Their wives and kids followed.

"G'day, Terry Watkins here to see the mayor," Terry told the young receptionist.

"Do you have an appointment?" the girl asked, looking at the calendar in front of her. "I don't see your name."

"If he didn't put it in the book, that's his fault, but since he asked us here you need to tell him we're here. Off you go." He pointed to the door leading to the mayor's office and waited while the frowning girl tottered off in her ridiculously high heels to see her boss.

"A Mr Terry Watkins is here with a bunch of people. Said you called him."

"Who?" Mayor Larry Dumphrey screwed up his face in thought, holding his phone to his chest to blank out the conversation. "Oh, right. Yep, send him in." Larry clicked his fingers as he remembered the name and went back to the call. "Mum, Mum, the people are here to catch the person doing all the crime around town. I have to go. Yes, yes, I'll make sure they know about your cat." He watched the two families walk in and wondered why there were so many people. "Yes, Mum, I'll let them know. Gotta go." Hanging up, he stood. "Which one of you is Terry?"

"I am." Terry stepped forward and introduced the family. "My wife Kath, my brother Adam and his wife Sally. We're all zoologists and animal behavioural specialists. Our kids help us out." He laid a hand on his son's head. "My boy Ben and daughter Sophie. Adam's boys Alex, George, Henry and Charles. They help us out by laying traps."

"Fascinating." Larry nodded at each family member, noting the kids looked to be about two years apart in age. "Okay, take a seat and I'll give you the run down."

He waited while the adults took their seats and saw Sophie sit on her mother's lap, while the boys stood behind their parents, before launching into the list of crimes that had been happening around town. He recounted the stories of his citizens as they had been told to him. The list was long, and with every detail, it took up an hour. "And now my mother says her cat is missing. She doesn't think it ran away, but was stolen. Me," he shrugged and sat back in his seat, "I think he ran away. It was a hateful cat."

"Was fur found at every scene?" Terry asked, scribbling in his notepad. "Fingerprints, shoe prints, hair, DNA, anything else?"

"No, and that's what's baffled the police," Larry said. "No human prints, just smudgy looking things. No shoe prints, just scuffy marks. And the only hair, as you know, is what we sent to the forensics lab who told us they sent it to you. So…" He leaned forward and placed his elbows on his desk. "What does it mean? Is it a person or an animal? Real or a prank? Adults or kids? People from town or out-of-towners?"

"We'll need to see each crime scene." Adam glanced at his brother who nodded. "Take pictures, measurements, look for the way in or way out. That will tell us if it was human or animal. We need a map of the town so we can pinpoint the crime scenes to see if there's a pattern to them. We'll need to speak to the victims, the townspeople in general, to get the vibe from the locals, and we'll need maps of the area to pinpoint wooded areas, caves, junkyards, cemeteries; anywhere the animal or human may be hiding." He finally stopped for breath.

"Done, done, and done," Larry said. "All at the police station. They have detailed maps of the area. Victims' statements, and a map of the crime scenes. Follow me, it's only two doors down." He left his desk and walked into the sunshine, with the Watkins family following. They passed a doughnut shop and stepped into the police station. "Nathan, the specialists are here," he bellowed.

Sergeant Nathan Belden hauled himself up from behind his desk and walked out of his office. "What are you bellowing about, Larry?" He was fifty and had been at this job a long time. Meandering over to the counter to see the mayor and two couples with kids, he eyed them suspiciously. "And who are these folks?"

"The animal scientists the forensics lab sent the hair you collected to," Terry said and introduced them all. "We need to see what you've done, and need a map of the crime scenes."

"And what do you want those for?" Nathan chewed thoughtfully on the toothpick in his mouth. He was trying to give up smoking for the umpteenth time and figured something else in his mouth would be helpful.

"Oh, for heaven's sake, Nathan. Just give them what they want so we can stop this crime wave in its tracks and get back to normal," Larry snapped.

"Mmm." Nathan eyed Larry's terse expression, flipped up the counter, and waved them through, then led them over to the board with maps pinned to it. "Here, the red pins are for the crime scenes, the blues for no evidence, greens for some evidence, and yellows are for ones we solved."

Adam took photos of the maps while Terry went through the victims' statements. Kath and Sally took notes, and the kids sat quietly, taking it all in for later.

"We're going to need the addresses of the victims. We want to talk to them. We'll take photos and what not," Terry mumbled absentmindedly while reading a statement. "Has anyone set a trap?"

Nathan glanced at Larry. "Why would we do that? And how would we know where to set one?"

"Is there CCTV through town?" Adam asked, turning from the board. "I can see straight away the crimes are all on one side of town, most in the one street, and that's the side closest to the Lake Forest district. A good fifty miles of bushland with a lake attached. Perfect for someone or something to hide. Do you have any known caves in the area? Wells, mines?"

Nathan rubbed his chin in thought. "We do have a few abandoned mines, decades old. Boarded up as far as I know."

"When was the last time you saw them?" Kath typed away on her laptop.

"About three years ago," Nathan muttered. "Haven't needed to check on them. Town's mostly full of old people who wouldn't think of, or need to go down there. Most youngins leave once they're old enough, and the oldies aren't about to pull pranks like this on each other."

"We don't think these *are* pranks," Terry told him. "But we do need to talk to the people it happened to, and the people in town in general. Get an idea of what's going on. And then we'll need to check out those mines to see if they're still boarded up."

"I can send a constable down there." Nathan stuck his fat thumbs into his belt loops. Not to be outdone by a group of outsiders, he didn't need them giving orders, or messing up his job. And it was a cushy one at that. Fifty grand a year clear and a home at the back of the station while he was there. The town had next to no crime until recently, they only had two constables, and now he had these do-gooders here messing up his plans.

"And what if your constable is hurt because he doesn't know what he's doing and comes across a wild animal? If it *is* an animal doing this," Adam said, sensing the sergeant's ire. "Give us copies of everything we need and let us get to work. It's already afternoon, and we need to take pictures of the crime scenes."

"Mmm," Nathan mumbled and reluctantly handed over copies he'd already made. "Here. They won't talk to you."

"Thank you, sergeant." Terry took the papers and the family left. "Kids, get your cameras; you'll be taking pictures while we do everything else. Divide and conquer. Adam, you take all the houses on the left side of Vacant Street, and we'll take the right. Kath, you and Sal talk to the tenants, Adam and I will take measurements. Everyone ready?" With nods all round, they got into their four-wheel drives and drove off.

House to house to house they worked with the precision of an army corps. The boys took photos of the scenes, their fathers took measurements and notes, while their mothers sweet talked their way into the houses to speak to the victims. By dusk, they had visited twenty crime scenes each, as many were as simple as knocked over rubbish bins that required no more than ten minutes of surveillance.

They met at the only motel in town, and Kath and Sally went inside to rent rooms while Adam and Terry stayed with the kids. Once booked in, they unloaded their cars and trailers, and hauled luggage and equipment into their rooms, making sure their cars were safely locked and so were their motel room doors.

Staring out the window into the night, Terry noted how barren the town was. "It must have everyone scared if no one's out after dusk. Not even the pub's got customers." He eyed the empty pub across the road, able to see most of the windows were dark and not a single soul was out.

"The sergeant probably has everyone running scared." Kath tapped the keys on her laptop and finished entering the last of her husband's notes. "There. Done." She hit *print* and the paper churned out of their portable printer. "So, do we know what it is yet?" She watched her husband close the curtains and lumber over to an easy chair. "Animal or human?"

"No bloody idea," he replied. "That hair was not human, not synthetic, and we couldn't identify it as animal. So, what the hell was it? So far, it's been all outside crime scenes. Rubbish gone through and turned over, plants knocked over, rattling doorknobs. It all sounds like pranks to me. But that hair..." he trailed off. "That's the kicker."

Kath piled the printed information into a folder and shut off her laptop. "Let's call it a night. It's late, and time for bed." She tucked Sophie into the single bed in their room, and made sure Ben and Alex were tucked into their beds in the adjoining room. After kissing them goodnight, she jammed a chair under the handle for extra security and closed the curtains tight. The other boys were with their parents in the room next door. Calling it a night, they got into bed and hoped for a good sleep...

That was rudely interrupted by their car alarms going off in the middle of the night.

"What the hell is that?" Kath leaned up on her elbow and checked the clock. "It's three a.m."

"And it's our cars. We've had a break-in." Terry slipped into his shoes and threw a robe over his shorts and singlet. He flung open the door and found Adam already outside. "What the hell's going on?"

"Someone tried breaking in," Adam replied, clicking his car key alarm to turn off the ear-piercing sound. Peace descended once more as the rest of the family gathered outside. No one else had turned up, just a few lights flashed on then off as people took a look and went back into hiding.

"Broken windows?" Terry circled the cars. "Lights? Doors?"

"Everything's fine." Adam scratched his head then peered closely at a door handle on the car. "Is that…?"

Terry leaned in to look. "Fur?"

They glanced at each other then told the kids to get their kits. Wearing latex gloves, they dusted the handle, took photos, and carefully collected the fur and sealed it in a bag.

"Think it's the same fur?" Ben asked his father, collecting weird shaped pebbles on the ground around the cars.

"Possibly." Terry shut his kit. "Okay, everyone. Back to bed. We've had our turn at the hands of the town's prankster, so let's get some sleep. We need to be up bright and early to get to the mines." After ushering the kids back to bed, they locked the doors and jammed the chairs under the handles.

*****

Early in the morning, after a hearty breakfast, they met the sergeant and his two constables at the station.

"Right, which one of you wants to escort us to these mines?" Terry asked.

The two constables fearfully looked at each other and backed away.

They can't be more than twenty, Adam thought. *Way too young to be doing this job properly.*

Nathan, not to be outdone by the out-of-towners, volunteered. "There's three of them about three k apart, about three k in from the road. It's a long walk. You up for it?"

Are you? Ben thought. *He's so not going to be able to keep up with us.* He hid his giggle with a cough.

The family smiled indulgently at the sergeant.

"I have a feeling we'll do better than expected." Terry took in the sergeant's portly rounded figure from years of sitting and doing not much of anything.

"Solved the crime?" Nathan sneered as he passed the family.

"Considering we only arrived in town yesterday, no," Terry replied, following him out.

"Any damage to your cars? I heard there was a break-in last night." Nathan thought he had them and flung the door of the police four-wheel drive open.

"No break-in," Adam told him. "In fact, nothing at all except for my alarm going off. It's been a bit dodgy lately. I really should get it fixed."

"Mmm," Nathan grumbled. "Come on, I don't have all day."

He drove off with the family following and parked off the dirt road at the first mine. "It's a walk from here. This way. Watch your step, it's an overgrown path."

"Why can't we drive to it?" Ben asked, taking a video of everything he passed.

"Too overgrown," the sergeant replied, already huffing.

It took half an hour to make it to the first mine which they found intact. The boys took photos, Kath and Sally made notes, and Terry and Adam made measurements and looked for fur. They tested the wood nailed across the entrance, and looked for other access points.

"This one's all right," Terry declared. "Let's get to the next one."

They repeated the process at the second and found the same. Everything was nailed shut and there was no other access. At the third, they found broken planks and a hole big enough for an animal or small human to fit through.

"Well, howdy doody." Adam knelt beside his brother and shone his torch into the shaft. "Big enough to gain entrance."

"But not for a full grown adult." Terry pushed at the wood and more fell away. "Think we should go in?"

"Better not. If the ground gives way we're screwed," Adam told him. "Kids, give me a camera."

Henry handed over his and watched his dad take photos while his uncle stood or knelt beside it for measurements to show if a human could fit through.

The boys continued taking photos, and Sophie wandered over to the pretty gathering of pink flowers near some shrubbery. "Ooh, pretty." She pulled some up. "This will make a nice bunch for Mummy," she told her pretty dolly that went everywhere with her, and pulled at some flowers. They wouldn't give way, so she tugged harder, finally freeing them from the ground. Gripping some more, she tugged and saw a patch of fur underneath that moved. Startled, she froze.

"Sophie, come on, sweetie, time to go," Kath called to her daughter.

Gulping, Sophie turned and ran back to her mother.

"Aw, what'ya got there?" Kath asked.

"Flowers." Sophie shoved them at her mother. "For you."

"Ooh, azaleas, how pretty. Thanks, sweetie. Come on, time to go." They made the trek back to their cars and drove to their hotel rooms to complete the data, where, finally, Sophie told them what she had seen.

"Are you sure it was fur, luv?" Terry asked his wide-eyed daughter.

She nodded, still shaken by the incident. "It moved."

"Could have been a rat, a cat, any sort of animal burrowed under a bush," Adam said. "How big was the bush?"

"Largish," Kath said. "I saw it briefly when I called out to her. But it was large enough for an animal."

"Well, there you go, sweetie." Terry tickled his daughter's chin. "It was just an animal. You hungry? Let's go and eat."

They had dinner at the pub which allowed children in the dining room only, and discussed their case in detail. Unable to come up with anything substantial, they headed back to the hotel. The sun had gone down and lingering traces of light scattered across the horizon, making it dark. They got out their hotel keys and kept the kids between them as they walked across the road, always on the lookout for anything or anyone. They checked their cars and trailers, and unlocked their doors.

Hearing a low growl behind her, Sophie turned around and came face to face with a hairy beast that towered above her. The scream that came out of her could have shattered glass.

The family turned around just in time to see the beast sweep Sophie off her feet with his big hairy arms and run.

"Yeti!" the boys yelled in surprise and took off after it.

The adults grabbed shotguns and cameras and ran after them.

"Ah!" Sophie's screams pierced the night and the yeti growled, its left arm around her waist, its stinky breath making her wave her hand in front of her face. "Ew, you stink. You need to brush your teeth and gargle." She sniffed, and added, "And maybe have a shower and use soap and deodorant. Didn't your mother teach you hygiene?"

"Argh." The five boys caught up and launched themselves at the yeti, attacking its legs to bring it down. Jumping on its back, they pummelled it with their fists to make it let go of their sister and cousin.

"Ow, it's heavy," Sophie complained, having partially landed under it when it had fallen.

The yeti let out an ear-deafening growl and threw the boys off as it leaned up on one hand.

"Stop right there," Terry slammed his rifle into

the beast's face. "Don't you dare move."

The yeti stopped, surprised by the long cylindrical object in its face.

"Sophie." Kath slowly pulled her daughter into her arms, never taking her eyes from the beast's eyes. "I don't think it's human," she told her husband.

Adam cocked his rifle into the back of the yeti's head. "Don't you dare move or I will blow your brains out."

"Anyone getting photos?" Terry asked.

Sally's flash went off. "Certainly am."

"And we've got fur." The boys held up their hands.

The beast cowered, its left hand in front of its face, its legs ready to launch itself off the ground. He'd only ever seen humans from afar, but knew these were different. Not like the ones in town.

Terry stepped closer and peered into the yeti's eyes. "I don't know if you can understand me, but you will do exactly as I say. You will get out of town and never come back. You will not seek food, knock over rubbish bins, break into people's homes or cars again. You will go back to where you came from and find food somewhere else. You will never come here again." Moving back, he lowered his rifle. "Now go." He nodded toward the road that would lead the yeti back to the woods. "Get out and don't come back."

The yeti, not quite understanding, but getting enough of the point, slowly climbed to his feet, cautiously glanced at the family, and took off down the road.

"You got the photos?" Terry asked once more.

Sally checked the camera. "About a hundred. I can't believe that's all we'll have of the infamous yeti. I can't believe you just let it go."

"And you let the million dollars go," Ben piped up, gobsmacked at having seen a real-life yeti and not capturing it for the reward money. Ah, the things he could have done with a million dollars.

Terry shook his head. "Neither can I. Come on, Bubba." He lifted Sophie into his arms. "Let's get you inside."

ABOUT THE AUTHOR

T.K. is a children's TV show veteran who loves watching disaster and creature/zombie movies and TV shows, but not at night.

T.K. started writing many a year ago back in primary school, but only started her author career in 2015 with the release of her first three stories and anthology. She will write and release stories until there are twelve *Bones* books and a special edition numbered 13...

T.K. lives in Australia, loves extra cheesy cheeseburgers and chocolate, and gets a kick out of watching funny dog and cat videos.

T.K. Wrathbone is the kid's/tween pen name for author Tiara King. You can find more about Tiara on her website; follow her on social media, or visit her publishing house, Royal Star Publishing.

SOCIALS

tkwrathbone.com

tiaraking.com.au

royalstarpublishing.com.au

Sign up for *Tiara's* Newsletter…

Make sure you're always in the know and never miss free exclusives, the latest news, book updates, and so much more with newsletters from…

tiaraking.com.au

HAVE YOU READ THESE?

Next Top Mannequin
Cinderfella and Princess Charming: Witch Hunters
www.badluck-youredead.com
The Bones of Wrath: Changes
One Bone: Anthology 1

The Orphanage
Hantel and Gresel: Food Critics
Mirror, Mirror On The Wall
The Bones of Wrath: Haunted
Two Bone: Anthology 2

The Howler
Shadow Walkers
Faded
The Bones of Wrath: Ghosts
Three Bone: Anthology 3

I Spy With My Little Eye
Knock, Knock…Who's Dead?
It Creeped At Midnight
The Bones of Wrath: Monsters
Four: Anthology 4

OR THESE?

Trick Or Treat
All Hallows Possession
They Rise On A Blood Moon
The Bones of Wrath: Horrors
Five Bone: Anthology 5

All Clowns Must Die!
The Demon Resides
Infestation
The Bones of Wrath: Terrors
Six Bone: Anthology 6